METAS

RAE LOUISE

Black Rose Writing | Texas

ISBN: 978-1-68433-239-7
PUBLISHED BY BLACK ROSE WRITING
www.blackrosewriting.com

Printed in the United States of America
Suggested Retail Price (SRP) $18.95

Metas is printed in Chaparral Pro

ACKNOWLEDGMENTS:

In memory of Rob, Merlin and Dante.

This book is dedicated to my sister, Lizzie, with a special thanks to all of my family and friends that have encouraged and supported me throughout this difficult life. Gratitude to readers, old and new, and everyone involved in making this book happen. Last but not least, much love to my fantastic fur babies.

METAS

PROLOGUE

It was his toes that deadened first. No matter how much he wiggled them, the circulation wouldn't come back. Damp was breathed up from the ground into the air, particles nipping at him like icicle-toothed piranhas. His shivers were imperishable and could be heard in every breath and sniffle that departed his body. Even the luxury of clothing wouldn't have fared well in warding off the invading chill; it got to the point where any embarrassment at his state of exposed vulnerability was insignificant. The abduction, his imprisonment and even the achy spots all over his bashed up body: he'd withstand it all over again if it meant a relief from that savage cold.

He heard shuffling from up ahead. Rats, maybe?

His head jerked up, eyes roving pointlessly in the dark. He might as well have been wearing a blindfold and had wondered on more than one occasion if he'd lost his sight.

No more movement, although he was certain that he wasn't alone. He hadn't heard anyone entering his prison, wherever that may be, but consciousness came and went like night and day; every minute, every hour merging with the next. *How long had it been now?* He didn't know the answer. There wasn't much he was aware of apart from the fear that encased his heart and slammed against his ribcage like a wrecking ball.

"H-hel... hello?" Another futile act as far as obtaining a response went. He'd lost count of how many times he'd tried – begged, even – and now it had become a habit. The want to hear anything that wasn't silence. Something to ground him, assure him that he was still his physical self and not lost in some hellish limbo.

Clip... clop... clip... clop.

Footsteps. He'd know a woman's strut, blind or deaf. It was the only thing to have killed his shivering. His head moved to follow the sounds. He wasn't sure how far away they were, but a couple of metres at a guess.

"Who's there? Pleas'... Miss?"

Next it came from behind him: a high-pitched, bubbling laughter. He turned and twisted from the shoulders up as it seemed to ricochet around him. Echoes, perhaps... or madness. Maybe he was in fact alone in the dank dungeon, mind conjuring the same demons that exploited his desires until sexual became sinful and he turned his back on the ethics that he'd vowed to abide by. Now it was his turn to play the victim.

As if it had materialised from nowhere, a giant paw clouted him across the face so hard that the chair he was bound to almost lifted off the ground. He capsized with it onto his side and was unable to stifle a yelp. His entire skull felt bruised and he winced at the taste of blood in his mouth, spitting it out onto the concrete. Waggling his tongue around, he found a couple of upper molar teeth that had come loose from their sockets. Though the pain wasn't unbearable, he hoped they stayed in place with a view to healing rather than have some sadist in scrubs probing his mouth – ironic, considering his own profession.

He began to cry then, broken snivels that sounded pathetic to his own ears, never mind anyone else's. This was made all the more apparent by the voice that projected from somewhere in the distance. Further back than his attacker, but in the same vicinity as where he'd heard the footsteps a moment ago. So far he'd counted three presences, but he felt the paranoia of a hundred eyes.

"You know why you're here, don't you, doc?" The words revealed nothing apart from what he'd already known: it was, indeed, a female.

"Pleas' –" he tried again, but she cut in tersely.

"Don't you?"

"No..." Yes, he did. But the prospect of any more torture was worth a thousand lies to save himself. "I never do any of these terrible t'ings. I'm a professional. People try to damage my reputation for money and attent-ion."

"We both know that isn't true. Perhaps you need an incentive in order to admit to your crimes. A chance of freedom – you'd like that, wouldn't you? To see the sun, inhale the fresh air and sleep in your own bed..."

He did. In fact he was so desperate that, for a second, he was outside of his confinement as though the proposal had triggered a case of astral projection, whereby his soul or conscience was on another plane. More likely it was a dehydrated, psychologically traumatised delusion; either way, he cracked.

"Any'ting. I do any'ting. Pleas'..."

Another screech as the chair was hoisted back into its vertical position, his twelve-stone frame but a feather to whoever – presumably a male – the strapping arms belonged to.

"It won't be easy," the woman cautioned. "You're going to have to tap into a place that sinks deeper and darker than what you thought existed or were capable of. Then again," her tone became scathing, "a man like *you* might enjoy it."

For the first time, he was thankful for the darkness that shrouded his guilt. Shame was too strong a word because if it wasn't for his predicament, he'd have felt neither. Although more uncertainties were raised once he'd gathered himself long enough to question how his captors were able to move freely without the impairment of blindness.

"So, what'll it be, doc?" The woman spoke again. "Are you ready to atone for your sins by giving up your eternal salvation?"

"Yes." No hesitancy this time. "Tell me – any'ting you ask, I do."

"Good."

The relief shook his body in a rapid expiration. He might have smiled if it didn't hurt every time he opened his jaw, wobbly molars leaking blood all over his chin.

"Thank you, thank you."

"Don't thank us yet."

Us... Of course he'd known there were others, but to hear confirmation not a few inches from him – a deep, masculine whisper and moist breath on his face – caused a static effect with the hairs on his body. An electrical surge that left him tingling from the outside in, penetrating him with a gut-clenching dread.

When light finally endowed the room with life, he couldn't shut his eyes quick enough. It scorched through them to the back of his skull, leaving him with an explosive headache. His eyelids fluttered before opening and in that instant, he wished that he actually had gone blind. It seemed to take forever for the scream welling in his throat to eject from his body but, now unable to focus on anything but the abomination before him, all of the terror and pain that he'd endured shattered the silence in one long, unremitting howl.

CHAPTER ONE

Leafless branches rapped against the glass, stark silhouettes etched into the moon's luminous shine. Their gentle swaying created an aqueous effect with the light that poured through the window, drenching the bed.

Violet Kendal let out a moan as the hand slipped out of her unbuttoned nightshirt, gliding down her stomach and further still. Those cool white rays shed an illusion of beauty upon everything they touched and felt simultaneously soft yet tingly at the same time, like running a silk scarf over her milky flesh.

"Don't stop," she whispered, in between husky breaths. "Please..."

She raked a hand through her lover's hair, clutching it in her fist. She heard him groan but didn't know whether it was an expression of pleasure or pain.

"I want you, Dean," she purred. "I want you *now*."

Violet's legs were already open when Dean's hand slid between them, burrowing into the mound of dark hair. She drew him closer to her, fingernails gnawing into his scalp. She thought she heard him speak but the words were drowned out by the sound of her gasps.

"I love you, too," she replied, on the off-chance. "Do it to me. Now, Dean... quick."

Violet could barely feel his fingers for the juices seeping from her entrance. Her whole body perspired and it looked like she'd been showered with crystals in the moonlight. She closed her eyes, sucking her bottom lip in between her teeth and biting down gently.

"Violet..." Dean's voice again.

"Dean," she whispered back.

"*Violet*." She felt his hot body pull away from her, and by the time she'd opened her eyes, he was already sitting up.

"What is it?" She spoke querulously.

Dean had his hand raised in front of him, and in the darkness it looked like he'd dipped his fingers into thick black paint. Violet shot up and reached over to the lamp on the bedside table. The silvery night was engulfed by a lambent glow, and she gawped down at the crimson puddle beneath her and the blood that slathered the inside of her thighs.

"Shit." Violet peeled herself free of the sticky bed sheets and clambered over Dean, who cringed at the trails she left on his legs like some kind of menstruating snail.

"Babe, are you okay? Where are you going? Violet!" He watched her hobble from the room with one hand cupped under her crotch. She locked herself in the bathroom opposite and yanked the toilet roll, knocking over the chrome holder so it clanged onto its side.

"Damn it," she hissed, unravelling the tissue until all that remained was a cardboard tube. She made a wad in her hand and dabbed away the blood dribbling down her thighs, followed by that which coated her backside. There was knocking on the bathroom door and she dropped to her knees in a panic, attempting to mop up the drips on the tiles but only managing to smear them with the sodden toilet paper.

"Violet?"

"Give me a minute," she called.

"I just wanted to say that it's okay. I mean, there's no need to be embarrassed. Shit happens." Dean's voice sounded muffled through the wood between them.

"I'm not embarrassed, I'm cleaning myself up. I'll be out in a bit."

There was no reply from outside. Violet dropped the bloodied tissue into the toilet, dampened a hand towel and then finished scrubbing the footprints off the floor. Once it was clean she left the towel, along with her soiled nightshirt, in a heap by the bath before rinsing herself down in the shower. By the time she was dry, the bleeding had stopped and she felt no discomfort – which all but soothed her. At least the accompaniment of cramps would have afforded some form of explanation.

With a towel secured around her torso, she wandered back to the bedroom where Dean was stripping the bed in his underpants. He stopped when he saw her to ask, "Is everything all right downstairs?"

Violet assumed it was a reference to her vagina. "Yeah, I'm fine. I don't know what happened."

"I thought you'd already had your period this month?"

Violet shrugged, adopting an air of nonchalance. "So, I had another one. It's perfectly normal, you know."

"That much blood, though?"

Violet followed his gaze to the mattress. The stain that had soaked through the under sheet was about the size of a cushion. When Dean spoke again, she knew that her hesitancy had been noted.

"You don't think... I mean, is there any possibility that you could be..."

Violet reasoned, "If that was the case then we've definitely just saved ourselves a trip to the clinic."

Dean frowned, an expression that never seemed to fit his smooth, placid features. "That's sick, Vi."

She chuckled and went over to give him a kiss on the cheek. "Sorry, but I'd know if I was up the duff and we're always careful. It's probably a one-off." *Another lie.*

"I'm just saying, you haven't been yourself lately. You seem... I don't know... different."

"Because you knew me so well before, didn't you?" It sounded more scornful than intended, but Violet felt a hot flush boiling to the surface that was becoming harder and harder to contain. Five months together and Dean already thought he knew every fact there was to know about her: how many zits she'd had as a teenager, the name of her favourite childhood pet and the sum of her life's savings.

"You could try letting me in a bit more," murmured Dean.

"We just tried that, it ended in a mess."

"There you go again – dismissing everything I say rather than talking to me like an adult. I don't mind being your punch bag as long as I have some insight as to why."

"Man, I was only kidding." Violet huffed while slumping down onto the edge of the bed. She let her hair fall loose from its bobble and worked the vibrant lengths through her fingers. Dean came and sat next to her.

"Is this about Isabelle?" he said.

"No," replied Violet. "Maybe... I don't know."

"I'm no doctor, but it might explain why your body's all over the place. I won't even try to guess at what you're going through, but I can see that it's torturing you. Maybe we should get away for a while, take some time out – or just yourself if you need a bit of head space. What do you think?" Dean traced his fingertips down Violet's spine, his hand settling on her minute waist. She looked into his dusky eyes and felt tears scalding her own.

"I think I don't deserve you," she said.

"Good job I'm a sucker for gals with freaky hair, then, isn't it?"

Violet laughed while flicking her mane showily over her shoulder. Dean kissed her on the lips before standing up. "Got any bleach? We'd better tackle this stain before it dries out."

"Just flip the mattress for now, it's late and I'm in enough bother at the office. Are you staying here tonight?"

Dean hesitated, probably because it was the first time she hadn't slung him out after being satisfied numerous times. He soon gathered himself, as though there was a time limit on the invitation. "I'd like that," he said.

"Cool, I'll go and fetch some clean sheets."

On her way to the door, Dean asked, "Did you mean what you said earlier?"

"When?"

"Before we were... interrupted. It kind of took me by surprise."

"I don't know. What did I say?"

Dean was quiet, his eyes searching her face all the while. He reminded Violet of a puppy that had been condemned to the kennels. The truth was, she remembered using the 'L' word while snared in the jaws of passion. An even sorrier truth was that she'd have said anything, probably to anyone, in order to quench the raging lust that almost frightened her.

Finally, Dean shook his head. "Never mind."

His gaze remained on her despite himself and he was a puppy once more, pining for the love and affection that had been denied to him. Violet gave him nothing.

CHAPTER TWO

Slouched over her desk, forehead nestled in palm, Violet struggled to resist the weight of her eyelids. The tapping of keyboards, constant drilling of phones and half-formed conversations all merged into a cacophony of noise. A bang from beside her sounded like someone clapping their hands next to her ears, the gust of air blowing wisps of hair across her cheek. She jolted upright and stared firstly at the stack of files that had magically appeared next to her, and then up at Tina Woodcock's pugged face.

"Haven't you got a bed at home?" her colleague said smartly.

Yeah, and it's probably half the size of yours, lard arse... Violet sneered at her own derogatory thoughts, which quickly morphed into a grin of pleasantry.

"Are these to be filed away?"

"They're for the archives." Tina spoke matter-of-factly. "Two of the doctors have been accepted for permanent positions, one's AWOL and the rest have closed their accounts with us."

Violet thumbed through the folders that contained paperwork and documentation for the mentioned clients of the medical recruitment agency: copies of identification, qualifications; registration and CRB checks. One name in particular stood out and she slipped the file out from the rest.

"Otis Yans – wasn't that the GP who got done for sexual harassment?"

"Allegedly," Tina pointed out. "Innocent until proven guilty, I say."

"So, what's the deal? Have you contacted him?"

"I've tried ringing a few times, but it keeps going to voicemail. Guess he's keeping a low profile until things have been straightened out."

"Or he's done a runner." Violet tucked the folder back into the pile. "I read about it in the newspaper a few days ago but couldn't figure out where I'd heard the name. One patient steps forward and then more victims start cropping up – that's a classic case of pervert-itis if you ask me. Maybe you should keep his details to hand in case the police show up."

"What could I possibly tell them that they don't already know? I was his consultant, I met the guy once."

"All right, I was just saying. Was there anything else you needed?"

"Not right now."

Tina was soon waddling back to her desk, her legs poking out of her pencil skirt like two flumps. Violet levelled a hand in front of her eyes and made a gun shape with her fingers, popping the air between her lips as the imaginary bullet burst through the back of Tina's throat. Smirking, she returned to her computer screen and saw that she had one new email from Lucy Smith. She opened it and read the line:

'Who ate all the pies?'

Violet giggled into her hand, attracting several glances from her co-workers. She replied: *'Tina did! Drinks tonight?'*

The next email came through in seconds. *'Yup.'*

Violet threw a cursory glance across the office. She and Lucy exchanged a facetious grin and then carried on with their work.

***

The absinthe seared the back of Violet's throat, setting her taste buds alight. She felt it rushing like acid down her gullet and into her empty stomach.

"Whoo!" Violet slammed the shot glass onto the bar, signalling the tender to bring over a second one.

"Steady on, Vi, it's still early," Lucy cautioned, in her light-hearted manner.

It may have only just gone 9 p.m., but it was Friday night and Cherry's Bar was filling up fast. Piss-cheap beer, along with the free-shot-with-any-cocktail deal, made it a popular venue for university students; especially those psyching themselves up for Derby City Centre's bigger pubs and clubs. Although the cocktails themselves were more juice than alcohol, and Violet had learned from experience that once you got over the excitement of free booze, it was fairly counterproductive.

"Where to after this?" she yelled, over the thudding beat of chart hits. "I'm in the mood for some serious boogying tonight!"

"Carry on the way you're going and you won't be able to stand up, let alone dance around your handbag." Another admonishment from Lucy.

A fresh shot glass filled with slime-green liquid was plonked on the bar in front of Violet, along with a milky-looking cocktail.

"I didn't order this," Violet told the barman.

He pointed behind them to the seating zone that ran alongside the main window. Violet was only able to identify the mystery man because he was sitting alone. Slouched in a chair, one elbow draped over the back of it in a lackadaisical fashion, a dark-haired stranger had them in his sight. His face rippled with colour beneath the disco lights, which cast surfing rainbows over his black shirt. The scene induced a hallucinogenic kind of dizziness, and in the end Violet had to look away.

"He bought this? For me?" she asked the barman, who clarified with a nod. She offered him some change to pay for the shot, but he waved a dismissive hand.

"Call it a freebie with the cocktail," he said.

"What cocktail is it?"

"Er, Screaming Orgasm."

Violet and Lucy glanced back at the stranger, then at each other. They erupted into unrestrained giggles.

"You're not going to drink that?" said Lucy, once the barman had disappeared.

"It'd be a waste not to." Violet took a slurp of the creamy liquid, then licked her lips and smiled sweetly at her friend. Lucy rolled her eyes while sipping her mojito. Her pink lipstick left a smudge on the rim of the glass, but with her natural good looks, it was virtually all the makeup she wore. Her fair hair was arranged into an elegant bun – a total contrast to Violet's unruly waves.

"Let's do some more shots," Violet suggested, while scraping together the loose coins that were floating around in the bottom of her handbag.

"You haven't finished that one yet." Lucy referred to the absinthe.

"Come on, I'm celebrating."

"Celebrating what?"

"Isabelle – she'd have been nineteen today. Wasn't much of a drinker, though. No doubt she'd be on the Tropicana if she was here now." Violet's laughter was loud but short-lived.

"Yeah, Dean mentioned that her birthday was coming up." Lucy spoke softly. "You know he's worried about you?"

Violet peered at her friend, her eyes almost disappearing behind the thick, smoky makeup that she wore. "Been gossiping about me, have you?"

"He's my cousin, we talk. You guys hooking up makes keeping friend and family matters separate kind of difficult, you know?"

"What exactly has he told you?"

"Nothing I didn't already know. Dean's a sensitive guy, he gives his heart out way too easily. Neither of us wants to watch you self-destruct, so if you need someone to scream at then do it and don't feel guilty about it."

"What's the point? I could scream and shout until my vocal cords explode, but it won't bring her back. That's why I'm doing the partying for her."

"By getting leathered, is that really what she'd want?"

Violet sobered a moment. "I know she wouldn't want me moping about, that's for sure. Tonight is about celebrating my sister for the life she had, not the pile of ashes sunk at the bottom of the Lake District."

Violet's temper burned as hot as the tears in her eyes. Her little sister was dead and she couldn't even afford a burial service. Dean had driven her up north where they'd said their final goodbyes together, a modest yet meaningful affair that had evoked many childhood memories. Violet stretched her thoughts back to eighteen years ago. To the urn in her mum's arms, nursed close as if it was a baby. Isabelle in her pushchair, spared the misery by youth and sleep. In the end it had been Violet who'd emptied her father's remains, the cool breeze scattering them into a grey mist that dispersed into the river below – a river that she'd played by more times than she could count. Violet's only consolation was that, by laying Isabelle to rest in the same location as her father, their souls would be forever united.

It was Lucy's fingers caressing her arm that brought Violet back to the land of the living. "I'm sorry, Vi."

"Don't be." Violet sniffed. "Now, are we going to bicker all night or shall we go ahead and have some fun?"

"I vote fun. You are looking kind of peaky, though. Have you eaten since lunch?"

"Does an apple count?"

Lucy frowned. "No, it doesn't. Why don't we grab some food and then move on to Walkabout, deal?"

"Sounds good to me."

"Cool, I'll just nip to the loo and then we'll head off."

Lucy guzzled down the dregs of her mojito and then mingled in amongst the crowd on her way to the ladies'. Violet peeked over her shoulder to find that Mr Screaming Orgasm was still watching her.

"Same again?" the barman asked, while collecting Lucy's cocktail glass.

Violet shook her head and attempted to close her bag, fingers fumbling with the zip as if it was coated in oil. The alcohol had rendered her useless and it wasn't even an hour into the night. When an elbow jabbed into her back, she was thrust into the edge of the bar and knocked the shot glass with her arm. It skidded before toppling onto its side, contents spilling over the wood. Violet swung around, mouth brimming with unspoken curses, but the groomed face staring down at her was like something off a men's fragrance advert.

"Sorry, darlin'." Violet couldn't tell if his accent was local over the noise, but his crisp suit was as wasted on Cherry's Bar as if he was in the middle of the Sahara desert.

"Where did you come from, the House of Parliament?" Violet jibed.

"Business meeting, actually." The man's smile didn't wane despite her mockery. It seemed a little *too* practiced.

"You don't come around Derby often, do you?" Violet said.

"How did you guess?"

"Take a look around, this place is half packed with students." It wasn't until after she'd answered that Violet realised he was being sarcastic.

The man squeezed up beside her and scanned the medley of bottles shelved behind the bar. "Any recommendations?" he asked.

Violet shrugged. "It's all cheap crap that they try to pull off as the branded stuff. Wouldn't you be better off in a swanky wine bar or something?"

"I'm only in town for the night. We thought it'd be quieter here than in the centre."

"Hmm, I thought you looked too old for a clubber."

The man regarded her for a good while. There was a rigidity in his eyes that even his curls couldn't soften, and Violet wasn't sure whether he wanted to gut her or grope her.

"What's your name?" he said, at last.

"Izzy." It came out so naturally. So morbidly.

"How old are *you*, Izzy?"

"How old do you think I am?"

"Twenty-one."

"That's a safe bet. Is that the kind of guy you are?"

"What?"

"Boring. Afraid to take risks. As stiff as that suit you ironed this morning."

The man fixed one side of his mouth into a grin, partially amused. "Why the hostility?"

"Why the questions?"

"You asked me the first question, remember?"

"It was rhetorical."

"Fair enough. Who have you come out with tonight?"

"A friend." Violet took a slow swig of her cocktail, prolonging his curiosity. "Are you single?"

"Yes."

"So is Lucy. I reckon you'd like her."

"What makes you think I'm looking for someone?"

"I can smell it."

"Smell what?"

"Testosterone. Call it a sixth sense."

The man had no response for this, aside from the infinitesimal flexing of a brow. It was at that point Lucy returned to the bar.

"Ready to go?" she said.

"Change of plan," Violet replied. "Meet my new friend... What did you say your name was?"

The man locked eyes with Lucy, neither his manner nor his expression giving any inkling of his feelings. "Matt," he introduced himself.

"Um, hello..." Lucy smiled shyly as they shook hands.

"This is Lucy, the friend I told you about," Violet informed Matt. "If you need someone to help you loosen up then she's the woman for the job."

"Vi!" Lucy elbowed her in the side, but Matt was unfazed.

"Why don't you ladies come and join me and my associates? If you think I'm stiff then wait until you meet them."

Violet sniggered at his phrasing. Lucy just went red.

Matt got a round of beers in, then they zigzagged through the crowd to a table where three other blokes, all ranging from their mid-twenties to early thirties, sat in wait. It wasn't until Violet had settled down that she realised Mr Screaming Orgasm had vanished.

***

The taxi rolled up to the curb. Violet tugged open the back door before clamping her hands either side of Lucy's face and planting a sloppy kiss on her lips.

"Ugh, get off me!" Lucy shoved her away playfully, and Violet almost went over in her six-inch heels.

"Love you, baby!" she slurred, as Lucy crawled into the taxi.

Violet waved her arm uncoordinatedly over her head. Across the road, a group of lads were just exiting a takeaway restaurant. They waved back at her with a barrage of sleazy comments.

"Piss off!" Violet shouted, half laughing.

"Are you sure you're going to be all right getting home?" Lucy asked.

"Stop fretting, Mum, there'll be another cab in no time."

"You could always come back to mine. I'm sure my parents wouldn't mind if –"

"No way, your mum still hasn't forgiven me for throwing up on the cat – never mind the time I tripped over your dad's shoes and bled all over the new carpet. You need to start looking for your own place, woman!"

"Fine, but make sure you text me when you get home, okay?"

"Don't I always?" Violet blew a series of kisses as the taxi pulled away and prepared to take a left turn at the traffic lights.

After leaving Cherry's Bar at around ten thirty, she, Lucy and the guys had moved on to a club on Wardwick in the centre of Derby. Violet had laughed more in a single night than in the last three months subsequent to Isabelle's death. She'd felt bad about it at first, like she was betraying her sister in some way, but socialising with people that knew nothing about her seemed much easier than being around those who did. The guys had been so refreshing, so laid-back and jocular without feeling the need to tiptoe around her. Especially the tubby one... *What was his name?* Violet couldn't even remember.

She didn't have to wait long before another car parked up ten yards down the road with its taxi light beaming. She made a move before anyone else spotted it but could only manage a precarious trot in her stilettos. The town was swarming with drunkards that would readily crawl over broken glass to catch a ride home, hence why Violet stuck to the side streets that tended to shorter waiting times. She'd have shared a taxi with Lucy if they didn't live on opposite sides of town.

Violet approached the car from the rear and was halfway there when she went to signal her presence. Her arm was seized from behind and twisted up against her back. A hand smothered her mouth, muting her squeal. Writhing and groaning, she was manoeuvred into a dingy alley that ran alongside a boarded-up chippy. Keeping up with the assailant's strides was a struggle in itself and left her heels scraping the ground.

Out of view from passers-by, the figure let her loose. The alcohol coursing through her veins seemed to have replaced the five-odd litres of blood, making her reactions sloppy and delayed. Stumbling against a wall, she spun around with her fists clenched in a pathetic boxing stance.

"Surprise!" cheered the stranger. Though little more than a silhouette in the unlit passage, his voice was enough to eliminate the panic that caused Violet's entire chest cavity to seize up.

"Matt!" she exclaimed, once her normal breathing was restored. Fists uncurling even though it took all of her restraint not to swing for the man. "What on earth do you think you're playing at?"

"Just taking a risk. Isn't that what you like?"

"I didn't say that I wanted to be scared to death, you big plonker! What if someone had seen?"

"I'm not stupid." Matt came towards her, arms encircling her waist. She allowed him to pin her against the alley wall, his sturdy body warming her from the chill; but the stench of piss that had long seeped into the brickwork made her want to vomit even more than she did already.

"What are you doing?" Violet murmured. "You know I'm seeing someone."

"He's not here now, though, is he?"

"I thought you liked Lucy?"

"I like you more."

Matt's hands slithered up her dress, tugging the waistband of her knickers. He could have been a completely different bloke to the one she'd met in Cherry's Bar, and not just personality-wise. The flaps of his shirt hung loosely over his trousers, with the top buttons undone to flaunt his smooth pectorals. The cologne that had been so fragrant earlier was now barely detectable, diluted by his own bodily fluids. *Must have been from all the dancing*, Violet mused. He'd had some slick moves on him, and he and Lucy had looked so natural on the dance floor together.

"Stop," she whispered, her friend's image stark in her mind. Matt kissed her neck, moistening her flesh by licking and sucking, before moving up to her lips to silence her protests. His tongue wormed its way into her mouth and for a while she reciprocated, her body not reacting to the signals from her brain. In fact she was repulsed by her actions, but the man's lust was infectious; a love potion of pheromones.

"Matt..." She twisted her head to evade his persistent lips. "Don't – I mean it."

"Come on, Izzy." He breathed, alcoholic fumes choking her. "Who's the stiff one now?"

"You, by the feel of things. And stop calling me that, it's my sister's name."

"Kinky."

"My *dead* sister."

Matt ceased his advances, searching her face for an indication that she was joking. "What are you, some kind of necrophiliac?"

"I guess I just... wanted to hear her name again. To feel like she's still around," Violet confessed. *Why was she telling him this?*

"Yeah, I understand." Matt sought her lips again, but Violet broke away.

"Don't you want to know my real name?"

"Violet – just like the hair, right?" He drew her locks through his fingers, clutching the roots and arching back her head until she was unable to avoid his penetrating stare. "I heard Lucy call you by it several times. No more games, eh? The truth is, I know *what* you are, and no name is going to change that."

Matt curled his hand around the back of her thigh, hitching up her leg so it was wrapped around his waist. She heard the other fumbling with his belt buckle and attempted to squirm free. "Matt –"

"Shut up!" he hissed, frustrated by the inability to see what he was doing. "You've been teasing my dick all night. I know you want it."

"I haven't, and I don't." Even as Violet's lips moved, even as the words hovered in the air, her body still craved to be satisfied. She didn't doubt that he'd already felt the moistness between her legs.

Matt unzipped his flies and yanked her knickers down over her butt cheeks. A few more seconds and it wouldn't just be her dignity in ruins, but her relationships with the only two people on this earth who cared about her as much as she did them.

"I'll scream," Violet threatened.

"I'll make sure of it."

"Just stop!" Her arm flew up with speed, and there was a loud crack as her palm connected with his fleshy cheek. Matt stilled his panting, easing his weight from her. Violet walloped him again, this time using her shoulder to power the blow.

"You little slag!" Matt forced her arm against the damp wall. Suffocated her with what was too ferocious to be a kiss, pinching her bottom lip between his teeth like a clumsy teenager.

Violet groaned as the whirring sensations in her crotch journeyed upwards to her chest and into her drumming heart. Lust bloomed into a desire that sank deeper than her consciousness could reach, but it wasn't for sex. It burned her from the inside like a demon fighting to be set loose. A hunger that had to be satiated.

With an uncontrollable surge of strength, her head lurched forwards and she dug her teeth into Matt's shoulder, not realising how deep she'd gone until his roar thundered through the passageway. Gripping a handful of Violet's hair, Matt used it to wrench back her head and then swiped the back of his fist across her face. The momentum sent her flying onto her front, limbs splayed over the concrete like a human starfish. She hadn't much fat on her to cushion the descent, but the alcohol acted as a natural painkiller.

Violet rolled onto her back, half expecting Matt to force himself on her there and then, but he was more concerned by the gushing wound on his shoulder.

"You crazy whore!" he screamed. "Look at what you did to me!"

The metallic smell of blood contaminated the air, filling the alley like a gas cloud. Even more incredible than this heightened perception was the fact that she'd managed to bite through his cotton shirt.

"Bitch, you'd better not have AIDS," Matt continued to rant, while pacing the narrow space. This prompted Violet to check her split lip, but damage from the kiss was minimal and the blood wetting her chin wasn't her own. She retched up a puddle of multicoloured vomit onto the floor beside her.

"Ugh – fuck this, I'm outta here. Goddamn skank!" Matt turned and stormed away. His footfalls echoed down the alleyway, blending with his curses.

Violet tried rising to her knees, but the abrasions on them were too raw to bear. Whatever adrenaline had aided in her scuffle had served its purpose, which was more than could be said for Matt's cheap shirt. She reached into her handbag, which she didn't remember dropping, and rooted through it for a tissue to dab her mouth with. The aching in her cheek came secondary to the sticky film on her tongue, and all she could think about was rinsing the revolting taste away.

Violet wasn't sure what prompted her to look up, but there was no escaping the sensation that she was being watched. Straight away, she perceived the tall, narrow silhouette blocking the entrance to the alley. At first she thought it was Matt coming back for another go and scrambled to her feet; but as she receded he drew nearer, as if they were connected by a length of rope. The alley opened up to some kind of yard to the rear of the opposite buildings – quite literally a dead end. It seemed as though the two of them were in a standoff for hours, like wild animals anticipating each other's reactions. If they were the predator then she was undoubtedly the prey.

Once Violet was better able to focus, she saw that the figure was wearing a trench coat, but details beyond that were camouflaged by shadow.

"You're worth more than this, Violet. So much more..." A man's voice travelled down the passageway, not that their gender came as a surprise to Violet. She narrowed her eyes to sharpen her vision, but the restricted lighting made it impossible.

"Who are you?" Her words carried an echo, making her sound bolder than she felt.

"You might know me as Mr Screaming Orgasm. It's a pleasure to finally meet you."

"Y-you're that creep from the bar?" Violet stuffed her hand into her bag and felt for her keys, gripping them in her fist like tiny daggers. "Have you been following me all night?"

"Yes."

"Why? You weren't with that asshole, were you?" Violet referred to Matt.

The stranger chuckled, a brief but welcome interlude to his unnerving demeanour. "I think you already know the answer to that," he said.

"Well, thanks for the help. Get a kick out of seeing women being roughed up, do you?"

"Actually, it wasn't *you* that I was worried about." The man took a solitary step towards her, pausing when she recoiled. "If I was going to hurt you then, trust me, you wouldn't know about it until it was too late."

That's comforting, Violet thought. She relaxed her grip on the keys, which were still secreted in her handbag. It wasn't that she trusted the man but, rather, her own instincts seemed to be driving her now. Whoever he was and whatever his motives, that intrusion of threat had dissipated as soon as Matt had left the alleyway.

"So, what's the deal? Are you some kind of stalker or...?"

"You wouldn't believe me if I told you," the man replied. "I just wanted to make my presence known so the next time we meet won't be as... tense, shall we say."

"Next time?" Violet managed a coarse laugh. "You need to work on your chat-up lines."

The man didn't counter, but even in the gloom, she could feel his grin on her.

"We shall meet again," he enforced. "And when the time comes, you'll be the one seeking me out. No one can help you like I can."

"What makes you think I need help?"

"You feel like you're losing control. Like there's a monster inside of you, and while you fight to cling onto your humanity, a part of you yearns to explore that deepest, darkest layer of yourself."

"Oh, I see." Violet crossed her arms brazenly over her chest. "Getting inside my head is the easiest route into my pants, right? Don't try that psychoanalytic crap on me. I might be hammered but I'm not helpless."

"We'll see." The man tucked his hands into his coat pockets, an action that threw Violet into defence mode again. As he turned sideways to leave the alley, the street became visible behind him and civilisation resurfaced. Violet watched him shrinking towards the opening and forbid herself from calling after him, no matter how much that voice nagged in the back of her mind.

"By the way..." the man stopped, "you're going about it all wrong."

Violet couldn't help herself. "What?"

"These urges that you've been having: no man will be able to satisfy them. Bringing your frustrations out onto the external will alleviate those blazing within you, for a short period at least. Next time, try doing it without hurting anyone."

Matt's image crowded her thoughts, memories of teeth burrowing through skin bringing a dreaded sense to the man's riddles. A mind devoured by hatred had eliminated not only her arousal, but every scrap of common sense and regard for what was deemed as normal human behaviour.

Violet saw the man take a right turn out of the alley and tottered after him. "Hey, wait! Who are you? How did you know my name?"

She emerged onto the street seconds later, eyes sweeping the route that he'd taken, but the area was deserted. There were no cars on the road, and even the taxi that she'd tried flagging down earlier was gone. Squawks of merriment could still be heard from the main street around the corner and, folding her arms to envelop herself in her own body heat, Violet headed briskly back to civilisation. Only when the clarity of her thoughts returned did she wonder how the man could have possibly heard her and Lucy nickname him Mr Screaming Orgasm.

CHAPTER THREE

The March air was still keen from the remnants of winter, despite the sun trying to peek out from behind drifting clouds. It wasn't enough to provide much warmth, but still a pleasant day for a stroll through Darley Park, situated a short bus ride away from the city centre. The picturesque park was a hotspot for families and tourists with its nature reserve, wildlife sites and various activities that Violet paid little heed to. She made the familiar hike along a walking trail that ran alongside the River Derwent, inhaling the freshness of nature and absorbing the sights, smells and sounds that it offered. It was invigorating – the best hangover remedy that she'd come across in years. It was hard to believe that the busy city lay upon the banks of this very river.

Violet started humming, the clomping of her pumps against the parched dirt like a backbeat to her invented melody. Oblivious to her surroundings, she only spotted the couple coming towards her at the last second. Huddled together against the breeze, they graciously swerved out of the way.

"Thanks," Violet mumbled.

The woman flashed her a smile, but it was the sympathetic kind. Violet pulled up her hood to obscure the red blotch on her cheek from where Matt had struck her last night. With her sickly complexion and under-eye bags, she didn't blame the woman for having assumed the worst. Violet had skipped her grooming routine that morning and could easily be mistaken for a crack addict.

A couple of minutes later, she approached her destination: a wooden bench nestled amongst the tree line. Immediately catching her eye was the bunch of daffodils tied to the back of it with a tatty piece of string. Violet slumped down beside it, her legs as weary as the rest of her, and rifled through the flowers for a card – not that the sender was any mystery to her. Daffodils were her mother's favourite.

Violet leaned over to sniff their sweet scent. They were relatively fresh, so Beverly must have been in the area over the last day or so. Violet had an urge to rip them from the bench and launch them into the river, but desecration wasn't in her nature.

"I see Mum's finally shown her face," she uttered, as if Isabelle was sitting in place of the flowers. "Nice of her to pay me a visit. I haven't seen her since..."

Violet refrained from mentioning the funeral, having blocked out memories of it for the last two months. Most of that day was snippets playing back in her mind, as if she'd watched it through a faulty television set. What she couldn't forget was the hysterical lamenting coming from the crumpled form of her mother on the floor – talk about milking it. Violet hadn't felt a shred of sympathy for the woman; if anything it was resentment, for that was the point at which she'd had to accept that she would never see, hold, cry or laugh with her sister ever again.

"I'm lost without you, Izzy," she whispered. "All those years I spent looking out for you, trying to be the protective big sister, but now I realise that you'd have been fine on your own. I needed you a whole lot more than you needed me."

Violet gazed up at the sky, waiting for answers that she knew would never come. Sometimes a bird would chirp or a leaf would rustle and she'd convince herself that it was a sign from Isabelle – that if she listened attentively enough, one day, she'd be able to understand the language of the dead. Violet plucked a daffodil from the bouquet and tossed it onto the ground where Isabelle had taken her last breath. Despite the coroner reporting that death would have been relatively quick after losing consciousness, the pain must have been incomparable to what any ordinary person had experienced. Violet imagined her lying there, bleeding out. Wondered what she'd thought, what she'd felt; what she'd heard if anything. Looking at the scenery now, at the weeping willows dipping into the undisturbed river, the tranquillity of it all was polluted by a holographic hell.

Violet closed her eyes, allowing the tears to slide down her cheeks. Isabelle had been six years her junior and studying for her first year at university. A born artist, Violet had always encouraged her to pursue her dreams. *Does that make it my fault?* It was a question that she often asked herself; after all, she was the reason for Isabelle having been there in the first place.

'It'll be good to get some quiet inspiration,' she'd urged. 'You go ahead, I'll meet you after work and treat you to a Chinese.'

The sun had been unusually bright considering that winter was underway. Violet could hear the children playing in her thoughts: innocent, mirthful laughter that would later metamorphose into ghastly wails of dismay. As soon as Violet had seen the police blocking the entrance to the park, she knew in her very core that Isabelle was dead. The next couple of hours were like an incomplete jigsaw puzzle. Much like the effects of intoxication, chunks of time were inaccessible; although, ironically, she hadn't had a sip of alcohol that day. Was it possible to be grief drunk?

"It isn't fair." Violet's voice quivered. "It isn't fucking fair!"

She hammered the base of her fist down onto the bench, the wood creaking as if in pain, yet it was her wrist that bore the impact. She clenched her teeth, jaw muscles bulging beneath the flesh; breaths confined in her throat.

Why her? Why Isabelle? She'd spend all night smashing the bench to splinters if it would relieve an iota of the hurt that crippled her every second of every day, but the only thing that might partially satisfy her was getting revenge on the psychopath who'd expunged Isabelle from this godforsaken planet.

Violet shook her head before flicking the teardrops from her cheeks. Re-evaluating everything was pointless: no one had any answers then, and pulverising her knuckles would serve to piss her off even more. She didn't know why she kept coming back to that site, for the police and forensics had combed the entire park for evidence and witnesses that didn't exist. Somehow, it was as if Isabelle's essence was still there, and that tiny granule of solace was all that kept Violet on the border of sanity.

After leaving the park, she walked back into town and stopped by at the local Boots store to purchase some items. It was a half-hour trek, but she had nothing better to do and the fresh air seemed helpful in alleviating her nausea. She took a bus back to the village of Littleover, where she occupied a semi-detached property that had effectively been chopped in half to create two compact flats. Violet had moved in at the age of seventeen after receiving her first paycheque, and she'd remained a happy tenant ever since. Quite often, Izzy would turn up seeking refuge from their drunken mother.

Violet typed in the key code at the main entrance and then trudged up the staircase that led from the reception hall to the first floor. She let herself into her flat, guzzled a glass of water and then emptied the pregnancy test out of the pharmacy bag. She didn't need to read the instructions – it was the second one she'd bought over the course of a few weeks – and instead she plodded wearily into the bathroom. Five minutes later, she was sitting in the open-plan kitchen-living area staring at the 'not pregnant' sign in the display window. Same results as always.

Violet stuffed the evidence into her bag to dispose of on her next outing, somewhere that Dean wouldn't be at risk of finding it. Then she swung her legs up onto the sofa and flumped back against the cushions, closing her eyes in an effort to blunt the thumping ache behind them. That's the last thing she remembered.

***

The knocking was faraway, yet persistent enough to wake her. Violet opened her eyes, and the sound came whooshing into the room as if to greet her. She went from flat to vertical in less than a second, the dizzy sparkles blending with her surroundings to give no clue as to her whereabouts. The one thing she was certain of was that, beneath the duvet, she was absent her clothing.

Perhaps out of habit, she reached for her bedside lamp and was relieved when the bulb shed its warmth over her glacial hand. At least she was in the comfort of her own bed and not that of a random stranger – then again, it wouldn't have been the first time.

The knocking became more insistent. Violet glanced over the empty space next to her while scrambling out of bed, concluding that Dean must have locked himself out of the flat. She made a gap in the curtains to see if his van was parked outside and was surprised to find that the sun was only just beginning to set.

"Hang on a sec!" she yelled, scanning the floor for some clothing to throw on. In the end she grabbed her silk dressing gown from the back of a chair and, with no time to ferret through her underwear drawer, she slung it on while making a dash for the front door.

On her way past the bathroom, a glimmer from her peripheral vision yanked at her ankles like invisible tethers. She paused just ahead of the doorway, then took two strides backwards. The mirror above the sink was a spider web of jagged fragments trimmed with blood, as if something had been propelled into its centre. Not only that, but the clothes she'd been wearing earlier were strewn across the floor. Almost with a sense of apprehension, she glanced down at her right hand and gasped at the sight of her split, bloodied knuckles.

The rapping on the front door started up again.

"Fuck's sake," Violet cursed, before yelling down the hallway, "Who's there?"

"It's the police."

The police? Violet nearly shrieked the words out loud. She pulled the bathroom door to and then scurried down the hall on her tiptoes like some kind of insect. Peeking through the spy hole in the front door, the high-visibility jackets were unmistakable.

"Shit." As the thoughts and fears hammered away at what was left of Violet's nerves, she tied her robe at the front and let loose her hair in the hopes of disguising her bruised cheek. She ran a finger over the tender flesh, wincing at the swelling that didn't seem to have reduced at all since her encounter with Matt.

After scanning for anything else unusual, she went to unlock the door but found there was no need to. The locking mechanism was loose and the entire handle came off in her hand when she pressed down on it. There wasn't much she could do as the door opened by itself and a curious face regarded her through the widening crevice.

"Violet Kendal?" said a slight blonde woman, who looked as menacing as a dormouse.

"Yeah," Violet replied.

"I'm PC Young, and this is my colleague, PC Richards."

Violet angled her neck so she could see the second officer through the gap in the door. She wondered if she should ask for ID after the succession of weirdos that she'd attracted of late, but with the absence of a door lock, she'd have been powerless to prevent them from forcing entry into the flat.

"We just need to ask you some questions in regards to a gentleman that was reported missing yesterday," PC Young informed Violet. "May we come inside?"

"Er, sure." Violet opened the door to make room for the officers. Once they were inside, she pushed it shut while wiggling the handle back into place and praying that it would hold.

Not wanting her visitors there for longer than necessary, Violet didn't invite them into the lounge. The three of them stood facing one another in the claustrophobic hallway until Violet could tolerate the male officer's rigid stare no longer.

"So, who's gone missing?" she asked, rather flippantly.

"Matthew Brody. We've received information that leads us to believe you might be one of the last people who saw him. Can you tell us about your whereabouts on the night of Friday 17th March?" PC Young waited patiently for an answer, but Violet was still trying to process the snippet of information that she'd been given.

"You mean... Matthew as in *Matt*?" Violet wanted to clarify, despite the fact that there must have been hundreds of 'Matts' in Derbyshire alone.

"According to Matthew's friends, you met in Cherry's Bar on Friday night," the officer prompted her.

"Missing as in abducted?" Another delayed response.

"That's what we're hoping to find out. Can you confirm that you were with him?" The question was more pressing this time.

"A group of us hit the clubs together, but we weren't friends or anything. He said he was only in town for the night. We got chatting and things moved on from there. I went along with it because he and my mate –" *Ah, crap, now she'd dropped Lucy into it as well.*

Before Violet could backtrack, PC Young produced a notepad from one of her pockets and flipped through its pages. "Are you referring to Lucy Smith?" she said, glancing up at Violet.

"Yeah. Did Matt's friends mention her as well?"

"We've already spoken to Miss Smith. Can you remember what time you left the bar and where you went to afterwards?"

"Umm..." *Nope, nothing.* "I guess I was pretty wasted. I know that we circulated around some of the usual hotspots – Walkabout was definitely one of them."

"Okay. What time did you leave town?"

"Just before closing time, around 2.30 a.m. or something. Haven't the others already given you this information?"

"Yes, but we still need to corroborate. Where did you go after that, and was anybody with you?"

Aware that her answer could impact the whole investigation, Violet tried to deliberate without causing a lengthy hesitation. The only thought rotating in her mind was why Lucy hadn't warned her that the police were sniffing about.

"I remember getting into a taxi," Violet told the officers. Withholding information may have been a crime but, morally, it wasn't as bad as lying.

"On your own?" enquired the female.

"Yeah, Lucy and I live on opposite sides of town. We don't travel together unless we're staying over at each other's houses."

PC Young scribbled something into her notepad, while the male officer gazed idly around the hallway. Thankfully, he didn't look like he had too much going on behind the eyes. He reminded Violet of Lurch from the Addams Family.

"Who left first, you or Lucy?" PC Young went on to ask.

"Lucy, I waved her off myself."

"And when was the last time you saw Matthew?"

Time to say goodbye to those morals, Violet's conscience spoke. "Just before heading home. We – Lucy and I – said our goodbyes and that's the end. How did you get our details anyway?"

"Lucy's number was in Matthew's mobile contacts. One of his friends handed it over to us."

"Why did they have his phone?"

"Apparently, he left it in one of the clubs. His colleagues claim that he went outside for some fresh air and never came back. What taxi firm did you use?"

"I don't know, whichever was free at the time. But I assure you that I *was* alone," Violet stressed. This was feeling more like an interrogation with each second, and she wouldn't be surprised if her paranoia was putting her under even more suspicion.

The PC continued to jot things down while adding, "Can you remember anything else that might help us with our investigation? Any suspicious people or activity at any time during the night?"

"Like I said, I was wasted." Violet gulped. "Anyway, don't folk have to be missing for more than twenty-four hours before you guys will follow it up?"

She hoped it would deflect their queries long enough to give her some breathing space and almost thought it had worked when PC Young separated pen from paper. "Yes?" It was a question rather than a statement.

"Well, if he's only been missing since last night then what's to say that he hasn't copped off with some girl? He was far from sober, maybe he thinks he's lost his phone or something."

"You do realise that today is Sunday?" said PC Richards. Violet didn't know what astonished her more: the fact that he'd opened his mouth or that she'd managed to sleep an entire day away.

"Oh, yeah, so it is." She finished with a stilted chuckle.

"Well, thank you for your time." PC Young swapped the notepad for a card out of her pocket, which she handed to Violet. "Here's my email address, along with some contact numbers should you have any further information. If something comes back to you then please get in touch, no matter how insignificant it seems. Remember to quote the case reference number as well, I've made a note of it for you."

"Thanks. Should I expect to hear from you again?"

"Not at this point. We have your contact details anyway."

"Cool." Violet dived in front of the officers before they reached the door, carefully manipulating the handle in order to disguise the vandalism.

"Sorry I couldn't be of much help. Hope you find him safe." It was all she could think of to say.

"Yes. Thanks again, Violet." PC Young smiled.

"Goodbye," added PC Richards, following his colleague out of the flat.

Violet watched them descend the staircase, waiting until she heard the main door clang shut before retreating into the flat. Down the hallway she ran, into her bedroom where she searched in vain for her mobile phone. After some time, she gave up flinging items of clothing around and went to check the living area.

The hunt led Violet to her handbag on the coffee table, where the pregnancy test box was still concealed. She tried to calm her mind enough to locate the last twenty-four hours' worth of memories, but it was as though the contents of her skull had been evacuated. She found her mobile in her bag and wasn't surprised to discover that the battery was dead, so she returned to the bedroom to charge it. The missed call notifications popped up instantly, and her message inbox was cluttered with texts from Dean. She skimmed through them, her eyes settling on the last received:

'Coming over, I'm worried.'

Violet compared the time the message was sent to that on her clock. There was a two-hour interval, and it took Dean less than twenty minutes to drive over from his place. If it was him who'd broken the door then where was he now?

"Oh, crap." Violet remembered the discarded clothing in her bathroom; the fractured mirror and the fact that she'd woken up starkers.

She placed the phone onto her bedside table and brought a hand up to her mouth, chewing her nails. "No," she mumbled. "I never told Matt where I lived... did I?"

He could have followed you.

It was as if another entity had spoken from inside her. Violet leaped off the bed and made hurriedly for the bathroom, where she eyed the heap of clothing as if it might come to life and smother her. Reluctantly, she bent down to inspect the garments. She held her hoody up by its sleeves to find that everything was intact, and then did the same with her vest. Light peeked through the four slits in the centre like sunrays through open blinds. Not those characteristic of scissors: they were too rough-edged. Rather, it looked like it had been clawed by something... something much bigger than any domestic animal that she could think of.

Violet chucked down the clothing and staggered backwards, clinging onto the doorframe to prevent herself from falling through it. Slowly, she dragged her gaze across to the hand that was latched around the wood. To the grazed knuckles that she'd previously matched with the cracked mirror. None of it made sense, and the multiple scenarios flying around in her skull like a game of tennis almost set her off balance again.

Once her legs had reclaimed some equilibrium, she dashed back to the bedroom and found Lucy's number in her mobile contacts. The first dial tone had barely reached completion before her friend answered, as if she'd been waiting with the phone in her hand.

"Lucy, I think something terrible has happened!" Violet exclaimed. "I just woke up and the door to my flat was busted open. I had no clothes on and... there was blood. Shit, I can't remember anything!"

"Slow down, Vi. Are you at the flat now?" Lucy sounded unnaturally calm given the circumstances.

"Yes – I'm freaking out, Luce!" Violet twisted to face the doorway, almost yanking the charging wire out of her phone. Any moment, she expected Matt to spring out of a shadowy corner and finish what he'd started in that alley two nights ago.

"It's okay, don't panic," Lucy tried to reassure her.

"How can I not panic? The police woke me up banging on the door. I thought it was frigging Saturday!" She quietened her voice, as if PC Lurch and his colleague might still be loitering outside. "What if someone broke in and drugged me? You hear about these things all the time. I'd know if I'd been raped, right?"

"You haven't been raped. It was Dean."

"What?"

"Neither of us could get in touch with you. When the cops showed up at my place this morning, I convinced myself that something bad had happened. Dean had no choice but to break in."

"Oh... thank God!" Violet exhaled into the phone, the heat from the battery causing her palm to sweat. "Where's Dean now? Why didn't he wake me?"

"He wanted to make it to the DIY store before closing to get some bits to fix the door with. Your neighbour downstairs was going to keep an eye on things until he got back. Dean said you were out solid when he arrived."

"Yeah – sorry, I didn't mean to scare you. I was pretty hung over from Friday night. What with everything else going on, I guess my body just needed time to recuperate."

"So it had nothing to do with the empty bottle of vodka that Dean found next to your bed?"

"Huh?"

"You were drunk again, weren't you?"

Immediately aware of the reprimand, Violet flipped her brain over and upside down in search for an answer, almost to the point that it felt bruised. "I don't think so," she answered, honestly. "Did Dean say anything else?"

"Like what?"

Violet reverted to silence. It wouldn't have been the first time that she'd taken her frustrations out on furniture and homeware, or drunk herself to unconsciousness. The slash marks in her vest could have been made by anything with a sharp edge.

"So, about Matt... weird, huh?" She changed the subject.

"I don't want to talk about it, Vi."

"Me neither, I've had enough of it from the cops. You are okay, though?"

"Yeah, I will be. Listen, I've got some family stuff going on right now but if you want me to drop by later –"

"Don't worry about me, I'm fine. You've dealt with enough of my crap for one day. I'll see you at work tomorrow, yeah?"

"Okay, bye."

Violet didn't have time to squeeze in a farewell before the line cut out. She glowered at the phone as if it had disobeyed an order, then replaced it onto the bedside table. She scanned the floor for any clues as to what might have transpired in the last twenty-four hours. Apart from a couple of condom wrappers leftover from the last time Dean had stayed over, there was nothing of significance. Even the so-called vodka bottle had disappeared – no doubt Dean had disposed of it in case the fumes were too much of a temptation for her.

Violet slumped down onto the bed while letting out a few deep breaths. Assuming Dean had seen the state of the bathroom mirror, she still had time to conjure up an explanation. The truth was, as she sat trying to recall whatever memories had been blotted out by the hangover, all she encountered was an impenetrable wall.

CHAPTER FOUR

Violet entered the office building at 9.30 a.m., half an hour after she was due in. She informed her supervisor that the bus had been delayed rather than admitting that she'd overslept, just to add to her list of lies. Then she scurried over to her desk, stealing a quick glance at Lucy and attempting to catch her eye without success.

Violet found the Monday morning post in a tower that almost levelled the top of her computer screen. She cursed while sliding it to the side, convinced that someone had stuck it there deliberately. After draping her sodden coat over a radiator to dry off, she made a start on sorting through the brown and white envelopes.

It was a whole hour before the boss left her throne and vacated to the canteen for a coffee break. Violet slunk past the open door and headed over to Lucy with a couple of files wedged under her arm, so that at least her roaming looked purposeful.

"Hey, how's it going?" she whispered to her friend.

"Fine, I guess." Lucy's soft voice intermingled with the jumble of phone conversations in the background.

"Are you sure? You seemed kind of distant yesterday..." Violet swallowed the globe of shame in her throat. "You're not worried about Matt?"

"Why should I be? I hardly knew the guy."

"I know, but you two seemed to hit it off pretty good. I mean, you gave him your number so you must have wanted to see him again."

Lucy gave an unexpected cackle, bitter and without humour. Violet waited for a reply, but Lucy's attention didn't budge from her computer screen.

"Violet, have you finished sorting out the post yet?" Tina squawked from across the office, as if trying to alert everyone that she was away from her desk.

Violet waved a hand to signal that she'd be over in a minute.

"So, what did you tell the police?" she continued to quiz Lucy.

"I told them the truth: I don't know anything." Lucy looked Violet square in the eyes, her tone cutting. "Why, got something to hide?"

"No. Why would you ask me that?"

Lucy ignored the query. "You do realise that Dean thinks you want to finish with him? That he's the one making you unhappy?"

"Come on, I've apologised for what happened over the weekend. It was a wakeup call if anything – no more binge drinking for me. Besides, I can't afford to keep replacing all of the shit that I smash up."

"Huh?"

"Never mind." Violet shook her head. Dean might have been gullible enough to believe that she'd attacked her property in a fit of temper, but Lucy wouldn't be so easy to convince.

"Anyway," she said, "Dean and I are supposed to be taking it slow. He can't expect me to live in his pocket all the time."

"And that gives you the right to treat him like he doesn't matter? I might have been the one that introduced you, but if it's a bed buddy you're after then you need to make it clear and stop stringing him along."

"Where's this coming from? You know I care about Dean, he's been great these last few months."

"Great as what, a distraction? I can't begin to imagine what you're going through, but you can't hide behind Izzy forever."

"Violet!" Tina interrupted again.

"You should get back to work before you get into even more trouble," said Lucy. "Good luck funding your bad habits without a job."

"What the hell is that supposed to mean?" Violet raised her voice loud enough to attract a couple of half-interested stares from nearby colleagues.

"I saw you and him the other night." Lucy turned to face Violet, her chair almost pivoting with her.

"Who?"

"That creep, Matt. After I'd got into the taxi, I saw him come wobbling out of the club and it looked like he was following you. I practically leaped out of the car before it had stopped moving, only to find you down some back alley with your knickers around your kneecaps."

"I didn't –" Violet was conscious of her volume and modulated it before more heads raised. "Nothing happened, and if you'd stuck around long enough then you'd have seen why. Yes, he tried it on and I'll admit that, for a *second*, I thought it was what I needed. But I couldn't betray Dean like that, and I certainly wouldn't risk our friendship for the sake of a one-night stand. It's like my hormones are all messed up, I can't explain it."

"Well, you're going to have to if the police find out."

"You mean you won't say anything?"

Lucy sighed before shaking her head. "It's too late now anyway. Besides, you might be a psychotic bitch but I know that you wouldn't hurt anyone. At least, not deliberately…"

Violet wasn't sure if it was a question, but she answered as though it was. "I have no idea where Matt is or what happened to him. Look, I know I've screwed up but can we go somewhere for lunch and talk properly? Please, Luce, I don't have anyone else to turn to."

"You've got Dean."

"Like you said, he's a sensitive guy. The last thing I need is relationship issues on top of everything else."

"So it is a relationship now? Make your mind up."

"Oh, fine, if I'm such a pain in the arse then consider yourself unburdened."

Violet's vexation didn't improve when she turned and collided with Tina, who'd been standing behind her for God knows how long.

"*Wh-at?*" Dramatically, she split the word into two syllables. Better that than Tina's melon skull.

The woman's lower jaw dropped open and was nestled somewhere amid her double chin. It was a few seconds before she replied, in a less domineering manner than before, "I'm expecting some documents in order to register a new doctor. It's a special delivery and I need to confirm that they've arrived."

Violet could hardly focus on the words through that squeaky, nasal voice. It reminded her of the party trick, whereby the nozzle of a deflating balloon is pinched together and the air screams upon its release. Violet often envisioned choking the woman with her own vocal cords. As if to spare herself the bother, her fist struck out with such an explosive force that Tina's head snapped backwards until her neck cracked. Blood erupted from her caved-in nose, but Violet's dismay was halted by the amazement at her own strength. She held her hand up in front of her, not the least bit affected by her reddened knuckles. When she looked back at Tina, whose unscathed head had slotted back into its normal position, the shock sent her reeling backwards.

"Is something wrong?" Tina's concern was begrudging at most. Perhaps she was more bemused than anything.

Violet glanced at her knuckles again to find that they, too, had returned to their original condition. For a fleeting second, she was almost disappointed.

Tina might have said something else – Violet didn't know or care – but for the fear of the delusion turning into something more substantial, she barged past the woman and retreated to her desk. Tina didn't approach her for the rest of the morning.

***

Violet had decided to take a late lunch in order to avoid the midday traffic from retail staff and shoppers in the city centre, which was a couple of minutes' walk from the office. As always, roaming the streets during the day was a separate world to when the sun was replaced with neon from the bars and clubs. It even sounded different: lively chit-chat and laughter escalating into drunken cheers and profanity.

Before entering the familiar alleyway, Violet scoped the region to check for bystanders. There was a sprinkling of people up and down the little side street, but they seemed too focused on their various destinations to pay her any regard. At least there were no police officers lurking or, more importantly, no Mr Screaming Orgasm. Violet hadn't given the man much thought with all of the other drama that she had going on. In fact, it had only just occurred to her that he was quite possibly one of the last people to have set eyes on Matt.

Memories flashed before her like movie stills as she slipped into the grim, lonely passageway. It amazed her how much she shivered in her coat and trousers, as opposed to a few nights ago when she'd been wearing half as much. *What if Matt had collapsed from blood loss and died of hypothermia in a gutter somewhere?* she thought.

Violet's eyes traced the ground as she pushed forth, all the while casting anxious glances over her shoulder: she couldn't shake the feeling that she was being watched. The reek of urine grew stronger as she ventured further into the alley, and if that didn't make her vomit then the thought of Matt's grubby mitts pawing at her intimate parts would surely cause her stomach matter to ejaculate. She wrapped her arms around her front, hugging herself for comfort and warmth. Her environment was disgusting. *She* was disgusting.

Finally, she reached the exact spot in which the episode had taken place. Violet could tell from the chunky, dried-up splattering of puke on the ground; the bulk of it having been rinsed away by the previous night's rainfall. She recalled Matt's rants about catching AIDS and vaguely wondered if, should the police discover any CCTV leads and decide to sweep the area for evidence, they'd be able to detect traces of his blood in the rancid substance.

"Okay," Violet exhaled, "no one's been here yet. That's good. Clues..."

Violet figured that apart from Matt and herself, only two people were privy to their alleyway fumble: Lucy and the creep from Cherry's Bar. Something told her that Mr Screaming Orgasm wasn't the type of guy to talk to cops. Retracing Matt's steps seemed like the most practical way to uncover his whereabouts, and this was as good a starting point as any.

Lingering between the walls of the alley, the musty air was tinged with something a little more potent. Violet's nostrils twitched, first in curiosity at its sweetness, and then more purposively as the odour would repeatedly fade and intensify. She wasn't sure whether it was that or some other inclination that led her towards the far end of the alley, as if pursuing a trail of invisible breadcrumbs. There was no exit, just the back wall of a building marred in graffiti of the usual nature: obscenities, who shagged who and, of course, a giant penis.

Eventually, Violet came to a commercial dumpster that she presumed belonged to the restaurant on the opposite street to the one that she'd emerged from. Again, she didn't know what compelled her to peer inside, although the vision of finding Matt's disembodied corpse caused a slight hesitation. On top of the mound of bin bags and other loose matter that had decayed beyond recognition, a strip of cloth was laid out. Unable to read the sketchy, reddish-brown lettering, she leaned inside to pick it up. Somehow, she knew that it was meant for her.

'Gustro Bar, tonight, 9 p.m.'

Violet stared at the material – cotton, to be precise – with widened eyes. Though she couldn't believe what she did next, again, it seemed as though an inner force was governing her. A voice that she wasn't entirely sure came from her own subconscious.

With the rag clutched in both hands, she brought it up to her nose and inhaled. The unidentified whiff that she'd perceived earlier rushed into her nasal cavity, and the crusty substance used to paint the message became sickeningly clear.

Not only was she looking at human blood, but also a scrap of clothing with residue of masculine fragrance absorbed into it. At a guess, it was part of a shirt.

The same shirt that Matt had been wearing on Friday night.

CHAPTER FIVE

It was forty-five minutes before last orders at Gustro Bar and Grill. Violet had purposely walked in fifteen minutes later than scheduled, having been hiding in the bus shelter on the opposite side of the road to survey anyone who entered and exited the restaurant. There hadn't been any suspicious-looking characters, just couples and the occasional group of people. All the while she'd been debating over whether or not to go home and pretend she'd never discovered the gruesome message, but her curiosity was unquenchable. Earlier that afternoon, it had crossed her mind that Matt may have been toying with her – some kind of revenge prank for rejecting his sexual advances. In any case, it was a public place so whoever she was supposed to be meeting couldn't have wanted her dead. At least, not tonight.

Violet loitered at the bar a while, her eyes coasting over the diners as if she was on a blind date – not that her attire would suit the occasion. She looked like she'd just nipped in to use the loo, and she was beginning to get the same paranoid feeling as she had done back in the alleyway. While she wasn't unmindful of having caught the stares of two men across the bar, the sensation she had was more intrusive than that.

As the talons of winter grazed against her flesh, hairs stiffening on the back of her neck, Violet whirled around with a violent shudder. He was in her line of sight before she'd even realised it, her eyes knowing exactly where to pinpoint. The tempestuous waves in her stomach made her feel sea sick, and she had the legs to match. Tottering over to the booth in the furthest corner, she forced herself to a halt before the table edge did it for her.

"I should have known that this was down to *you*," Violet spat.

The dark-featured man stared up at her, lips peaking at the corners even though his face was square. The overhead lighting shone over his crown, the contrasting shadows eclipsing his eyes like shades. Violet remembered that weak-headed feeling upon first seeing him in Cherry's Bar, how she'd blamed it on a combination of the drunken spins and technicoloured lighting. Yet as she stood before him now, that same internal swirling threatened to set her off balance.

"Miss Kendal, won't you join me?" The man used his fork to gesture the padded chair opposite him. Violet noticed the red smears on the silver and glared distastefully at the slab of meat on his plate, bathing in its own juices.

"Why did you lure me here? Is this blackmail?" she demanded.

"*Take a seat.*"

Violet did so, not because she was commanded to but to avoid the embarrassment of collapsing in front of everyone.

"Didn't I tell you that the next time we met, you'd be seeking me out?" The man spoke again.

"I didn't really have a choice. Isn't this all a bit risky? The police are looking for Matt, which means they're also looking for you. At least, they will be when I show them the little gift that you left for me to find."

"What makes you so sure that it has any relevance or connection to our friend, Matthew?"

"He was wearing that shirt on Friday night, I recognised the smell." *And the blood*, Violet almost blurted out. If saying it made it any easier to believe then she would have done.

"That's quite a talent you have." The man almost looked amused. "However, it doesn't explain why you went back to the alley or how you came upon the dumpster in the first place."

"I was following my instincts."

"As you should do. Our instincts are never wrong, even when we think they are. Oftentimes, it just means that we haven't interpreted them correctly."

"Cut the bullshit. What did you do to Matt?"

"Me?" The man arched one of his brows to its highest point. "I wasn't the one that attacked him. I didn't take a chunk out of his shoulder after he tried to –"

"*Sshh!*" Violet glanced behind her, to both sides, and then back again. "Keep your voice down, damn it."

"Ah, so I take it the police are uninformed of your sordid encounter with the missing? Tut-tut, Violet."

The man started hacking at the steak, and Violet winced at the scraping of his cutlery against the porcelain. She caught him smirking, as though mindful of her discomfort.

"Want some?" He waved the fork under her nose, the sliver of beef weeping blood.

"It's practically still breathing." Violet gagged.

"When did you become vegetarian?"

"How did you..."

"Your colouring," the man said, before she could finish the question. "There's a lack of iron in your blood. Humans were designed to eat meat, it's what nature intended."

"My body seems to be rejecting everything recently – not that it's any of your business. I can't stand the sight of dead meat on my plate, ever since my sister –"

It was the man's unshakable, deep-eyed gaze that prevented Violet from saying anything else. She could feel him digging around in her mind like a parasite, as if he already knew everything there was to know about her.

"Look," she said, at last, "if I wanted to talk about my diet then I'd consult a nutritionist. I know when someone's tormenting me for the hell of it, so why don't you –"

As Violet started to rise, a hand closed around her wrist in a grip that was gentle and effortless, yet firm as glue. The only part of him that moved was his arm which, though shrouded by a long-sleeved shirt, it was more slender than stocky. Violet concentrated on his face as he leaned into the warmth of the lighting, and it was like looking at it for the first time. Gone were the shadows that created mystery and depth. Now he was just a man in his thirties, the curves of his cheeks adding a youth to those hardened eyes.

"My apologies. Let's start again, shall we? I'm Joe Carter."

Violet's backside reunited with the seat without any additional manipulation. She might have appeared charmed to some, but in reality it felt more like hypnotism.

"The last thing I want to do is mock you," Joe went on. "I was trying to get a feel for your personality, see what makes you tick. Call it a habit if you like, but spontaneous reactions are usually the most genuine – you understand?"

"I understand that you're a dick," Violet retorted.

"I prefer the term 'bastard', but for you I'll make an exception."

Was that sarcasm? Violet wondered. She'd always had a knack for reading people, understanding their intentions and motives, but with Joe Carter she got nothing.

"You must have tracked Matt down after he left the alley," she continued to probe. "Are you saying that he willingly handed over his shirt, why, because you said 'please'?"

"The state he was in, I could have taken a lot more," mumbled Joe, before changing the subject. "What intrigues me is why you're so concerned for a man who tried to sexually assault you."

"Morals aside, I don't particularly like having the police on my back," Violet answered. "And like I said, I've still got the piece of evidence that you left for me. Consider it as leverage."

Joe shrugged, finally letting go of her wrist. "Do what you wish, it's not my fingerprints that they'll find all over it."

"So, you were watching me earlier – I knew it!" Violet made a swift recovery. "You know what I think? You went to Cherry's Bar on Friday night with the sole purpose of catching a fish. You thought I looked vulnerable and decided to try your luck at grooming me. I mean, why else would a grown man be drinking alone in a predominantly student bar? What are you, a pimp or some sadistic pervert that gets his kicks out of toying with emotional women?"

"Neither. I'm not that kind of man. I'm nothing like Matthew."

"Well, you obviously think I need saving. Maybe you decided to teach him a very permanent lesson."

It didn't take long for her implication to sink in, as was evident by Joe's cocky simper crumbling to reveal the steely foundations that made him the ominous presence that he was.

"The shirt was to attract your attention, nothing more. If you believe otherwise then walk out of that door right now." He nodded towards the restaurant's entrance. "Go on, run to the police and tell them everything. There are witnesses and CCTV all around us, I couldn't stop you even if I wanted to."

With a huff, Violet flopped back against the chair and folded her arms like a petulant child. Joe's smirk reappeared as promptly as it had faded.

"I thought not. I just want to help you, Violet." Joe brought the fork up to his mouth and inserted the meat as delicately as a surgeon performing an operation. He'd scarcely chewed it before swallowing, and Violet swore she heard the macerated chunk slide down his gullet.

"Prove it," she said. "Tell me what the hell is going on or else I swear I'll go to the police. I don't care what happens to me, I've got nothing left to lose."

"That, I can believe." Joe smiled sympathetically. "It says a lot about a person when they fear not death, but life itself. Yet the very fact that you're here seeking answers tells me that there's at least one thing keeping you on this earth."

"Maybe. But I assure you that I'm *not* the reason."

"So, you don't wish to know what's happening to you: the sickness, the rage, the blackouts? Why this succulent piece of cuisine gets you wetter than the sight of a man's cock?"

In ordinary circumstances, the statement would have seen Violet rolling off the chair in a paroxysm of giggles. As it happened, her taste buds were standing on end and she suddenly felt more ravenous than she had done in a long time.

"See what happens," said Joe, "when you stop fighting nature's intent? As my father used to say: 'He who stands at the top of the food chain is God; everything else is already dead.' Wouldn't you agree?"

"I-I don't know what game you're playing but..." *so juicy, so tender*, "... I don't need you or anyone else to tell me how I should and shouldn't be feeling." Violet swallowed a mouthful of saliva. "I'm going crazy and that's all there is to it. The doctors say it's grief –"

"Fuck the doctors." The words were curt enough to rip Violet from the daze that she'd found herself in. "You're changing, Violet. You're becoming who you were born to be, and no amount of counselling or medication is going to prevent the inevitable. The longer you delay it, the worse it'll get – not just for yourself, but for everyone around you. We can give you a reason to live again."

"We?" It was the only word that Violet could focus on.

"There are others like you and me. People that I've guided, and who have come to trust me as I hope you shall, too, some day."

Joe wiped his mouth with a serviette before producing a twenty-pound note out of his trouser pocket. He tucked it beneath a wine glass that was still half-full and then stood up, slinging on his trademark trench coat. Violet had to cock back her head to take in his lofty form, and she realised that he wasn't as puny as she'd first thought.

"Coming?" he said, while flicking up the collar of his coat. Violet wasn't sure whether the action was done out of habit or for show; either way, it was annoying.

"Where?" she asked him.

"If you keep on firing questions, how do you ever expect them to be answered?"

"I'm not going anywhere with –"

Joe was already leaving the restaurant. Seconds later, Violet followed him.

***

The night was dense from the invading shadows cast by the trees that fenced the park. Violet and Joe had been walking in silence for a good ten minutes since leaving the restaurant, mainly due to the distance between them. Violet tailed along several feet behind so at least she had a head start if a chase was to break out. That voice of reason was screaming at her to turn around and go home, and the further they got from the main street, the more she wished that she'd listened.

She allowed another half a minute of silence to elapse before impatience kicked in. "Are you going to tell me where we're going anytime soon? I'm freezing my tits off here, and this is getting weird –*er*," she corrected herself.

"It's not like I have you on a leash."

"Not a physical one," Violet mumbled. "I told people where I was going tonight, so if I disappear then they'll come looking."

She heard Joe snigger, as if he knew it was a lie and that she hadn't disclosed to anyone her plans for the evening. Perhaps because she'd only resolved to go through with them a few minutes before walking into Gustro Bar and Grill.

Joe took a packet of cigarettes out of his coat pocket. "My dear, I watched you tear through a man's flesh using your teeth. Which one of us is more dangerous, I wonder?"

"That was the adrenaline; plus, alcohol thins the blood. Don't you know your biology? Did you even go to school?" What began as sarcasm turned into genuine interest.

"I thought we had an understanding? If I wanted to hurt you then I've had plenty of opportunities – when you were spying from the lonely bus shelter, for example."

"You saw me? How the hell –"

When Joe stopped walking, Violet almost recoiled at the thought of him whirling around with an extended fist. With a cigarette wedged between his lips, he exchanged the packet for a lighter. The flame sparked to life, bringing a temporary glow to his features. He sucked on the filter and then blew out a steady plume of smoke into the frigid air. Violet made a point of coughing – for all of her bad habits, smoking wasn't one of them.

"You were right about one thing: you *are* a bastard," she grumbled.

"Finally, we agree on something."

Violet's forehead was beginning to ache from the scowl. Joe glanced past her to the middle of the park, causing Violet to turn her head. The grassland was a giant square with a footpath cleaving through its centre. There were numerous benches dotted around and strategically placed streetlamps on the other side of the hedge. Violet knew the area well and often picnicked there during her lunch breaks. On weekends, it would be packed with kids playing football and teens trying to look cool with their cans of Red Bull. Tonight, it was deserted.

"Showtime." Joe's voice interrupted her mental wandering.

He grasped her arm loosely and guided her to where the row of bushes ended. They ducked behind the leafy barrier so they were out of view from the park, although Violet had seen nothing to warrant the stealth. At his full height, Joe was able to peer over the top of the hedge; but even on her tiptoes, Violet only came up to his neck.

"What's going on?" she said, a little too loudly.

Joe pressed a finger to his lips. Violet sidled back to the verge of the obstruction and poked her head out just enough so that she could see into the park. She had to squint a while before she was able to confirm that the shape moving in their direction was human. They emerged from the opposite entrance to the park, the clip-clop of heels against the path hinting at a female. She was perhaps a couple of bus lengths away when Violet asked herself how she hadn't dropped dead from hypothermia in the miniskirt and tank top that she was wearing. She looked to Joe, disturbed by the excited flare in his eyes.

"I don't know what this is, but I don't like it. Did you hear me?" Violet surprised herself by prodding him roughly in the shoulder. "Weirdo, I'm out of –"

An intrusive screech caused Violet to blindly leap out from behind the bushes. The woman was no more than several yards from them, but now she wasn't alone. A black figure grappled for her handbag in a tug of war, almost as if this person had been birthed from the shadows themselves.

"Bitch, give it to me!" a man's voice growled from beneath the bandana that was knotted around the lower half of his face.

The next thing Violet heard was the smacking of flesh hitting flesh, its echoes biting through the night. The female was flung onto her back and the assailant almost tumbled with her, still attached to the straps of her handbag, which the woman clutched onto as though it was her child.

"Oh, God." Violet gasped, terror for the woman lurching inside her. Joe gripped her elbow as if predicting her intentions, and she turned to meet his unswerving gaze.

"Are you crazy? She needs help," Violet insisted.

"Stop it, please!" the victim wailed. "Somebody help me!"

"Fucking shut up!" The man stomped his foot down into her abdomen, muting her at once.

Violet couldn't bear it any longer. "Oi, leave her alone!" she yelled, while trying to twist out of Joe's hold.

With no idea that he was being observed, the mugger glanced around wildly before spotting them by the hedge. It seemed to enhance his frustration, and he was soon wrestling for the bag as though it contained the Crown Jewels. The woman yowled again after receiving a kick to her side, but still she refused to surrender.

"My friend is a black belt in karate," Violet goaded. "He'll kick your ass all over this place. Come on, pussy, pick on someone your own size!"

The man turned and hissed something that sounded like verbal abuse.

Amazingly, he tired of the blonde and stormed over to them with his arms swinging by his sides. Violet looked to Joe, the grin sliding from her face when she saw him glowering back at her. Releasing her arm, he took a last drag on his cigarette and then stubbed it out – on his own *hand* – before flicking it to one side.

The mugger advanced swiftly, hood drawn over his head, and the stench of marijuana was so strong that Violet expected to see fumes coming off him like in the cartoons. She glimpsed the shimmer of a penknife in his right hand and started to shuffle backwards. She looked fretfully between him and Joe, who was still gazing down at the extinguished cigarette like a mourner at a graveside.

"Such a waste." He sighed.

"Come on, karate kid," snarled the mugger. "You want some, eh?"

Joe lifted his head unhurriedly, then pointed to the ground behind the aggressor. "You dropped something."

The man took his eyes off them for the most fleeting of seconds. Joe zipped forwards, clutching his hoody in both hands. Violet watched his body being craned up off the floor and hurled the full distance between themselves and the cowering woman. The man screamed as his arm cracked beneath the weight of his body, which missed the concrete path by inches. Rolling onto his back, his crooked posture indicated that the tumble had jarred his ribcage. There was no sign of the weapon, which must have fallen amongst the grass somewhere.

Joe stalked after him with a hefty tread, and the mugger raised a defensive arm as if he expected the blows to come raining down. Joe used this against him by grabbing him in a wristlock, and the crunching that followed caused a feral scream to tear through the night.

"Jesus – stop!" Violet's words almost spilled out in an expulsion of vomit when she perceived something that resembled split wood protruding from ragged flesh.

"Why?" said Joe, seemingly impervious to the man writhing on the ground beside him. "I didn't see him stopping when begged to do so."

"But you can't just... I mean, this isn't right!" It wasn't that Violet felt particularly sorry for the bag thief, but she had no idea what Joe was capable of.

"I'm calling the police." She shoved a shaky hand into her jeans' pocket, where her mobile was tucked away.

"What good will they do? He'll be out of prison within a couple of years, free to pick up where he left off. I should break both of his wrists."

Violet glanced at the mugger again and saw that the bone was stained red from the blood spewing from his mangled wrist. She scanned the park for witnesses, more for their own sakes than hers.

"You fucking psycho, I'll have you done for this!" howled the man, causing Violet's pity to recede even further. "Just you wait and see!"

"You heard him." Joe spoke again. "He has no remorse for what he's done. Once the lawyers get involved, I'll be the one paying him compensation. That's my reward for aiding a fellow citizen – where's the justice in that?"

By now, Violet had typed triple nine into her mobile and her finger hovered over the dial button. She was already on the police's radar and knew for a fact that this would hinder her situation.

"Please, just let him go," she begged.

"Where's the fun in that?" another voice came from behind Joe.

Violet hadn't seen the woman rising; in fact she'd forgotten all about her until she drew up beside Joe. Now that Violet could see her close up, she didn't appear as youthful as previously. Perhaps it was the outfit that trimmed off a few years, but she'd gone from early to late twenties in a matter of seconds. Though shorter than Joe, her athletic physique gave her the kind of toughened exterior that suggested she was more than capable of taking on a lone mugger. What's more, she seemed unfazed by her earlier beating and didn't have a mark on her that wasn't grass or dirt coloured.

"Y-you planned this?" Violet looked from the victim to Joe. "*Both* of you?"

"It was for your own good, sweetheart." The woman propped an elbow onto Joe's shoulder, leaning into him slightly. Even in the darkness, her tawny flesh contrasted against the pastiness of his face.

The mugger doubled up on his side, sobbing and whining like an infant. The woman reared back her leg as if in preparation for a penalty kick, but Joe stopped her.

"*Camilla*." His voice was stern but controlled. The blonde didn't question him.

Joe cocked his head while eying the mugger, eventually crouching in front of him on the balls of his feet. "You don't recognise me, do you? Too busy prowling in the shadows, wasted out of your skull. Stalking young women and waiting for the right time to pounce. You picked the wrong one this time, my friend."

Camilla sniggered, as if the conspiracy between her and Joe was for fun rather than revenge or whatever misguided operation that they'd embarked on. Violet couldn't tell if the mugger's snivelling was a reaction to Joe or his own suffering.

"You think this is the first time that he's done something like this?" Joe asked her. "According to local papers and neighbourhood gossip, Camilla must be his third victim at least. All female, all alone, all in this area. You've heard of honey traps, whereby people catch out their unfaithful spouses? This is along those same principals. All it takes is research, patience and... what was it you said earlier? Ah, yes – instinct."

"That doesn't make what you're doing excusable," Violet countered. "You're no better than he is."

"Admittedly, we laid out the pieces, but no one forced him to play the game. He thought he'd singled Camilla out, but in reality it was she who reeled him in like vermin to squalor."

Joe's observation fell to the mugger, contempt rumpling his features. "Theft is merely a by-product of what gets his pulse racing. I sensed a perversion in him and I exploited it, the same way you tuned into Matthew's darkness."

"I'm nothing like you. I never set Matt up. That was a stupid, drunken mistake; this is madness!"

"What's madness is you not accepting that, like Camilla and I, you have a gift. Call it instinct if you like; a sixth sense or even enhanced versions of the sensory faculties that we use every day. Humans in their most primal form are not so different to animals."

Violet shook her head in large, exaggerated motions. "You're fucking crazy."

"I don't know why you think this bitch is so special," Camilla broke in, with a derisive snort. "We're wasting our time. I suggest we dump this piece of scum and get the fuck out of here before she calls the cops."

"She's not going to do that – are you, Violet?" Joe's grin failed to disguise the threatening undertone in his voice. "You tell them about us and the whole story will unravel very quickly. You've already lied to them once, which means your word won't count for anything. The purpose of tonight was to show you that there are ways of unleashing the beast inside without hurting those undeserving of it."

"By playing vigilante?" Violet spoke incredulously. "You could try anger management like everyone else."

"You remember that feeling when you tore into Matthew's flesh? It was like a drug, an incredible high; and now that you've had a taste of it, it will call to you again. He may have been a snake of a human being, but aren't there more deserving people? Murderers, paedophiles, *thieves*..." Joe's eyes lingered on the mugger for a few tense moments. His face was pressed into the grass, wrist clutched to his abdomen, the odd whimper escaping him. Violet guessed that he was close to passing out, if not from the pain then the shock.

"So, what's your plan?" she said. "Kill him and then walk away? Where does that leave me?"

"To kill an unarmed man in cold blood is a coward's game. I can see that you're not ready to come around to our way of thinking yet. As a token of trust and respect for you, we'll call it quits right here and now."

"I may be willing to keep your twisted secret, but are you really going to take that chance with him?"

"Believe us, there are ways of silencing someone that don't involve murder," Camilla chipped in.

Violet's thoughts tumbled over each other. A drone of voices passed by from the street beyond the park, alerting her to the density of trees to their left. They were all that screened them from potential bystanders, but her concern wasn't shared by the others.

"No... I can't be a part of this." Violet closed her eyes as if to dismiss everything she'd seen that night. Not because she was afraid of her new acquaintances, what they'd done or what they might do; because she was terrified of her own desires.

"There's a payphone around the corner," she said. "I'm calling an ambulance and then I'm leaving. I'll make it anonymous and as long as you leave me the hell alone, it'll stay that way. Stop me if you want, but I'm going to try."

As Violet turned from the abysmal scene, she waited to feel two pairs of hands yanking at her shoulders from behind. It turned out that physical force wasn't necessary to stop her.

"What would Isabelle say?"

Feet nailed to the ground, every emotion and every dark, sadistic image that had branded her mind was flushed away by the mention of her sister's name. Violet had had an inkling all along that Joe had known her or, even more confounding, she knew him.

With a fractional twist of her head, she asked, "What do you know about Isabelle?"

"I know that she deserves to be avenged for the deplorable crime that was committed against her." Joe spoke with that everlasting equanimity. "If you won't join our cause for yourself, then do it for Isabelle. Isn't that what she'd want?"

"It doesn't matter what she'd say or want. She's *dead*."

Violet pivoted in one motion, her impulse to shake the facts out of the man suppressed only by his unpredictability. Joe didn't look like much on the outside – no more dangerous than any other guy that she passed in the street on a daily basis. Yet everything she'd witnessed made her believe that he was, indeed, something more. Something worse.

"You know in your heart that you'll never fit into this life or the people that you share it with," Joe persisted. "Join us and we can offer you vengeance and, more importantly, peace."

"Isabelle's death was all over the news and the local papers – anyone could have tracked me down. Either you're screwing with me or you're involved on some level. If I find out it's the latter then the police will be the least of your worries: that's a promise."

Camilla was poised diagonally in front of Joe, almost as if in guard of him. Her legs were at shoulders' width apart, fists curled by her sides. Her flinty eyes didn't stray from Violet, and a 'ready when you are' grin hovered across her lips.

"I suggest you're gone by the time the ambulance gets here," Violet warned.

With a belly of unease and a head overflowing with uncertainties, she turned and ran from the park. Though not wholly convinced that Joe would keep his word and spare the mugger's life, once she was back in the safety of the street, protected by lamps and the vigilance of passers-by, she hoped that prior events would retreat to a dusty corner of her mind; cached but never forgotten.

CHAPTER SIX

Violet arrived home later than anticipated, having decided to take a detour on the off-chance that she was being followed. It hadn't occurred to her until shuffling through the main entrance that Joe already knew where she lived, and had been keeping her under surveillance for Lord knows how long. As she plodded up the stairway to the first floor, every question that had arisen throughout the night was like a tentacle trying to drag her back to the park. At the forefront of her mind was that, while aiding a man who'd stab someone for the sake of a few quid may have been the right thing to do, was it the *best* thing? Once the shock had loosened its grip on her, Violet realised that if such events had unfolded behind a television screen then she'd have been cheering Joe on like drunkards at a footie match.

The sight of Dean sitting slouched against her front door brought an abrupt end to her musing. "Er... hey, I thought you weren't coming over until later?" Violet asked automatically.

"Me and the lads got all of our jobs finished up early, so the site manager sent us home. How come you didn't answer your phone?"

"Must have left it on silent. Sorry, I went for a walk and lost track of time."

"No worries." Dean didn't probe any further than that.

Violet took her keys out of her jacket pocket, her hands trembling so they jingled together. After multiple attempts at inserting one into her front door, she realised the key was upside down.

"Are you okay?" asked Dean.

"My hands are frozen, that's all." Under Dean's watchful eye, the tremor became even more uncontrollable. Finally, the key turned in the newly fitted mechanism and Violet pushed her way through the door.

"Stick the kettle on, will you?" she said, on the way to her bedroom. "I'm just going to get changed. Mine's a coffee."

She heard Dean utter something in acknowledgment but wasn't sure what. After kicking off her shoes, she flumped onto the bed, snatched up a pillow and buried her face into the foam. Her despairing groan was muffled enough not to have alerted Dean in the kitchen.

"Bollocks," she hissed, once the release was over. "If you're listening, sis, then please give me a sign. Tell me what I should do." She turned her face to the ceiling, waited a few seconds, then shook her head and chuckled.

"What am I saying? Of course you'd want me to confess everything to the police because you're not a fucking idiot. But what if..." Her eyes found the ceiling again. "What if this is the only chance I'll ever get to find out the truth?"

The vision of Joe snapping the mugger's wrist like a matchstick was so vivid that Violet heard the gruesome sound all over again. It must have taken considerable force to cause such damage, or perhaps skill in Joe's case. Even if it healed, it was unlikely to return to its original state. *At least there'd be no more nicking handbags*, she thought grimly.

"I know that what they're doing is immoral, but I can't fault their logic," Violet resumed the one-sided conversation. "Mum always said there was a darkness in me, so maybe this is the path that I'm meant to take. Your death doesn't have to be meaningless after all."

Seconds ticked into minutes, and the silence in the room seeped into her thoughts until all she could hear was the kettle rumbling on the other side of the wafer-thin wall. She changed into her jog suit and went to join Dean in the living area.

"Have you eaten tonight?" he asked, from across the room. Violet shook her head.

"Shall I make you something?" Dean offered.

"Nah, just bring over some biscuits for us to nibble on."

Dean poured a splash of milk into each mug before stirring in the sugar. Violet winced as the spoon clanked against the china; it felt like her eardrums were being used as a piñata.

"Cut it out," she snapped, shielding her ears with her hands.

Dean glanced up at her. "Cut what out?"

"That! Are you trying to crack the damn mugs or what?"

"Sorry."

Dean left the spoon in the sink, placed the milk back into the fridge and then carried the mugs over to the sofa with a pack of custard creams tucked under one arm. He set everything down on the coffee table and then lifted Violet's legs so he could slide himself beneath them. Violet moaned as he started to massage the sole of her foot between his fingers and thumbs.

"You might be an idiot, but you are good with your hands." She held him in her heavy-lidded gaze, using her other foot to rub the bulge in his jeans. In that moment, nothing else seemed to exist but the tingling in her groin, yet Dean was as unresponsive as his flaccid member.

"You're not sulking because I was late back, are you?" Violet kept her tone light.

"No. I was worried if anything."

"Why?"

Dean absorbed himself into the massage, the pressure on Violet's foot increasing to a vigorous kneading motion. She noticed a flush to his cheeks, a shallowness to his breaths. Exactly how or why she'd picked up on these fluctuations was outweighed by Dean's silence.

"You're afraid." Violet withdrew her legs from his lap and straightened herself into a sitting position. "Dean, for Christ's sake, talk to me."

"I don't know how to. You've been all over the place recently, I feel like I'm treading on eggshells."

"Just be honest." *Hypocrite.*

Dean looked at her sideways, the hesitation still in his voice. "Yesterday when I found you unconscious, I didn't know what to think. All kinds of things were going through my head, and when you wouldn't wake up..."

"You thought I'd topped myself?"

"I was seconds away from calling an ambulance. I saw your bag on the side and checked it in a panic – you know, for pills or something. It wasn't until afterwards that I found the vodka bottle and figured you were just sleeping it off."

"I told you, I don't even know where that came from. It was probably an old one that had rolled underneath the bed or something."

"This isn't about the vodka. It's about the pregnancy test that was hidden in your bag."

"Oh..." Violet's eyes fell ashamedly to the floor.

"Call me a snoop if you want, but you can't blame me for being curious."

"No, it's my fault. I don't mean to push you out, and if the results had been different then of course I'd have said something sooner."

"Could it be wrong? You hardly eat, and even when you do, it usually comes up again. Your mood swings are getting worse –" Dean elevated a hand as if to quell her forthcoming argument, "I know that you've been through a lot and the symptoms are all intertwined. But what happened at the weekend... it wasn't normal, Vi."

It had already occured to Violet that hypersensitivity could be associated with pregnancy: the smell of Matt's shirt, the blood and the spoon clashing against the mug. She'd even heard of psychic ability enhancing as a result of carrying a child.

Violet shook her head, mainly for her own benefit. "Look, I'm sorry that I didn't tell you about the test but it was for peace of mind more than anything. We've never had any accidents, you know as well as I do that it's impossible."

"Yeah, well, maybe you should see a doctor anyway. Randomly losing consciousness at home is one thing, but what if it were to happen in the middle of the street?"

The notion was almost as sobering as the desperation in Dean's fluid-filled eyes. Unable to bear the weight of his anguish on top of everything else, and too exhausted to argue, Violet relented with a sigh.

"Okay, let's see how I am after a week of sobriety. If there's no improvement then I'll go ahead and make an appointment with my GP."

"Really?"

"Uh-huh. Don't say that I never do anything for you."

Dean rested a hand on her thigh, a comforting act more than a sexual one. Violet wished that he'd lust after her instead – anything to distract herself from the stress and consternation of the last few days.

"I am trying to pull myself together," she said, "but I know this isn't what you signed up for. If you wanted to walk away then I'd understand. I can't make any guarantees that what we have will work out after... you know."

The sadness that Violet was so acquainted with extended deeper than tears could reach. She'd cried for hours, days – months, even – but the relief turned out to be emptiness in disguise; a void to be replenished with more misery. A part of her wanted to let Dean go, to free him from the darkness that poisoned everyone around her. Yet the words would never come, and she couldn't work out whether it was down to the fear of being alone or submerged feelings for him that she couldn't recognise beneath the murky ocean of her mind.

"If our relationship is putting pressure on you, then I'll back off as much or as little as you want." Dean spoke gently. "All I ask is that you don't shut the door completely. Maybe I'm being selfish..."

"No," Violet said. "You took a chance on me – several, in fact. Just do me a favour and stop running to Lucy whenever there's a problem. Come to me, okay?"

"Sorry, I'm just terrified of fucking this up. I'm as close to Lucy as I am with any of my lad mates – hell, we used to take baths together."

"You took baths with a bunch of guys?"

"No, you cheeky –" Dean lunged across the sofa and began tickling her below the ribs. Violet squealed and wriggled, eventually prising his hands away.

"Are you sure I can't make you something to eat?" Dean was serious once more. "No offence, but if you get any thinner then I won't have anything left to cuddle."

"You never know, I might find my appetite along with my marbles some day."

"You're not crazy, Violet. Crazy would be not feeling a thing."

Dean kissed her cheek before hauling himself out of the sofa. Violet reached for her coffee and took a sip, feeling the liquid warm her insides. The park had left a chill upon her that wasn't entirely physical, and while Violet hoped never to find herself in the shady presences of Joe or Camilla again, she had a feeling that she would.

"Man, your fridge is depressing. This yoghurt went off weeks ago."

"Huh?" Violet looked around to discover that Dean was back in the kitchen with the fridge door wedged open. "Oh, just stick it in the bin."

As Dean dropped the tub into the peddle bin, Violet said, "Can I ask you a hypothetical question?"

"Of course."

"If you were me and you got your hands on the person that killed Isabelle, what would you do?"

Dean paused. "You mean would I want revenge?"

"Yes, *hypothetically* speaking," she reminded him.

"Uh... I guess what I'd want to do and what I'd actually do are two different things. It's hard to predict something like that."

"It still doesn't make sense to me."

"What?"

"The way it happened. Even a shooting would make more sense than a fucking arrow through the chest. I mean who were they, some kind of Robin Hood wannabe out on target practice?"

"As I keep telling you, right now you need to come to terms with what did happen rather than why it happened. I don't know what else to say, Violet."

"No one ever does."

Neither of them pursued the conversation. Dean closed the fridge and headed back to the living area. He fumbled in his jacket pocket that was sprawled over the back of the sofa and pulled out his wallet.

"Going somewhere?" asked Violet.

"Tesco, I should make it there before closing. I'll pick up some snacks, but I'm taking you shopping tomorrow even if I have to drag you there. You'll be okay while I'm gone?"

"Yeah, but isn't it a bit late? I've got work in the morning."

"Then, I'll make you a packed lunch instead."

"You don't have to fuss –"

She was silenced by Dean's soft lips smacking against hers. Violet kissed him back, her resistance forgotten.

"I'll be back soon, okay?" Dean whispered.

Violet nodded, then found his lips once again. She let her hands glide over his stubbly cheeks, holding his face, paying no mind to his attempt at withdrawal. The kiss was more sensual than she'd ever known a kiss to be; it seemed to last a lifetime, but even that wasn't enough. Violet heard his wallet plop onto the carpet as she reclined against the cushions, dragging him down with her.

The dominance shifted as Dean pinned her down with the weight of his body. He nuzzled her neck, the skin so sensitive that it made her squirm. His hand slid expertly down the front of her bottoms and into her knickers. She parted her legs a little to allow the manoeuvre of his fingers but, sensing her eagerness, Dean held back to prolong the anticipation. He shuffled down to the opposite end of the sofa while tugging her bottoms over her hips and thighs, his tongue leaving a slick trail over her abdomen. He paused at her knicker line, flicking his tongue back and forth to tantalise her further. Violet moaned at the shame that burned through her, which Dean mistook for pleasure and began to lick more passionately.

Isabelle's dead, and here you are in the midst of ecstasy, her conscience scolded. Memories of Friday night mingled with those of her sister. The grubby alley and the beer-infused breath on her face; thick fingers probing her intimate parts. The last person to have stimulated her had vanished, and Violet had no idea to what extent, if any, that she was involved. What if the same thing happened to Dean?

"I can't," she murmured, over the sound of her crashing heart.

As Dean continued to pleasure her, the protests clogged in her throat. Her thoughts became corrupted by vicious scenes of death and bloodshed that she couldn't differentiate between reality and imagination. Young, milk-white flesh reposed beneath a crimson shower. Isabelle's deathly peaceful face, glazed eyes riveted to the heavens. Interfering with these visions were other features, so transient that it was like flicking between television channels. Black, gleaming orbs that might once have been humanoid; blood trickling through ivory prongs like a cascade of Merlot wine.

A yowl from Dean shattered the trance like a rock slung through a window. Violet opened her eyes to find tufts of hair clutched between her fingers. Dean was standing up, rubbing his neck as though the muscles were sprained.

"What the hell? I thought you wanted to..." It was spoken more in confusion than anger as he stared down at her, the snake in his jeans rapidly shrinking.

"I... I'm sorry." Violet pushed herself up, strands of hair glued to her cheeks with perspiration.

"I didn't mean to get carried away," Dean apologised.

"It's fine, honest. I've just had one hell of a fucked up day." Violet was glad that he kept his eyes averted.

"I'll, er, go and get the food before it's too late." Dean picked his wallet up off the floor and stuffed it into his back pocket. "Won't be long."

In the time that it took Violet to say goodbye, he was already gone. Once she'd heard the front door closing, she pulled up her bottoms and let her head sink into her hands. She dug her nails into her scalp, punishing herself; yet the physical pain was much easier to process. It was uncomplicated and somehow relieving. It sprang to mind that this might also have been the case with the bathroom mirror, but she was either too hung over or exhausted to recollect it.

What other explanation was there?

***

It tore off in her mouth like a chunky rasher of bacon. Warm, dripping flesh adhered to a tasty layer of subcutaneous tissue. The meat was no match for her needle-like teeth, elongated canines slicing through it like cheese wire. Violet rolled the masticated flesh around with her tongue, the coppery juices stimulating her taste buds to incite a hunger-induced orgasm. She swallowed it in one, savouring the feeling of it sliding down her gullet. She licked her lips with a blood-wet tongue while gazing ravenously at her meal. At the mangled throat, where fleshy ribbons and severed veins protruded from the bloody grotto like the roots of a mutated garden plant. Violet stuck a pinky finger into the gash, hooking her razor-sharp fingernail behind a carotid artery and hacking it in half so that bright red blood jetted from the tube. She always did like a lot of ketchup with her steak.

Sucking the vital force from her finger, she took a few moments to study the body that she straddled in the bathtub. His torso was stripped down to the bone in parts, leaving viscid walls of muscle tissue and fibres. What blood hadn't coated her naked form had either trickled down the plughole or splattered the tiled wall. Violet couldn't remember dragging the corpse into her bathroom, for the hunger had overwhelmed her to the point of possession. Even after the scrumptious feast, her gut rumbled for more – she was starting to wonder if she'd ever be satisfied.

Violet was about to chow down on a juicy pectoral when she had the sensation of being watched. She glanced across to the doorway and was surprised to see a couple of figures standing there, one male and one female.

"What the hell are you doing here?" Violet said, unabashed by the crimson cloak that was painted upon her exposed breasts.

"Don't you remember?" replied the blonde woman. "You let us in, just like you did the other night."

"Why would I let the likes of *you* anywhere near me?"

The man answered next, "As I keep telling you, we're the same. Feeling better now, are we, after your snack?"

Camilla sniggered then, her green eyes moving across to the deformity that was crammed into the bathtub. "Is he as tasty as he looks? I bet you never imagined that, one day, you'd be eating your lover in quite a literal sense."

"Huh?" Violet's gaze fell upon the corpse. To the rigid features and sightless eyes with lids half-drawn; pallid lips and flesh that were speckled with blood. The discharge in her stomach spewed forth in a fountain of maroon-coloured mush.

It was as if she was witnessing her meal for the first time, that her hunger had created some sort of inebriated haze. Now that she could see Dean's once handsome face with the utmost clarity, Violet expelled a long, howling scream.

***

"Violet!"

Dean's voice reached her before the sweet, rusty odour. She felt something being snatched from her hands, and as consciousness returned to her, she was blinded by the kitchen spotlights.

"What?" she croaked, squinting her eyes.

Dean slammed something into the bin as though it had a contagious disease. Violet felt stickiness on her fingertips and looked down to see redness. She became aware of the irony taste in her mouth – a taste that she recognised from the very nightmare that she'd woken from.

"Oh, God!" She spun around to the sink, leaned over and retched, but her stomach wouldn't release the macerated meat.

Dean held back her hair while she spat out what was left in her mouth and slurped handfuls of tap water, rinsing and spitting until it ran clear.

"Better?" said Dean, handing her a tea towel to dry off.

"What the hell was I just eating?" Violet coughed.

"Frying steak."

"Steak! Why would you put that in my fridge?"

"Sorry, it was going cheap. It's not like I was going to cook and eat it in front of you. How was I to know that you'd start sleepwalking?"

"I don't sleepwalk... do I?"

Would that explain the blackouts? she wondered. Not the sudden craving for raw meat, though.

"You've been having nightmares all week," Dean told her. "I know you don't like me fussing, but this is getting beyond a joke."

"Can you see me laughing?" Violet snapped. "Maybe the nightmares have acted as a trigger or something. You know, like that sleep eating thing you hear about."

"Must have been some nightmare."

Violet was scarcely able to look at him without seeing the carcass in the bathtub. She even found herself checking his limbs for teeth marks.

"Sweetheart –" Dean opened his arms to embrace her, but she swerved the endeavour.

"Sorry, I'm so grossed out right now that I can't even..." She shook her head, wordless and bewildered.

"Can I get you anything?"

"No, you might as well go back to bed. I'll be fine once I've cleaned up and brushed my teeth."

"Are you sure?"

"Positive. I know where you are if not."

Dean plodded back to the bedroom without saying anything more. Violet scrubbed all traces of blood from her hands and face until the skin felt as raw as the steak that she'd savagely consumed. After brushing her teeth, she curled up beneath a blanket on the sofa. Light from the television screen flickered in the darkened room, and gradually the pictures became harder and harder to focus on. The next thing she knew, she was woken by the melody of her mobile phone's alarm clock. Violet rubbed her eyes before they tracked the sound to the coffee table in front of her. She stuck an arm out from under the blanket to silence it, figuring that Dean must have placed it there to ensure she didn't oversleep. She noticed the piece of paper that it had been resting on and leaned forwards to read Dean's handwriting.

'Dinner tonight, no arguments x.'

Sinking back into the cushions, Violet heard her stomach rumbling for the first time in months

CHAPTER SEVEN

Violet crammed the last slice of ham into her mouth, gobbled it up and then licked the flavour off each of her fingers. She'd already devoured the packed lunch that Dean had made her, but the craving for meat had enticed her to take a detour past the supermarket on the way to work that morning. At least one thing Joe had said made sense: it must have been some degree of anaemia that had been making her feel so weak and lacklustre. The more she ruminated over last night's sleepwalking, the more she believed that it was her brain's way of taking back control.

With a bloated stomach, Violet trashed her rubbish and had just finished washing her mug when Lucy sauntered into the canteen. They exchanged a partial smile, which was an improvement on the lack of eye contact over the last day.

"Hey." Lucy was first to speak, while taking her lunchbox out of the fridge. She headed over to the table that Violet had been sitting at, and Violet perched on a chair opposite her.

"Hey, how's things?" she asked genially.

"Not bad," Lucy replied. "You?"

"Same." Violet watched her friend piercing her drinks carton with the provided straw. "This is stupid. We're still best buds, right?"

"Of course we are. The only reason I get so pissed off is because I worry about you."

"I know, but I've had a heart-to-heart with Dean and I think I've figured a few things out. It's not just my body that I've been starving; it's my mind, too. It's made me confused, angry – delusional, almost. I've cut out the drinking, and my appetite is already coming back. Everything seems a lot clearer than it did yesterday."

"I'm glad to hear it. You're stronger than you think, Vi."

"I'd have lost my shit a long time ago if it wasn't for you and Dean. For the first time in my life, I feel vulnerable. People seem to be able to sniff it out, too."

"Are you talking about Matt?"

Violet hadn't spared a thought for Matt all morning and, truthfully, he was the least of her worries. "I think drink got the better of both of us. It's not like I was fighting him off with a stick."

Lucy placed a hand onto Violet's forearm. "I'm partly at fault for that night. I knew you were wasted and not thinking straight, but I ran off in a tantrum anyway."

"Yeah, well, it's in the past now." Violet wished that was true. "Fancy coming back to mine after work? Dean's cooking and it's been a while since the three of us hung out together."

"Are you sure he won't mind me playing gooseberry?"

"Nah, I'll text him and let him know. I'd better get back to work, I'm on reduced breaks until I've made up the time that I missed."

"All right, talk later."

Violet got up off the chair and withdrew from the canteen. She was halfway across the office floor when a poignant agony shot through her gut, as if someone had jabbed her with a cattle prod. She tried to latch onto a nearby desk during the descent, but only managed to knock off a wad of papers that fluttered about her like crazed pigeons. She heard more than a few sniggers from various corners of the office, which quickly died down when she didn't get back up. Within seconds, there was a cluster of bodies standing around her, their voices indistinguishable due to the sirens in her ears.

Violet moaned with both arms coiled around her stomach. Collapsing onto her side was unavoidable as the pain spread through her, and it wasn't until she looked up to the ceiling that she saw Tina's bright pink face peering over the edge of her desk. *Of all the places to have fallen!* she thought, in spite of her condition.

Her frustration didn't last for long. The walls of her stomach convulsed as if an entire machine gun round was being emptied into it. Her heart pumped at a rate that made it difficult to breathe. Even her eyes felt like they were spewing volcanic lava down her cheeks, and just when she thought she could take no more – that her body would sooner shut down than prolong the suffering – Lucy's soothing voice dragged her back to consciousness.

"Violet? Calm down, honey. Breathe..."

Violet concentrated on the words, sucking the air into her nostrils and blowing it out of her mouth as though she was in labour. As the oxygen began to circulate, her pulse dropped to a semi-regular speed and the fitting ceased altogether.

"Shall I call for an ambulance?" Another female spoke.

"How many fingers am I holding up?" A man this time.

"Can she even hear us?"

"You okay, Violet?... V-i-o-l-e-t!"

"All right," Violet groaned, "I'm not retarded."

"See, she's perfectly fine," came Tina's distinctive voice.

Violet attempted to rise, but frantic hands nudged her back down. "Don't move," Lucy ordered. "I think you've had some kind of seizure or panic attack. Give her some room, people, for Christ's sake!"

With a bit of squirming, Violet managed to flip onto her front. Her body felt limp, pins and needles tingling in her arms and legs. It took every one of her neck muscles to elevate her head until it was level with the front window, which ran the entire width of the office. Through the rows of desks, she saw a young girl staring back at her from the other side of the glass. She couldn't tell if her spectator was a child or woman; the only feature that stood out was the dark brown hair. Violet blinked rapidly, not completely trusting her eyes.

"Izzy..." She was distracted by a hand on her shoulder and looked up to Lucy.

"Vi, what's going on?" her friend worried. "Has this happened to you before?"

"No, I..." Her gaze darted back to the window. She pushed herself up onto all fours, eyes swivelling from side to side. "Where's she gone? Did you see her?"

"Who?"

"The girl, she was standing right outside." Violet crawled lethargically through the crowd, shrugging away the hands that tried to steady her. Eventually, she scrambled to her feet and wobbled over to the main doors.

People were everywhere, like multicoloured blurs as she wandered outside onto the street. The girl wasn't amongst them, perhaps she never had been.

"Violet!" She heard Lucy calling from the office doorway. "Please, come back inside. You need to get checked over by someone."

"I can't, I have to find her."

"Then, let me come with you. Just wait here while I get my stuff together... Violet!"

Violet continued down the street, turning in circles while scanning every doorstep, every corner for a face that she knew irrefutably that she couldn't have seen. Occasionally she'd bump shoulders with a member of the public, but whatever abuse she received bounced off her like bulletproof glass. Lucy's voice became fainter and was eventually swallowed up by the lunchtime crowds. Violet drifted aimlessly, the brisk air nipping through her blouse and pencil skirt. It was refreshing after the pints of sweat that she must have lost during the seizure, the dampened cotton sticking to her back.

Aggravating the stitch in her side, she slowed to a more leisurely pace but it had little effect. Her stomach felt stagnant and had been running on empty for so long that it'd probably forgotten how to digest. She needed to belch but held it back for the fear of her lunch voiding itself. Her hair felt wet against her face, so she wiped her sleeve across her forehead and found that the material was stained with sweat.

Violet didn't realise how far she'd strayed until she stopped to collect herself and saw Westfield Shopping Centre up ahead. As the bile churned inside her, she contemplated her options: vomit on the street in front of everyone, try to make it back to the office or duck into the nearest public toilets and pray that one was vacant.

Power walking through the shoppers, head bowed; hand covering her mouth, Violet passed by the mall and counted down the thirty seconds that it would take to reach the toilets. *Nearly there*, she urged herself, focusing on the concrete gliding past beneath her feet. This only seemed to amplify her dizziness; her head was so light that it could have been filled with helium. The stitch in her side was excruciating to the point of skewing her walk, and she was almost certain that she'd torn a muscle during the fall. Upon approach to the outdoor toilets, she scooted into the ladies' and shouldered through the nearest cubicle door like a stunt woman on a movie set.

With no time to lock herself in, Violet leaned over the toilet bowl and heaved violently. Nothing came up. She tried again, even ramming her fingers down her throat, but the relief wouldn't come.

"Goddamn it!" She thrust the palm of her hand into the wall in front of her, breath coming in gusts. "What the fuck is wrong with me?"

There were no sounds from the two neighbouring cubicles, assuring Violet that she was alone. She elbowed one of the sides as if to provoke a reaction, but the reverberations ended with silence.

Slouching against the opposite wall, she let her head roll back and closed her eyes. When she reopened them, she was surprised to see a dent in the metal that segregated the toilets, right where her elbow had smashed into it.

"Piece of shit." For the simple fact that she could, Violet drew up her knee and then extended her leg as hard and fast as she could. The metal rattled and shook beneath the kick. She lifted her skirt for less restriction and then repeated the action, again and again until the thunderous bangs sparked a headache. It was as though all of the tension in her body had shot out of her foot, and the destructive force inside her had unleashed itself onto the cubicle wall. The damage presented itself in the form of a small, circular indentation created by the heel of her shoe. She half expected the structure to collapse for how shoddy it must have been. She inspected her ankle for swelling, but if anything it felt stronger – powerful, even.

Without hesitation, Violet fisted her hand and then drove it, full force, into the metal. A twinge of discomfort streaked up her arm, and then nothing. She glanced over her knuckles, almost childlike in appearance, yet her skin must have been armoured like Kevlar.

"What-the-hell...?"

Violet struck out a second time, the knot of muscles in her jaw unwinding into a maniacal grin. She didn't care how, she didn't care why. Relief turned into euphoria, and euphoria became a drug. Even if every bone in her hand was to simultaneously shatter, she was determined to keep those feelings alive for as long as her body allowed it.

Violet boxed away at the cubicle wall: right, left, jab, jab...

The sounds boomed through the chamber, and she could hear the adjacent door clattering on its hinges. Flecks of red splattered the metal, but she wasn't aware of any soreness in her knuckles. Her adrenaline was coursing at such a rate that it must have desensitised them somehow. She grunted as all of her anger and hostility accumulated in her fists and was then blasted out with each punch. It was just as Joe had explained: there was a way of refocusing those negative emotions without hurting anyone, including herself. She'd almost forgotten how close to death she'd felt a few minutes ago.

By now, the dent in the cubicle wall was so thin that it was beginning to bend like cardboard. She'd lost count of how many hits it had taken, but that didn't stop her from retracting her fist one last time so it was parallel with her head. As she propelled it forth, the steel caved to create a mouth of jagged teeth that left deep trenches in the back of her hand. Violet was unprepared for the stinging pain and swore through her teeth. She withdrew her fist carefully from the orifice and then shook it as though it was on fire, but it only served to agitate the wounds.

She gathered a handful of toilet roll from the holder and applied it to the lesions. "Jeez," she hissed, slightly regretting her outburst.

The blood saturated the paper, prompting her to add more pressure. It wasn't until she looked back to the destruction of the cubicle wall that she noticed a hazel eye peeking through the hole.

"Holy shit!" Violet bounded backwards with both hands clutched to her chest.

The eye disappeared, and she saw movement behind the manmade peephole. A couple of seconds later, the door to her cubicle slowly creaked open. Violet pressed herself against the wall, dreading who or what she was about to come face to face with. When the girl came into view, there was already a wide grin sculpted into her grubby face.

"Feelin' better now?" she said, in a thick Irish accent. Her elfin frame was swamped by the army jacket that she was wearing; the Dr. Martens ankle boots giving no lift to her shortness.

"Y-you..." Violet swallowed to lubricate her throat. "You're *her*."

"Actually, I do have a name, but pleased to meet y'e either way." The girl extended a hand, but if anything dissuaded Violet from shaking it then it was the black stains under her nails.

"You were at the office where I work," Violet persisted. "I saw you staring through the window. I thought you were... someone else."

"Uh-huh." The girl nodded, seemingly unfazed by having witnessed an eight-stone woman punch through a steel wall. Her bob moved as a single mass and, like the rest of her, looked as though it hadn't seen a wash or a brush in days.

"Who are you?" Violet caught a whiff of the girl's natural odour – nothing unpleasant, which was surprising given the state of her. It was almost... *familiar*, somehow.

"They call me Gypsy, or Gyp for short. It's not the name my parents gave me, that one didn't seem to fit anymore. Times change, you know?"

"What are you talking about?"

"Ignore me, I'm rambling again. Sorry for freaking y'out earlier, it wasn't intentional. No offence but you looked like you'd walked in on a ghost taking a dump."

Violet didn't share in the girl's amusement, but she couldn't deny that there was a pull between them. Perhaps it was because she reminded her of Isabelle, or because she looked like she'd been on the streets for some time. If it wasn't for social services, the few stints that Violet had spent in foster care would have been replaced with a cardboard box right next to this oddity of a teenager.

"You're with them, aren't you?" Violet guessed.

"Depends who you mean by 'them'."

"The delightful duo. I wasn't sure before, but I can smell them on you."

Violet would have laughed, but they weren't the most nonsensical words to have left her mouth that week. With her uninjured hand, she kneaded her tired eyes while saying, "Look, I know why you're here but my answer is the same. I may be a lot of things, but I'm not a killer."

"Every creature on the planet is born with that innate killer instinct: it's called surviving. Something I had to tap into a long time ago, otherwise I never would've made it alone in the big wide world."

"Good for you. Now, please, leave me alone."

"You can't pretend that last night didn't happen, just like you can't keep going about your business as if everything's normal. Denial is an exhausting facade to keep up."

"Better than the alternative," Violet mumbled.

Gypsy leaned with one shoulder propped against the cubicle wall. "I do get it, you know. I'm as much a stranger to you as y'are to me, probably more so. But the things I've seen... what I've been subjected to... they turned me into a monster long before Joe and Cammy got to me."

"So, what, I'm supposed to feel sorry for you? I saw firsthand what you people do for fun. You made it my business, and now that man's blood is on my hands as well. Is he even still alive?"

"Joe gave you his word, didn't he?"

"His word means shit, and so does yours. Besides, it doesn't look too good when people claim to know more about my sister's death than I – or even the police – do."

Gypsy must have recognised the gruffness behind the words, for her response was less bolshie than before. "Joe says that you're not ready to –"

"Joe isn't here, so if you know something then you'd better start talking or else it won't be a wall that I put my fist through next time." It perturbed Violet not that she'd threatened the girl, but at that moment in time, she'd have carried out the threat as if it was an everyday chore.

The main door to the ladies' squeaked open, filling the space with a buzz of voices from the street outside. Violet grabbed the front of Gypsy's jacket and yanked her further into the cubicle, nudging the door shut and snapping the bolt across. Thankfully, the footsteps passed by the first two cubicles and shuffled into the one that was furthest from them. As Violet looked back to Gypsy, she realised that her forearm was pressed to the youngster's chest, pinning her to the wall. Just like earlier, her face morphed into Isabelle's. The resemblance stirring feelings of sorrow and love that was so ingrained, she had no choice but to lay off the girl.

Gypsy remained stationary while Violet unlocked the cubicle door, as if anticipating another manhandling. "Go," she uttered quietly, "before I do something that I regret."

Gypsy didn't need to be told again. She made it through the door before turning, still with a chariness about her, and saying to Violet, "Even if I did have all the answers, it's not my place to give 'em to you. But if you come with me now then I can show you."

Violet knew better than to ask where, for these people dealt in actions rather than words. As the toilet in the end cubicle was flushed, she took a moment to ponder while the woman washed her hands and then left. Violet wasn't sure if she had the brain capacity for more questions, nor did she have the energy to keep searching for truths that were potentially being offered to her. But it came at a price that she wasn't willing to pay.

"I've fallen for this spiel once already, and I'll be damned if I'm walking into another trap," she decided. "My whole life has been spent learning to rely on no one but myself. Whatever's happening to me, I'll figure it out alone."

"Well, good luck with that. At least we both know that you're capable of *handling* y'self, should the need arise."

Violet wasn't amused by the reference to her injury. She lifted the wad of toilet paper that had adhered to her hand with a gooey layer of blood. The soreness was less acute now, but it was too messed up to see the extent of the damage.

"I hope this won't need stitches." She spoke mainly to herself, although Gypsy was quick to reassure her.

"It'll heal. Why don't I give you my number, just in case you change your mind?" She produced a cheap-looking flip phone from her jacket pocket.

"I won't change my mind," Violet promised. "Besides, I left my phone in the office."

"Joe said that you were a stubborn one. I'm sure you'd rather we didn't keep bumping into each other like this?"

"Oh, fine, anything to get rid of you." Violet recited her mobile number, which Gypsy typed into the keypad of her mobile.

"I'll text y'mine, and then the choice is yours. You'll never have to see us again if that's what you want."

"Seriously? You'll leave me alone now?" Violet was skeptical.

"I told you, we never go back on our word."

"Good. Now, if you'll excuse me, I have to clean myself up before I get back to the office and try to explain what the fuck just happened."

"Chow, then."

Violet couldn't believe it when Gypsy exchanged the phone for a lollipop out of her pocket, then waltzed from the toilets with the sweet sticking out of her mouth. She waited for her to return, but was left oddly disappointed.

***

"Eeww!" Lucy's squeal brought the room back into focus. Violet thought the chortling was coming from the TV until she saw the new word that had appeared on the Scrabble board: faeces.

Dean delved into the mystery pouch to replace the letters that he'd used, while Lucy spoke again. "Your turn, Vi. What have you got for us?"

Examining the board in its entirety, Violet wondered when it had become so cluttered. She didn't remember half of the words staring up at her, and looking at the tiles on her stand was like trying to read a foreign alphabet. Her mind was so preoccupied that she'd forgotten basic spelling. The bleeping of her mobile prompted her to make her excuses.

"I've got nothing, you might as well take your turn. Anyone for another drink?"

Both Dean and Lucy declined, too absorbed in their game to query her lack of enthusiasm. On her way to the kitchen, Violet opened the text message that she'd received from the same number that Gypsy had given her earlier.

'Just checking in, hope you're feeling better. We're here for you. Any place, any time.'

Violet was about to delete the message when a frosty paranoia turned the hairs on the back of her neck into icicles.

'Where are you right now?' she texted back.

'Close enough.'

Violet placed her mobile onto the kitchen worktop facedown, as if hiding the messages would blot them from her memory. Lucy and Dean were chatting over the Scrabble board, some drivel that Violet paid no mind to. So as not to appear suspicious, she poured herself a glass of coke and sipped it thoughtfully. Her bandaged hand was feeling a lot better than earlier, when simply gripping her bus pass had caused seepage.

'It'll heal...' Gypsy's certainty had befuddled Violet ever since. She hadn't popped so much as a painkiller and already the tenderness had blunted. After some time, she picked up her phone and typed a final message to Gypsy.

'STAY AWAY.'

Violet moseyed over to the living room window, drink in hand, and peeked through the blinds. The night hindered her vision of the poorly-lit street, although she could see no figures weaving in between the shadows.

"Vi, you're going to miss your turn again."

Violet turned to Lucy, who was sitting on the carpet across the other side of the coffee table. "Huh?"

"Are you okay?" her friend asked.

"Yeah, just stretching my legs. Why don't you guys finish up without me? My eyes are getting tired."

"Oh, you should have said something. I'll get off home after –"

"No!" It was too late to disguise the urgency in her voice, but the thought of who might be lurking on the streets made Violet reluctant to let anyone leave. "I mean, it's still early. Stay, have fun; eat popcorn. I'll make a start on those dishes in the sink."

"You don't have to do that," said Dean. "Go for a lie down if you're tired. I'll drive Lucy home in a bit and wash the pots up when I get back."

"You are still looking peaky after that funny turn you had in the office," Lucy agreed. "You should have taken the afternoon off to see a doctor."

"What, so they can throw more pills at me like they did when Isabelle died?" Violet spurned the idea. "It was probably a panic attack like you said. I just got a little... disorientated. I feel fine now – great, in fact. Who fancies dessert?"

"Uh, I didn't think to pick anything up." Dean looked taken aback at Violet's restored interest in food.

"No problem, I'll nip to the shop. I could use the fresh air."

Dean glanced at his wristwatch. "It's almost nine o'clock. Besides, there's plenty of popcorn to go around."

Violet was already heading back to the kitchen. She plonked the glass onto a side unit, grabbed her phone and then fetched her jacket off the back of a chair. "I'll be fifteen minutes. Stick a movie on or something, yeah?"

Lucy began to stand up. "Hang on, I'll come with –"

"Guys!" Violet elevated her hands as a parent might do when settling a rowdy dispute between kids. Lucy and Dean stayed silent, awaiting whatever reproval came next. "I'm not an invalid, so please don't treat me like one. At least give me twenty minutes before forming a search party."

Her shot at humour wasn't acknowledged by either of them. Without further debate, Violet left the flat. The walk to Tesco was brisk and unsettling, yet it was worth it just to escape the claustrophobic atmosphere at home. Her head was continually turning as she observed and listened, convinced that she was being stalked – if not by the freakish threesome then by the night itself. Still, if one of them was to make an appearance then better she was alone than risk having to explain everything to Dean and Lucy.

Violet made it to the shop without incident, the fluorescent lighting welcoming her with safety and warmth, but not much in the way of people. She noticed a customer at the tills and one or two browsing various isles on her way to the desserts. Scanning the fridge shelves, it occurred to her that she wasn't even hungry, but returning home empty-handed would result in more interrogations.

In the end, she grabbed a box of éclairs and then headed to the tills. The customer that she'd passed a few moments ago was still there: a balding man wearing a tracksuit and sandals. Violet's amusement at his choice of footwear was spoiled by the cracked, fungus-infested heels poking through the straps, so she turned her attention back to the change that she'd dug out of her coat pocket. As she counted out the correct amount, she had one ear on the conversation – or rather, dispute – that was taking place between the man and the cashier.

"Come on, mate, give us a break," the bald guy slurred. "It's ten pence, you know I'm good for it. Can't you stick it on a tab or sommet?"

"Sorry, sir, but unless you have the full amount then I can't serve you," the younger male persisted.

"But I need my cigs, aren't there any cheaper ones?"

"Unfortunately not."

"What if you go halves with me and we can split the pack?"

"I don't smoke."

"Fuck's sake," Violet grumbled.

The man turned his head, his glazed eyes barely able to lock onto her. Violet glanced around to see if anyone else shared her impatience, but they were the only pair in the queue.

"I suggest you come back in the morning because the store closes in fifty minutes and there are other customers that need serving." The lanky youth spoke in a monotone voice that matched his bland expression. He couldn't have been much older than eighteen.

"Aw, you can't make me go all night without a fix," the man whinged. "At least lend me the ten pence and I'll pay you back with interest." He stuck an arm behind the checkout and began a half-hearted fumble for the cash register.

"Jesus, I'll give you the ten pence," Violet intervened, before security was called.

"Oh, you're an angel." As the man whirled around to thank her, he lost his balance and teetered to one side. Coppers and silvers slipped through his fingers as if leaping to their deaths in a bid to escape the boozy stench.

"Ooh, me pennies, me pennies!" he babbled, while bending over and scrabbling for the change. Violet swerved around him while he was distracted and handed over the éclairs so the cashier could put them through the till. Goods and money were exchanged within seconds, and the man was still collecting the last of his coins.

"Would you like a bag?" the youth asked Violet.

"No, thanks. See you." She tucked the box under her arm and hurried for the exit. She'd barely made it ten paces down the street before a familiar voice yelled after her.

"Oi, angel, what about my ten pence?"

"Go and choke on it," Violet muttered, too quiet for the man to have heard.

"Hey!" He adopted a brisk tone, but still she kept on walking. "You'd think some people had never heard of charity. Help out a fellow human being, eh?"

Violet was conscious of the footsteps blundering up behind her, but the hand on her shoulder came unexpectedly. In an unpremeditated strike, she wheeled around with both arms swinging outwards. The dessert packaging slammed into the side of his head, collapsing one corner, although Violet was more bothered about the destruction of the éclairs than his skull. The man's drunken reaction saw him cowering from the blow after it had happened, and Violet scrunched the collar of his jacket in a single fist before shoving him back into the external wall of the store. He didn't put up much of a struggle – the hand tugging at her arm might have belonged to a child – but Violet couldn't determine whether it was down to her enhanced strength or him being too pissed.

"Easy, angel." The man let go of her and showed his palms. "I ain't never hurt a woman before –"

The same hand that pinned him to the wall sprang up to his throat just below the jawbone, hoisting him up a few inches higher. She didn't hold all of his weight, despite being confident that her puny arm could take it.

"Listen up, you drunken cunt." Her voice was like stone, hard and unfeeling. "If I ever catch you making trouble here again, then I'll use those cigarettes to burn out your corneas before feeding your eyeballs to you through your asshole. You get me?"

Violet thought she heard the word 'yes' spluttering out in what sounded like an imitation of Donald Duck's voice, along with his frantic nodding.

"Maybe they were speaking sense after all," Violet told herself. "Someone needs to clean up the streets. People shouldn't be afraid to leave their houses after dark. Hardworking citizens shouldn't have to take crap from worthless scum like *you* on a daily basis."

"Jeez, lady, all I wanted was a c-cig." The man choked. "I never put a gun to no one's head."

"Not this time." Satisfied, and feeling strangely composed, Violet released her hold on him. The man gave a loud gasp for breath as his heels re-established contact with the pavement.

"Now, beat it," Violet ordered.

He took off like a horse on the racetracks, straight past the shop's illuminated front and out of sight. Remembering about the desserts, Violet checked the box to find cream smeared over the lid; other than that, they were still in one piece. She took her mobile out of her pocket and typed as she walked, knowing that any further vacillation would cause her to change her mind yet again.

'*Meet me tomorrow after work. 5 p.m., outside the toilets. Last chance.*'

She sent the message to Gypsy, receiving confirmation seconds later. By the time she got back to the flat, her skirmish with the drunkard was a distant memory.

CHAPTER EIGHT

It loomed before them like a relic from World War II: a shell of beaten bricks with grim and charmless bowels. Two storeys were distinguishable by the wooden boards nailed into rectangular slots. The only window that remained had a bullet-shaped hole in one of the gridded panels, although Violet suspected that it was more likely caused by a stone having been pitched at the time-weakened glass.

"Two bus rides and a twenty-minute hike down a woodland trail in these shoes, and this is what you have to show me?" Violet raised an unimpressed brow at her guide.

"You wanted the truth, didn't you?" Gypsy's response offered no more solace than the journey itself. She'd spent the whole time prattling on about the various towns that she'd hitchhiked through; the shelters she'd stayed in and all of the interesting people that she'd met. She seemed quite content with how her life had turned out and even referred to herself as a traveller rather than homeless. Violet had been expecting to hear some tragic back story, perhaps in relation to the so-called hardships that she'd faced, but Gypsy hadn't given so much as a whisper about life before the streets.

"What's so special about a rundown old mill?" Violet regarded the building again. It was about the width of two or three terraced houses, obscured from the road by a barricade of trees. She and Gypsy had taken a shortcut through a trail of undergrowth and brambles to the back of the mill. Violet had seen part of the River Derwent after stepping off the bus, which gave her some comfort in the knowledge that, if necessary, she'd be able to find her way back into town.

Gypsy proceeded to the building's entrance in spite of Violet's hesitancy. "Wait, you don't expect me to go in there?" she said.

Gypsy answered, "It's not what's inside that you should be afraid of. It's everything out here."

She pulled open the double doors simultaneously, the scraping of their ancient hinges amplified in the hollow structure so it sounded like a beast roaring in pain. The gloom appeared to devour her as she slipped inside and, left alone, Violet became aware of the eerie silence of nature. Not a single bird or cricket chirped, making her wonder if they were in hiding or had left completely.

With that in mind, she hurried after Gypsy. The cracks of light that filtered through the many crevices in the building looked smoky from the dirt that hung in the air. Violet felt the molecules scratching her throat with every breath, causing her eyes to water. Gypsy seemed immune to it as she trampled across the littered ground: debris of cans, food wrappers and split planks of wood, presumably those that had been prised from one or more of the windows in order to gain access. There was a staircase leading up to the first floor, but the tenebrous space looked neither welcoming nor safe. When she glanced ahead, she could no longer see Gypsy in front of her.

"Hey, where did you go?" Violet called, coughing at the dryness of her throat. She fanned a hand through the air in front of her as if to clear it.

"You'd better not be screwing around with me!" she warned.

"Over here." Violet traced the voice to the left and saw Gypsy poking her head out from behind another wall. She hadn't noticed the opening before, but as she plodded forth, she discovered that it led into a separate chamber towards the rear of the mill. It was much smaller than the main area, and with a single boarded-up window, the dank blackness prevented her from entering as though it was another brick wall.

"Gypsy?" Violet's voice echoed in the void. It was as though her companion – 'friend' seemed like too strong a word – had dissolved into the shadows. She suddenly felt very alone and very vulnerable, and she was a second away from retreating when a shock of light flooded the room.

Violet closed her eyes in a reflex, the luminosity still visible on her inner eyelids. She forced them open to find a figure slouched on the ground in the far corner, an LED lantern planted between his legs. Most of his face was curtained by the long, oily mane that ended just below his chest. She wasn't acquainted with this man, but clothed in oversized jeans and a skull shirt, he reminded her of a member of a death metal band.

The focus of Violet's scrutiny soon landed upon the three figures standing in front of her. In the middle, and by far the tallest, was Joe. Camilla, always his right-hand woman, was wearing a tank top and combats; her broad shoulders lending weight to those toned arms. Gypsy stood to his left, staring sheepishly back at Violet.

"Welcome to our lair," said Joe, phlegmatic as ever.

"Told you I could persuade her." Gypsy looked up at him, her enlarged eyes taking on the appearance of a child seeking a prize.

"W-what the hell is this? Who's he?" Violet glanced back to the silent stranger in the corner.

"We know him only as The Kid," Joe answered. "He doesn't say much, but his reputation as a backstreet dealer precedes him. Not a good reputation I might add, but you have nothing to fear. He won't bite unless commanded."

Violet disregarded the jest. "I thought I said no more surprises?"

"As I'm sure you're aware by now, some things must be seen to be believed. Whatever you feel in the next few moments – whatever you think – do *not* run."

That last sentence alone was enough to raise the breaks and hurtle out of there. She perhaps would have done if it wasn't for a shuffling noise from behind the three strangers, movement alerting her to what could have been mistaken for a shadow in the surrounding penumbra. Suddenly aware of a sixth entity in the room, Violet barged a gap through the bodies. A metal ring was bolted to the brickwork on the back wall. Dangling from it was a bulky chain, on which the other end was shackled around a man's neck.

Slumped on his knees, only his battered trousers cushioned him from the concrete floor. His head drooped forwards; short, scraggly waves clinging to his face, but it wasn't enough to disguise the fact that he was no ordinary human being. His ribcage looked like a xylophone, high and prominent, although there was no emaciation to speak of. His torso and limbs had a sinewy appearance with minimal fat to conceal the muscle definition.

"What... is..." *He? It?* Neither seemed fitting.

As if recognising Violet's voice, the man tilted his head up towards her. Through black, sweat-drenched tendrils, his raspy breaths grew louder as she approached. She felt Joe's gentle pull on her arm as he spoke in forewarning, "Don't be fooled by his apparent frailty. That chain has already been replaced several times."

Violet swatted him away as though she might do a fly, her unease of the prisoner now a tiny seed in the back of her mind. There was a familiarity between them that went beyond the physical, irrespective of his structure having mutated beyond recognition. Similar to when she'd first laid eyes on Gypsy, it was something very akin to a bond.

"Oh, God," she whispered. "Matt...?"

"*Grroooar!*" He thrust his arms out to their full extensions, fingers raking the air just millimetres from Violet's face. She bounded backwards into her three accomplices. If the numerous pairs of arms hadn't been there to support her, then her legs would have crumpled beneath her.

"Holy fuck!" Violet shrieked. "W-what the..."

While this abomination had once been human, only a creature of hell's origin would possess claws so wickedly forged. The hands were large and leathery, almost oversized. Tipped with thick, yellowish thorns meant for one distinctive purpose: slaughtering its prey.

"Some would call it a monster; others a consequence," said Joe. "Me? I see it as a victim of its environment. That is, the most primitive version of man that has ever – *will* ever – walk this earth."

Dumbstruck, Violet half twisted her head to look up at him. It was Camilla she heard next, as was evident by the disdain in her voice. "You parade the truth in front of her and she still reeks of confoundment. What a waste."

"No," Gypsy objected, "I've seen the power inside of her. Besides, you only have to look at the brute strength of that thing to know that she's special."

Violet didn't think she could be any more mystified until Gypsy pointed at the beast. "What's any of this got to do with me?" she said.

"Everything," replied Joe. "You made Matthew what he is today. Your blood runs through his veins, and now it's time to take responsibility for your actions."

"No. That's impossible... I-I never –" Violet remembered the bite. The kiss *before* the bite. Her own blood contaminating Matt's shoulder.

She shook her head. "I don't believe you. This is some kind of prank, and you're a bunch of sick fucks!"

"Enough!" With a burst of impatience, Joe manoeuvred her closer to Matt until she was just out of reach, like dangling a steak in front of a Rottweiler. Violet quailed as her gaze was forced to the monstrosity once more. His hands had moved up to the metal collar and chain, tugging savagely. The spluttering growls indicated that if he couldn't escape then he'd choke himself in the attempt.

With his head canted towards the light, Matt was hardly recognisable through the malformed features. The protruding brow bone and sculpted cheeks seemed to push his eyes higher and wider, expanding his peripheral vision in an animal-like fashion. The large, heavy-set jaw provided foundations to pronged teeth and elongated canines. All Violet could do was shut her eyes to him, tears forcing their ways through her lashes and dribbling down her cheeks.

"That night in the alleyway," Joe whispered into her ear, breath hot against her cheek, "you did what you thought you had to in order to survive. If we hadn't been there to clean up your mess, many people would have died as a result of your carelessness."

"I... don't understand," Violet wept. "I don't understand any of this."

"Of course you don't, because you've been lied to all your life. Put a lion in a cage, repress it of its basic needs and instincts and it'll drive itself into a frenzy of pent-up rage, making it more dangerous than when left to its own devices in the wild. That's what your parents did to you, Violet: they tried to domesticate you. The consequences of their actions have proven fatal for one innocent girl's life already."

"Isabelle? She has nothing to do with this. That wasn't my fault!" Violet glanced back at Joe, at the same time wondering why she was defending herself to a bunch of delinquents.

"It wasn't your fault that you couldn't protect her," Joe added. "If you're looking for someone to blame then you should start a bit closer to home. To the people that made you vulnerable in a world where you're the bullseye of many targets."

"But... I'm just a girl. A pathetic, messed up reject that spends her life chasing drink and men."

"Finally, she speaks sense," Camilla sneered.

"Sucks to be jealous, huh, Cammy?" Gypsy stepped forwards and placed a dainty hand onto Violet's shoulder. "We both saw what you're capable of back in the toilets, and Joe's told me how quickly your senses are advancing. I know it's scary, but we've got your back."

Even the girl's sweetest smile failed to dent Violet's consternation; rather, it made her wonder what kind of nut jobs that she was associating herself with. Violet glanced at each of them in turn, having almost forgotten about Kid in the corner, who hadn't moved or so much as grunted since her arrival. Clanking sounds resonated through the chamber, dust flaking from the brickwork that secured the chain. Bolts began to slip so the bracket was no longer flush with the wall. Without a single thought, doubt or question in her overwhelmed mind, Violet broke loose from Joe and ran. Even after departing the structure, she kept on running, heading in no particular direction as long as it was away from the freaks and their pet.

The path she took angled through the woods, tapping feet and vigorous breaths chasing away the inhabitants of nature. Twigs and overreaching brambles snagged her bare legs, dirt kicked up beneath her heels; but it wasn't long before she heard even louder, swifter footsteps from behind. They gained on her fast – so fast that she expected another, much larger body to pounce on her any second. Short of arming herself with a shotgun, turning around was not an option: she knew exactly who and what was hunting her. The afternoon sun was already low, and the canopy of trees gave the illusion of approaching night. Violet couldn't outrun him, although the thought of those shovel-like hands ripping her head from her shoulders as if she was a human Pez dispenser afforded some acceleration.

Somewhere, a trigger was flipped in the confines of Violet's mind. She skidded to a halt, heels grooving the earth. Then she crouched, being sure to shield her head from the impending collision. While Matt's knees slammed into her, there was nothing to obstruct his torso and both the weight and momentum sent him diving headfirst over her. His arms flailed like front crawl through a sea of air particles, and Violet heard the smacking of his skull against a tree trunk, followed by a roar that was fierce as it was painful. If she could split her body in half then she didn't doubt that one side would flee, while the other braced itself for the attack. Either way, the outcome remained the same: certain bloodshed.

Matt scrabbled onto all fours, nails sinking into the dirt. He shook his head a little before refocusing onto her. A deep growl rumbled in his throat, drool hanging like slime from the corners of his mouth. His entire face looked like some sort of mask or prosthetics, and the reflective film on his eyes hinted that his night vision was a lot sharper than hers.

"M-Matt..." Violet gulped, "is it really you in there?"

The beast snarled, making a snapping motion with its jaw. Violet could have been going into rigor mortis as every muscle in her body tensed up simultaneously.

"It's me, Violet – from the club," she mumbled, through stiffened lips. "You remember me, don't you? What happened between us... it was a misunderstanding. I know you never meant to –"

It was the bark that silenced her. She didn't have time to think as Matt launched himself in her direction, the spring in his back legs more than enough to cover the distance of a car between them. Violet wasn't sure if it was the collision or her own reflexes that ploughed her onto her back, but Matt's weighty bulk upon her left no room for manoeuvre. His jaw stretched so wide with roars that she thought he might swallow her head whole; the moist, foul-smelling breath almost as lethal as his canines.

The next thing she saw was a hand come swooping down from behind him, wrenching the metal collar around Matt's neck with such power that he emitted a strangulated yowl. Violet hadn't even noticed Camilla until the beast was prised off her and the feisty blonde swung him onto his front. She dug the sole of her foot into the area just below his shoulder blades to keep him pinned to the ground. Matt's arms thrashed and beat against the earth, forcing Camilla to pull harder on the collar to restrict his air flow. To see an ordinary woman overpowering the feral creature was enough to still Violet's trepidation a moment or two, flashbacks of the park swarming her thoughts. This demonstration of superhuman strength wasn't too dissimilar to the way Joe had propelled a fully-grown man into the air as if he was a blow-up doll.

"Someone get this thing on a fucking leash!" Camilla bellowed, with an unaccustomed strain in her voice.

Gypsy trotted over and hooked the missing chain around Matt's collar, clipping it into place. She handed the reins to Camilla and then stood well back.

"Easy, boy," Camilla attempted to mollify the brute. She looped the end of the chain around her hand and then hoisted his head and shoulders off the ground. Her biceps threatened to rupture as she brought Matt to his knees and, ever focused on Violet, he continued to gnash his teeth and make feeble swipes at her with his claws.

Camilla was generous with the length of chain, allowing enough pull to scare Violet into recoiling without Matt reaching her. She shuffled away on her elbows and feet until backing into an obstruction, then craned her neck to see Joe looming over her.

"You see how strong he is, despite being in a starved and weakened state?" he referred to Matt. "It's almost beyond controlling, as will you be if you don't give in to your desires."

"What the hell are you talking about?" Violet wailed. "Get that thing away from me!"

Matt's lips peeled back to expose the full lengths of his teeth, sputum spraying onto Violet's ankles. Grit and twigs had left mucky lashes in her flesh, and the sleeves of her blouse were smeared with dirt.

"Take control, Violet. Mould the fear into something useful." Joe's voice was more commanding. "It's merely a soldier; a beta. It's a creation and you are the creator."

The words held no comprehensive meaning to Violet, yet as her eyes connected to Matt's, as did her consciousness. She absorbed his wrath with each breath that she took, felt the heat on her skin as if sitting in front of an open fire. But instead of being projected at her, it was confined within himself like a moth in a jar. A tangled mass of frustration that Violet understood all too well – empathised with, even. As if receptive to her solicitude, Matt's panting slowed; still with a light rasp. Violet was drifting towards him without any memory of having stood up. Everything around them seemed stiller, the quiet almost hypnotic. The breeze had subsided and the trees no longer played their game of Chinese whispers. In that moment it was just the two of them, fixed in one another's gazes. Behind that monstrous exterior, all she saw was the soul of a man in turmoil.

Violet outstretched a steady hand. Her fingertips brushed over his wiry hair, not typical of human texture but more like a horse's mane. It had thickened and grown since that night in the alleyway, and what with his lean physique, one would think he'd been held captive for weeks rather than days.

Violet's movement continued past his ears and down towards the stocky neck. She used her forefinger to snap open the latch on the collar so the metal hoop clattered to the ground. What had possessed her to carry out the action was similar to the feelings conjured when seeing an animal in pain, but Gypsy's gasp from behind reminded her that this wasn't a duckling trapped in plastic beer can rings.

As if Violet had suddenly ceased to exist, Matt sprang around in a crouch. He was upon Camilla before any of them could blink, and all that remained of her were the screams shaking through the forest from beneath the beast. Violet could only stand and watch as his enormous jaw clamped around her collar bone, and there was a grinding crack as he bit through it like a stick of rock. She smelled the blood before she saw it, a feeling of sinking dread alerting her to the gruesome reality of what she'd done.

Joe marched hastily around Violet and, using both arms, brought a leafless branch crashing down onto the back of Matt's head. Violet winced at the thought of his skull splitting open like a coconut but, unbelievably, the branch took most of the damage and the lower half of it ricocheted into the air.

Camilla's howling terminated when Matt went limp and collapsed on top of her, a respite from the madness that Violet could only guess was temporary. As Camilla wriggled out from underneath him, Joe used his foot to nudge the motionless bulk to one side.

"Fucking bitch, look at what you did!" Camilla was already storming over to Violet, her chest coated in blood so thick that it looked like someone had spilled a can of paint down her front. The flesh around her collar bone was shredded by dagger-shaped teeth marks, and Violet was amazed that the woman was still standing at all.

In her stupefied state, Violet saw a blurry shape slash through the air in front of her. First, she was aware of the wetness dribbling down her face and neck as if it might never stop. Then came the searing pain, and her eyes fell to the stiffened talons by Camilla's side that tapered into hooks – the same ones she'd seen on Matt. Whimpers were all Violet could manage, for any stretch to her jaw enhanced the agony. She raised a hand to her face, the gloopy substance warming her fingers. There must have been three, possibly four trenches carved in a diagonal pattern across her face, the highest just millimetres above her left eye. It was by accident that her index finger slipped into one of the mushy slits, eventually feeling a hard object which she presumed was her cheekbone.

Violet looked back to Camilla towering over her as if she'd grown several feet, but when she felt soil beneath her knees, she realised it was her that had shrunk. Blood trickled into her eye, mixing with tears until she could see nothing. She swayed a little before keeling onto her side, strangely grateful for the natural painkiller of unconsciousness. She closed her eyes to encourage it, one last thought forcing its way free: please, don't wake up.

CHAPTER NINE

Images flickered like an old film reel. Chains, woodlands, teeth, claws and blood... lots of blood.

Violet shot upright, eyes open, yet the flashbacks continued as if she was witnessing the grisly scenes all over again. She screamed, her legs thrashing beneath the duvet until it was flung from her body.

"Easy, Violet." A voice soothed her. "You're safe now. Calm down."

Strong hands clamped her shoulders to prevent her from squirming, though they were nowhere near as sizeable as one would expect for such a hold. The ghastly projections from her mind dissipated like smoke to reveal a petite form resting on the edge of the bed.

"Isabelle..." Violet felt for the hands on her shoulders, squeezing them as if to make sure they were real. She could smell Dean's cologne but he wasn't beside her; rather, it was coming from the oversized T-shirt that she was wearing.

"It's me, Gypsy." The girl in front of her spoke again.

Violet blinked as the awareness slowly came back to her. "H-how did I get here? Where's Dean?"

"We brought you home." Gypsy let go of her. "I cleaned y'up and then watched over you while you recovered. As for Dean, you don't need to worry about him."

"What's that supposed to mean? What happened last –" Violet's hands jumped up to her face, patting motions turning into a frantic fumble when she found that the flesh was still intact.

"My face..."

"Let me explain –"

"*My face!*"

Anxious to get to a mirror, Violet was too impatient to take a detour around the bed and thrust Gypsy aside. She scrambled to the opposite end on her hands and knees, then dashed over to the free-standing mirror. Her reflection appeared as a stranger at first, but it wasn't the deformity that she'd expected. What she saw was even more shocking: a complexion that glowed with vitality. Wide, clear eyes glistening like sunbeams over an ocean. Flesh that was porcelain rather than pasty, with a flush of colour in her cheeks. Violet rotated her waist, studying herself from all angles to ensure that it was her in the mirror. She saw a smile on her ruby lips and touched them as if in confirmation. She'd never looked healthier in her life, even before abusing her body with drink and late nights.

Another face appeared behind her, and she met Gypsy's gaze in the reflection. "Why aren't I dead?"

"It's gonna take more than that hot-headed cow to put y'in your grave." Gypsy spoke facetiously.

"That hot-headed cow practically ripped my face off." Violet turned to Gypsy so there was no mistaking her gravity. "And you didn't raise a hand to stop her. None of you did."

"At least you know the truth now. That's what you wanted, ain't it?"

"Not like this! Besides, I can't remember anything after Camilla attacking me."

"Ever heard the phrase 'so hungry that I could eat a horse'? I never imagined that I'd see it in quite a literal sense."

As if Violet didn't feel queasy enough, she covered her mouth with her hand. It was like the raw steak all over again. "Oh, God, I didn't..."

"I'm kidding," Gypsy teased. "It wasn't a horse, it was –"

"Don't!" Violet raised a hand in gesticulation to stop. "Is that what the incident in the park was about? You hunt and kill people, pretending to do the world a favour, but in actuality it's just so you can get a meal."

"We're not cannibals, Violet. We gave you the sustenance that you needed in order to heal – to grow strong again. Don't you feel better for it?"

It was true. She felt invincible, energised. From streaking naked down the street to charging at the enemy on a battlefield, nothing was beyond her limits.

"First my senses go haywire, then I manage to punch through a steel wall; now the accelerated healing," Violet reflected. "What will it be next, sideburns and a monobrow?"

Gypsy gave a mocking laugh. "This isn't a movie, silly! It's a lot less daunting if you think about it in the sense that we're just a more primitive species of human."

Violet didn't know whether the girl's blasé attitude made her feel better or worse. "So, we're no different to Matt? Is that what I look like when..."

"Joe will explain everything. You might have healed from last night physically, but mentally it takes time. These blackouts that you've been having are a defence mechanism, like when people repress memories of abusive childhoods. The same thing happened to me after I was turned by Joe."

"Like I turned Matt, you mean?"

"Not exactly. You were born with your abilities, whereas the rest of us acquired them through the exchange of blood. That's why Matt's difficult to control. I guess you could say that he's purer than us."

Violet sank onto the end of the bed as her knees weakened, brittle laughter forcing its way past the lump in her throat. "Part of me wants to say that this can't be happening. I'd rather be insane than any of it be true, but I've always known that I was different. Isabelle and I were as close as sisters could be, but as individuals we couldn't have been more opposite."

Gypsy sat beside Violet, listening intently as she poured out all of the things that she'd never had a chance to say. "I was a loner growing up: the outcast at school, the troublemaker at family dos. You know, that kid who sticks chewing gum to people's chairs and sets fire to their sleeping uncle's hair."

Gypsy chuckled as Violet went on, "None of my family was perfect, but I always felt like the rotten apple. Isabelle never treated me like that, though. She was my anchor, and now she's gone."

"How old would she have been?"

"About your age. Despite the years between us, she was always the mature one. When I was fifteen, I got in with the wrong crowds and did a whole load of stupid shit. I didn't even like them, I was just sick of never having any friends."

"I know that feeling. My family moved to England when I was ten; whenever I did go to school, I was bullied for being different. My cousins were all married before they were seventeen, and the thought of spending my life knee-deep in nappies and beer cans was enough to send me running. I'm not saying that life on the streets was all fun, but I am and always will be a drifter. I'm not fussed where life takes me, as long as it takes me somewhere."

"This can't be where you imagined ending up, though." Violet looked wonderingly at Gypsy. "Does none of it bother you?"

"When I first met Joe, around a year ago, I'd just been caught shoplifting from a backstreet off-license. Granted, it wasn't the first time, but the owners laid into me like I'd committed murder or something. If they'd called the police like anyone else, then maybe one of them wouldn't be rolling himself around in a wheelchair right now."

"Jesus." Violet winced at the metal snapshot.

"Jesus had nothin' to do with it. It was Joe that came to my rescue. I'm safe with him and Camilla, and that's all that matters to me."

"You could argue that those guys were only doing to you what Joe does to other criminals. How come it's one rule for you and another for everyone else?"

"There are always exceptions to the rules. I know it's a lot to take in, why don't we go and get some fresh air? We could grab a coffee, see a movie or do some retail therapy – whatever it is that normal people do."

As Violet watched her flit about the bedroom, it wasn't only the girl's nonchalance that baffled her, but the fact that she seemed to know where everything was. From the jeans and tops in her chest of drawers, to the jackets hanging in her wardrobe.

"Why do I get the feeling that you've been in my flat before today?" she asked Gypsy.

"I've been watching over you all night. Too nosy for my own good, me."

"You wouldn't happen to know anything about an empty vodka bottle?"

Gypsy's delayed response told Violet all she needed to know. Red-faced, the girl returned to the bed and plonked a selection of clothing down next to her. "We had to make it look like there was a credible reason for your blackout to whoever found you. Taking you with us would have caused more harm than good."

"So you set me up instead? Everyone thought I was losing my mind – Christ, I thought I was losing my mind. How did you even get in?"

"You let us in, and it was a good job, too. You were out of control, tearing the place up. You were on the verge of transforming without having any clue of what was going on."

"But you must have been nearby... watching me." Violet made a face. "Do you know how creepy that is?"

"Creepy is a small price to pay for what might have happened if Dean was here."

Gypsy had an inarguable point – one that stirred a cauldron of dread inside Violet's stomach. She rested her forehead in one hand, concealing the top half of her face.

"I might not be as powerful as you, but I do have some idea of what you're going through," Gypsy added. "Joe helped me to control it, and he can help you, too."

Violet looked at her sideways through her fingers. "It's what he wants in return that bothers me."

"All he wants is your faith. What other options are there?"

It was a question that Violet had asked herself repeatedly since that night in the park, and her answer was always the same. "None," she murmured.

Gypsy clapped her hands together, startling Violet. "How about I make you a nice strong brew to wake y'up, eh?"

"Then, what? Go for a stroll down St. Peter's like nothing ever happened," Violet replied caustically. "Shit, what time is it? I've got to get to work –"

"Relax, you're taking a sick day as far as they're concerned. I sorted it all out for you."

"Oh... thanks, I guess. I should call Dean, though. He'll be wearing holes in his carpet from pacing around."

"Yeah, about that... I might have texted him from your phone last night pretending to be you."

"You did *what?*"

"I kept it short, just said that I – you – weren't feeling well and that you were going to have an early night. He's kinda clingy, ain't he?"

"He cares about me."

Gypsy surprised Violet by embosoming one of her hands in both of hers. "So do we. Come hang out with us, get to know the group better. Maybe then, you'll be ready to move on to phase two."

"What's phase two?"

Gypsy's characteristic grin broadened to show off her teeth. Violet wished she hadn't asked.

***

"Tell me again why we've had to come so far out?" Violet felt no less than exposed on the open stretch of Peak District, flanked by its mountainous terrain. A thick patch of trees to the front reached as far back as she could see. To the rear of them, the country road that they'd come from was just visible from their vantage point. The grass felt hard beneath her boots, not ideal for a romantic evening of stargazing; although she had a feeling that wasn't on the agenda tonight.

"Close your eyes," said Joe.

"Excuse me?"

Joe slunk up behind her and repeated, "Close your eyes and hone your senses. What do you hear? What do you smell?"

Violet shut her eyes, replying sardonically, "I hear the wind and I can smell the grass. I don't need to close my eyes for that, we're in the frigging wilderness."

"Listen *through* the wind and there's so much more. The scuttering of wildlife, the flapping of bat wings. Owls hooting, tree branches clashing against one another. You can taste the earth in the air: damp leaves and musty bark. The more you practice, it'll start to become second nature – like when you found Matt's shirt in the dumpster."

"All right, no need to remind me." Violet zipped up her camo jacket and folded her arms. Blasts of chilled air swept down from the mountains, spattering her with light, misty rain. Violet hunched against it, but the rest of the group seemed unaffected. A part of her couldn't quite believe that she'd climbed into the Jeep with the four deviants. Worse-case scenario, there was nowhere for her to run.

Feeling Joe's gaze upon her, she brushed away the strands of hair that whipped her face.

"I understand your apprehension." Joe kept his voice low, as if they were in a roomful of people. "But until you lose yourself, you'll never be able to find yourself. Remember what I said about an animal being caged, how they're driven to madness by the very boundaries that are built to keep them safe? Tonight, you're free to be one with the beast. You won't end up like Matthew, I promise."

"How can you be so sure? Matt's like a rabid animal, and I'm the source of that madness. If that's even a fraction of the monster I'll become..."

"The transformation is a magical thing. It awakens a part of us that is much more powerful than what the average human is capable of. The alterations to our skeletal structure, not to mention the surrounding muscles and organs, puts a tremendous amount of stress on the nervous system. Think of it as a mental breakdown or psychotic episode."

Violet raised a dubious brow. "You're not exactly selling this to me."

"My point is that there has to be an adaption period. Also take into account that males have much higher levels of testosterone than women, thus increasing aggression. The hormone plays a key role in puberty – the development from child to adult – and many of these physiological effects can be seen during our own transformations: muscle mass, bone density and even morphology, especially in the hands and skull."

"You're saying that a spike in testosterone turns us into flesh-eating mutants?" Violet shook her head before a response was given. "Biology was never my strongest subject, but it sounds to me like we're just a freak of nature."

"In some ways, you're absolutely correct. Not everyone survives the change, hence why there aren't more of us. Matthew's young and healthy, so there's every chance that he'll make it through this."

"What if he never goes back to the way he was?"

"It's possible," said Camilla, upon her approach. "I'm living proof of that."

"Wait, let me get this straight," Violet replied. "You were turned first, then you transferred it to your brother..." she turned to Joe, "and you passed it on to Gypsy and Kid? Christ, now I feel like an STI."

"To be fair, it was my only option." Gypsy spoke up. "Joe's blood helped me to heal after the shop owners assaulted me. I'll never be that helpless little girl again."

"What about... *that*?"

Violet nodded towards Kid. He was further back from the group, more engrossed by the whispering tree line. Crouched as always, he cocked his head as if listening to the sounds of the forest.

"Typical junkie, never was right in the head," Camilla explained. "Make no mistake, though – he's a relentless tracker and a good dog."

"Talking of which," said Joe, "let's get down to business and do what we came here to do."

"At last," uttered Camilla.

Before Violet could question them, she was slugged in the gut by a full-force uppercut. She thought she was at risk of vomiting her intestines and doubled over while staggering forwards. Camilla stepped aside so she ended up face-first on the grass. Violet rolled onto her back while cradling her stomach, tears blown across her cheeks by the breeze. For a while she was unable to speak, only gaze up at Joe as he leaned over her with his hands clasped on his knees.

"Like any species, pain is our primary weakness. But for us it's also an antidote, a deterrent to the change. Why? Because it connects us to our humanity."

"N-no shit," Violet grunted, as the ache in her stomach began to blunt. Just as soon as she felt that she could rise, Joe pressed the sole of his foot onto her chest to keep her flat.

"Fight through your emotions and tap into the rage that drives them. Adrenaline is the trigger: it increases speed, strength, awareness and reaction times – it even allows for a diminished sense of pain. You felt it the night that Matthew tried to force himself on you, did you not?"

Violet gasped for air as her ribcage caved inwards, pushing down on her lungs. She yanked at Joe's shoe but would have had more luck shifting a boulder from the ocean bed.

"S-stop, you're hurting me." Her voice was lost in the wind. She was sure that she could hear her bones creaking like old wood, ready to collapse at any second.

"Your abilities have been suppressed for so long that you've been rendered useless. If you can't defend yourself against me then you're going to die here tonight. Isabelle will never be avenged and her killer will go unpunished. Do you understand me?"

"Joe..." Gypsy looked nervous.

"Think back to that day," Joe continued. "You walked the streets, oblivious to the agony that she was enduring. The fear of knowing that she was going to die alone. How does it feel to have to pass by people every day and ask yourself, 'Is it him or her? Could they be the one that stripped the world of my beautiful sister?'"

"Stop..." Violet was scarcely able to mouth the word. Her heart slammed against the underside of Joe's foot, and his smirk convinced her that he could feel it.

"I bet they enjoyed it," he hissed. "I bet they laughed the evening away while you wept like an infant, unable to save the one person that you lived and breathed for."

"Pathetic," scoffed Camilla. "I say we do her a favour before the hunters get to her first."

Hunters? Violet wasn't sure that she'd heard her correctly. Blood rushed through her ears – or was it the wind? A desperate growl seethed in her throat as she kicked up between Joe's legs, her heel clouting his ball sack. As soon as she felt the pressure ease off her chest, she locked her hands around Joe's ankle, twisted outwards and then threw him backwards. Both Camilla and Gypsy broke into loud guffaws as he thudded onto his backside, legs flung almost over his head. Violet heard shouting from the girls, but it wasn't until her senses were restored that she realised they were cheers. They stood pointing and jeering at their leader like school kids in a playground, while Kid bounced up and down like a frog on speed.

"That's what I'm talking about!" Joe clapped his hands while jumping to his feet.

Violet's temper cracked, and the next second she was springing through the air towards him. Her body felt weightless, as though it was a trampoline beneath her feet rather than grass. She descended upon Joe's torso, looping her legs around his waist with enough muscle in her thighs to support herself. One hand balanced on his shoulder, while the other plunged down towards the arch of his neck. The flesh was tough, unnaturally so, yet her nails pierced it without resistance; blood welling up from the slits. Joe groaned, although it sounded more erotic than painful. He groped the back of her thighs through her jeans, keeping their bodies locked together as if they were in the midst of passion. Violet extracted her fingernails and held her hand in front of her, merely a silhouette in the darkness. She could make out the elongated fingers, pointed tips slowly retracting until they returned to their natural length and shape. Violet unclenched her legs and slid onto her feet, separating herself from Joe.

"Well, what d'ya know, the bitch finally grew a pair!" Camilla applauded from behind them.

Violet's eyes remained affixed with Joe's, the delight in them even more disconcerting than her own act of savagery.

"Can we go and play now?" Gypsy whined, having grown bored of the spectacle.

"Indeed," Joe replied. "Let's introduce Violet to our true nature. It is what she came here for, after all."

Gypsy and Camilla clasped hands and then skipped to the tree line as one. Kid sprinted after them with his ape-like gait, which looked uncomfortable but the speed suggested not. Their whoops of laughter grew as dim as the night sky, and soon there were no traces of any of them.

Joe drifted past Violet, twisting his head to say, "If you still have doubts then turn back now. The Violet that enters those woods will not be the same one that departs them."

He proceeded in the same direction as the others, knowing, as Violet did, that the time for turning back had already elapsed. Taking a deep breath, she trotted after him.

***

The thick clusters of trees were like great umbrellas overhead, sheltering her from the watery light of the misted sky. It was as though life didn't exist beyond the forest, and everything that Joe had spoken of – the sounds, the smells and even the taste of the air – was contained inside a giant fish tank. The ground was uneven beneath her feet, and the silhouettes of tree trunks persistently crept up on her.

"Damn it," Violet cursed, as her toe clipped a volcanic mound of earth. She pulled her mobile out of her coat pocket and activated the flashlight, at the same time noticing that there was no signal in the area. Her eyes left the ground momentarily to check that Joe was still ahead of her. She couldn't see the others, but the breeze carried their voices in waves every couple of minutes.

"Hey! Slow down, will you?" she called to Joe. "I can't see shit."

"Then, use your eyes," he replied smartly. "Your *other* eyes."

"You guys can see in the dark? Is that why Matt's eyes looked so... black?"

"Naturally, the pupils dilate to allow more light to enter when light is sparse, but the size and shape of ours is more akin to the visual organs of nocturnal animals and felines. The reflexive surfaces can make us sensitive to bright light, even in human form, but not enough to cause problems."

Violet nodded, both enthused and unnerved by this new knowledge. "I don't even want to think about what the claws are for."

"We have what only is... what *was*... vital for our survival many centuries ago. The source of our abilities dates as far back as the prehistoric man, before the time of education and technology. As humans evolve, they too are changing their environment; the result being that they're becoming less adapted to the world they create. Allergies, antibiotic-resistant bacteria, mental illness: the list is never-ending."

"But we all have a part to play. Times change and we change with them, that's how modern living works."

"Not for all of us," Joe refuted. "Two and a half million years ago, the creation of tools was a new invention: from stone to spears and the control of fire. What if none of that ever came to be? What if, rather than man changing the environment, the environment changed man?"

Violet stared at the back of Joe's head as they trampled through the woods. She wished that he'd turn around just so she could see whether or not he was joking. "I guess it's plausible," was all she said.

"If it wasn't, you'd have likely killed me back there. Healing is a natural process within every living creature's design. Without medicine or doctors, would it not make sense for our bodies to develop a heightened resistance or even immunity?"

"Well, more sense than some magical, airy-fairy bollocks, at least." Violet cringed at the blood that was still crusted under her fingernails. "I'm sorry about your neck, by the way. I don't know what came over me."

"No need for apologies, it only hurt for a second."

"Christ, I swear people would kill for these abilities."

"They would, and they do." The gravity behind Joe's words sparked an intrigue that, until now, Violet hadn't been ready or willing to explore.

"Is that what Camilla meant when she mentioned the hunters?" she asked him.

"There's a very powerful organisation known as The Clan that has been around for almost as long as our kind. They're hell-bent on controlling us, not just hunters but people of education and prestige: scientists, doctors, investors. What they can't control, they kill."

"How have they managed to keep everything so secret? And if we're neither human nor animal, then what the hell are we?"

"Metasapien or 'metas' is the official term that they branded us with, but now is not the time for a history lesson. At the risk of sounding patronising, it's a lot to process for an unsound mind. There are important things that I must teach you first."

"I think I've handled this pretty damn well so far. Besides, you don't have to spare my feelings because I've already worked it out."

"What is it that you think you've worked out?"

"My parents aren't my parents." Violet slowed her tread for a chance to regain her breath. Joe stopped while she caught up, and she shone the flashlight on him before adding, "That means Izzy wasn't my sister, right?"

Violet sensed Joe's reluctance in his silence, but a part of her was glad of it. To hear confirmation would make it all too absolute.

"It's kind of comforting to know that there was a reason for feeling unloved and resented all my life," she went on, as if to deflect any pity that came her way. "I can't say that I blame my mum... Beverly... for wanting rid of me, especially after my dad died. I was always closer to him."

"It sounds like she was and still is a great source of your self-hatred. Once we get justice for Isabelle, it will herald a new start for you. That is what you want?"

"I want answers. I want to know where I came from and how I ended up here. Were Beverly and my dad part of this Clan?"

"No, but not everyone within the organisation was loyal to it. This individual – a mole, if you like – was an acquaintance of the man whom you thought to be your father."

Violet sighed at the revelation. "That's why Izzy got caught up in all of this. Tell me straight, did those fuckers have something to do with her death?"

"I think you already know the answer to that."

The flashlight on Violet's phone chose the most inappropriate of moments to cut out. "Crap," she muttered, seeing the warning sign of a low battery.

"Hey, if there's a knack to this seeing in the dark thing then –" She glanced up to the empty spot where Joe had been standing not seconds ago. Thinking it was down to the sudden darkness, she extended her arm, using the screen to irradiate the area.

"Joe?"

Leaves rustled all around her, and half the time she couldn't tell whether it was coming from the trees or the shrubbery. She hadn't heard any sounds from the rest of the group for some time.

"Joe, stop messing with me."

Twit-twoo.

Violet drew back her arm at the visualisation of a man-sized owl swooping down and snatching it from her. It might as well have done, for the phone completely blinked out. After tapping the unresponsive keys, she slipped it back into her pocket and looked all around, stretching her eyes open and willing them to adapt to the gloom. Focusing on the outlines of tree trunks and picturing their features in her mind, hoping that it would somehow project onto the external. She only succeeded in giving herself a headache.

With unease circling in her gut and the cold stinging her throat, Violet blundered forwards; twigs snapping like firecrackers in the quietude. Several times she felt skeletal fingers raking at her hair, later realising that her imagination was turning harmless branches into lurking monsters. Preserved memories of the man she called 'Dad' entered her thoughts, perhaps as a distraction or because the reality of her situation was finally sneaking up on her. Beverly often complained about feeling like she was married to a hippy, with Kevin's trademark ponytail and the wispy rug on his chin – that was, during a time in which she'd taken pride in her appearance.

Pride... Violet nearly sniggered. That wasn't quite the right word to describe Beverly's low blouses and even shorter skirts. Still, her hair would be in rollers every morning and her makeup completed before anyone else had finished breakfast – not that she needed such embellishments. Twenty years later, the only thing that remained was the tacky wardrobe. Booze had contributed to the premature withering of her skin, and puffing on thirty cigarettes a day had turned her mouth into something that resembled a shrivelled asshole. She still had the foundations of a looker, and Violet had always believed that she'd inherited her slender frame from Beverly. She also thought she was doomed to follow the same path of self-destruction, so the knowledge that they shared no DNA had at least one advantage.

A cracking sound to her distant left interrupted Violet's reminiscence. She glanced around, even though it was futile in the dark. A rustling followed, like tiny feet scurrying through thicket. Her eyes, ears and even her nose were on alert, but the forest gave no discernible clues as to her stalker. Either she was trying too hard or it was some kind of performance anxiety. In the past, her enhanced senses had only come into effect on the spur of the moment.

Violet picked up speed, despite not knowing which direction she was heading or how dense the forest became. It could be daybreak before she reached the other side... *if* she reached it. After another couple of minutes of fumbling her way forwards, an orange glow danced between the trees. It was a little lower than ground level, and Violet assumed there must have been a gradient up ahead. The smell of smoke wafted towards her as she cautiously approached, not knowing whether it was Joe and the others; boozed-up teenagers or an unlucky case of wildfire.

Keeping behind a tree trunk, Violet peered down the dirt bank. The fire was no more than a few metres away, damp logs crackling and spitting; smoke clouds whirling up through an opening in the trees towards the starless sky. Shadows gyrated like spirits of the forest amongst three familiar figures. Closest to the flames, crouched down, the nude curves of a backside and thighs shimmered in the light. Violet identified the blonde hair as Camilla's, and in front of her lay a deer split open from neck to pelvis. Its entrails were spread in a viscid-looking discharge that had seeped around Camilla's bare feet. She held the intestine to her mouth, sucking and munching as though it was spaghetti; blood gloves running down to her elbows.

Paying no attention to his comrade was Kid, straddling a fallen tree trunk. He gnawed on something that resembled a limb, likely belonging to the deer; flesh squelching between his teeth as he tore every scrap of gristle from the bone. Gypsy was nearest to Violet, also with her back turned. She stood in her vest and knickers beside a heap of clothing and footwear.

Violet glanced back to the unfortunate prey and licked her lips, imagining the sweetness on them. A sight that would induce sickness and repulsion in most people, as it had once done her, causing a famishment that left her stomach gurgling. Drool bled from the corners of her mouth and sweat bubbled from her pores – whether because of the excitement or the roaring fire, she had no idea.

"Orgasmic, isn't it?"

Violet swivelled around to the sound of Joe's voice. He stood behind her like the others, stripped from the waist up. His torso was lean, the kind of muscle built up from running and climbing. She recoiled from the blood that painted his lower jaw, not in aversion but for the fear of wanting to taste it; to taste *him*.

"Give in to it, Violet," Joe said, as if reading her thoughts. "Let go of your inhibitions. What happens in the forest stays within the forest."

Violet's lips were slightly apart, giving a slur to her words. "I... don't want to be like this. How do I stop it?"

"You can't. You can only repress it, and look where that's got you so far."

"Last time I ate raw meat, it nearly killed me. The other day at work, I felt more pain than I've ever endured in my life."

"It was your body resisting the change due to the fortifications as set by your mind. Feeding encourages our natural habits, thus strengthening the connection to our inner being."

As Violet continued to back away, Joe drew further into the light. Soon, she could see the flames blazing in his eyes as though they were blackened mirrors. The structure of his face had shifted to present the same characteristics as Matt: the heavy brow bone and large jaw, with crafted cheeks to allow a more tensile stretch. She assumed it was the leathery skin that allowed them to acclimatise to the cold so well, as with Matt's rapid hair growth.

Joe was so close that Violet could feel his blood-tainted breath on her face. Her taste buds were like popping candy, alive with little explosions of eagerness. A meteoric wave of hunger almost knocked her legs from under her. Joe noticed her unsteadiness and looped an arm around her waist, squashing their bodies together. Violet felt the organ in his trousers pressing against her as he dipped his head, pausing when their lips were millimetres apart, as if trying to tempt her the rest of the way. It felt as though all of the blood in her body had drained to the curse in between her legs, and it took most of her restraint not to slip her hands down his boxers and work him to stiffness.

Violet closed her eyes, chest rising and falling. Her tongue slithered out of its burrow like an earthworm, the tip licking the stickiness off Joe's lips as if they were drizzled in syrup.

"Violet."

She opened her eyes and turned to see Gypsy beckoning her over to the campfire. Joe detached himself with a stride backwards, though his gaze drove deep into her.

"Go," he whispered. "Enjoy the bond of true family for the first time in your life."

Violet felt as though she was floating towards the fire. Towards warmth, companionship and understanding. These people... these creatures... may have been strangers to her, but the bond that Joe had spoken of was as real as the situation that she'd found herself in. Whether it was something as tangible as blood or transcendental as the soul, she didn't know. It didn't even matter to her.

Violet allowed Gypsy to unzip her coat and ease it back over her shoulders. She lifted her arms to aid the removal of her sweatshirt, without questioning or resistance, and they stood facing one another in their semi-naked states.

"You're so skinny." Gypsy's eyes wandered over the breasts cupped in Violet's bra and down to her waist, which ran in parallel lines to her hipbones. Violet shivered without the extra padding.

"I'm cold," she murmured, at the thought of losing her jeans, too.

"You'll get used to it. Besides, this gets kinda messy and clothes are harder to wash than skin. Not to mention that they weigh us down, and shoes aren't stealthy for hunting."

"Hunting? I-I can't..."

"Once you get a taste for it, it'll become second nature. Trust me."

Gypsy took Violet's hand, the smile embedded into her face somehow reassuring. As she was led to Camilla and the slaughtered deer, Violet took a final glance at Joe. Still he observed her from afar, silent and inscrutable. A history of secrets that Violet didn't doubt rivalled her own.

CHAPTER TEN

The muscle was shredded from bone with blade-edged teeth: rich, lean and slimy with blood. The gristle had felt strange at first. All she wanted to do was spit it out, but before long it was sliding down her oesophagus with everything else. Violet had spent most of the first night observing the others. As parts of her anatomy began to change, she ascertained that her molars weren't built for grinding and chewing. Their sole purpose was for tearing through flesh, bone and everything in between.

The second night was less inhibited, and watching the others mindlessly devouring their prey without wastage had exacerbated Violet's hunger. The third night felt like an orgy, all basking in the pleasures of themselves and each other. If anything it was the fur that Violet disliked the most: bristly fibres sticking between her teeth and irritating her throat, not to mention the thought of fleas and other parasites. She did her best to avoid it by using her sharpened nails to dig beneath the epidermis, although it didn't seem to bother anyone else.

Violet had felt an awakening that deepened with each feast, a transition that was internal as much as it was external. Every nerve was like a tiny spark working to revive her exhausted body. She recalled glimpses of her kin, human yet not human, hunched over various carcasses with sinewy physiques that reminded her of fleshless bodies. As their bellies filled, their behaviour became more beastlike and carnivorous; features more disfigured. Perhaps it was Violet's fear that had caused such imaginings, for everything else seemed irrelevant compared to the need to feed. From the perplexity of her circumstances to her own physical transformations, everything was caught in a mental blizzard. For a few passing moments, even the anguish of losing Isabelle was lost.

CHAPTER ELEVEN

Violet awoke to the sounds of her own dreamy moaning. She yawned with her arms stretched over her head, then flipped onto her side and draped herself over the warm body next to her. As consciousness found its way through the haze, she opened her eyes and raised her head off the pillow. Dean's face had a restful kind of serenity that prompted her to lay a hand on his chest to confirm that he was still breathing. Relieved, she rolled onto her back so she was facing the ceiling and brought the same hand to her forehead, as if trying to extract the missing memories from the last few nights. It was as though she'd had an out-of-body experience, and in the snippets that she did remember, she could easily have been watching someone else.

Dean stirred beside her, the movement having roused him. His eyelids opened just wide enough so that he could peek at her. "Hey," he croaked.

"Hey." She graced him with a mechanical smile. "What time is it?"

Dean brought his arm up from beneath the duvet and squinted at his watch. "Almost seven."

"In the morning?"

"I hope so, or else we're both out of a job."

Violet decided against asking him what day it was, although she could make a guess. Dean shifted onto his side, and Violet felt a hand slither over her belly, lightly brushing the top of her pubic hair. "That was one hell of a surprise, you turning up here out of the blue last night. I wasn't prepared for things to get so... wild, shall we say."

Violet's head left the pillow a second time, her torso swiftly following. She hadn't even realised that the bed she lay in wasn't her own. "Oh, man," she groaned.

"Hey, I'm not complaining." Dean propped himself up on one elbow, combing back her lengthy tresses and kissing her shoulder. "I've missed you these last couple of nights. I get that you needed some downtime, and clearly you're feeling re-energised. Maybe give me a warning next time you plan on ripping the shirt off my back, anyone would think you're in heat."

Though it was meant in jest, it made perturbing sense to Violet. Looking into Dean's innocent face, she fleetingly wondered how he'd react if she was to blurt out everything that had transpired during the last week. As if to stop herself, she kicked back the duvet and scrambled out from underneath it.

"I have to go," she said, half crawling around the floor on the hunt for her underwear.

"What's the rush?" asked Dean. "You can shower here while I rustle up some breakfast. I'll drive you home for a change of clothes and then drop you off at work."

"Work?" The thought hadn't even crossed Violet's mind. "Oh, er... I have a doctor's appointment this morning. Sorry, it completely slipped my mind."

"I was beginning to think I'd have to drag you to that place in a straitjacket."

"Better I get it over with, especially if it's going to stop you guys from worrying." Violet preoccupied herself by fiddling with her bra strap, hoping to disguise the shame of more lies.

"Well, I wish you'd told me sooner. I could have taken an hour off work and come with you," said Dean.

"Don't worry about it, I'm a big girl."

"At least stay for breakfast, you must have worked up an appetite after last night. I know I have."

Violet had an impulse to laugh. She'd eaten more over the last few days than an average woman would eat in a week. "Haven't you got some plugs that need rewiring or lights to fix?"

"All right, I get the message." Dean whipped back the duvet and swung his legs out of bed. As he rotated his neck to loosen the muscles, Violet's eyes fell to the inflamed lines that crisscrossed his back. Not deep enough to scar, but definitely symbolic of claws.

"Dean..." Violet finished wriggling into her jeans before leaning across the bed and tracing her fingertips over the angriest of welts. "Did I do this?"

Dean strained his neck to look back at her, raising an amorous brow. "Told you it was a wild night."

"I didn't hurt you, did I?"

"If you did then it was in all the right ways. To tell you the truth, I was more worried about hurting you."

"What do you mean?"

"Well, we've never done it that rough before. I guess you're right about being tougher than you look." A pause, before he asked cynically, "You do remember all of this?"

"Of course, I must have got carried away in the heat of the moment," Violet lied.

"You just seem a little..."

"I wasn't drunk if that's what you're implying."

"I never said that."

"Good."

After dressing herself, Violet scooped up her shoulder bag and then made a beeline for the bedroom door. "So, I'll call you later, yeah?"

"Don't I get a kiss?" Dean stared across at her from the bed, the duvet barely obscuring his manhood. Violet swallowed, knowing that one step towards him would result in locking lips, hips and everything in between.

"Something for you to look forward to later." She winked, hoping it didn't look as feigned as it felt.

"You tease. Why do I feel like I'm being blown off?"

Sure that he would approach her any second, Violet plucked her keys from her coat pocket and unhooked one of them. She tossed it to Dean, who caught it in a reflex. "That's the key to my flat, come over after work if you want. If I'm not back then let yourself in."

"Really?"

"Don't get too excited, it's not a marriage proposal. I keep a spare key in my bag anyway, call it paranoia." While it was mainly a distraction to get out of there, Violet couldn't deny the feeling of security that he offered. Links to her old life were becoming sparser by the day, and if Lucy turned her back then Dean was all she had left.

"Thank you." Dean's voice was as tender as his smile, and Violet felt for the door handle without turning around.

"You're welcome. See you later." After backing out of the room, she fled the house.

***

"Hello?" The walls threw back the echoes of Violet's call, welcoming her into the abandoned mill. The sound waves disturbed a pigeon that had been nesting on the upper floor. Violet ducked as it soared over her head, wind whipping through its feathers as it flapped towards the entrance that she'd emerged from. For one ridiculous moment – or perhaps not so ridiculous – she wondered if it had sensed her predatory nature and absconded for the fear of being gobbled up.

Violet crept further into the mill, eyes roaming all around her. "Hey, guys! Anyone here? Gypsy...?"

Even with the doors wedged open and light squeezing through the boarded-up windows, it looked as if the sun was setting in the dingy space. A breeze moaned through the shattered glass towards the back of the building, causing Violet to shudder at her loneliness. Knowing there would be at least one other person in the mill – a person that she'd given no thought to until now – she entered the adjoined section that served as Matt's holding cell.

The metal collar and shackle were firmly in place, with the bracket having been re-embedded into the brickwork. Matt was recumbent on his side with his arms out limply in front of him, shoulders engraved with claw marks. Though the blood appeared dry, his wounds were unhealed. The same scarring was visible on his chest, which bobbed with each scratchy breath. Violet refrained from sweeping his hair back off his face at the risk of losing a hand or worse, and instead she knelt by his side, hoping in some way that her presence was comfort enough.

"What have they done to you?" she whispered, remorse choking her words. "What have *I* done to you?"

Violet tried to convince herself that if it wasn't for the restraints, Matt wouldn't hesitate to rip her flesh from her bones. That even in his enfeebled state, such barbarity was so ingrained that it overpowered any vestiges of human thought or emotion. But all she saw was a victim of her own rage, a connection to the piece of her that she was too afraid to unleash. For that, she felt no animosity towards him; only pity.

Violet laid down her bag and shuffled closer until she was half an arm's length away. "Matt, can you hear me? I'm so sorry for what I've put you through. You don't deserve this."

Matt offered no acknowledgment that he'd heard or understood what she was saying, but the tiny hint of relief that came from making some kind of peace was worth pursuing. "I promise you that I'm doing everything I can to make this right. I'll fix you just as soon as I figure it out. Please, just hang in there... Matt?"

"You're wasting your time."

Violet was on her feet instantly. She turned to find Joe in the doorway, hands in his pockets; that usual sangfroid demeanour.

"Sneak up on me much?" she scolded, though her vexation was aimed more at Matt's treatment than her own.

"If you'd been concentrating like I taught you, there'd be no opportunity for sneaking in the first place," Joe riposted.

"That's kind of difficult when half of my days are a blank. I feel like I'm permanently drunk, and it's not limited to the transformations either."

"Meaning?"

"Let's just say that, according to Dean, our bedroom activities are verging on S and M."

Joe grinned. "Lucky man."

"It's not funny! You know what I'm capable of."

"Rest assured that your mind and body are starting to balance themselves out. If I thought you were a danger to the people around you, then you'd be in chains right next to your prodigy there." Joe indicated Matt.

"Chain me up and use me as a punch bag, right? Are you even feeding him?"

"If an animal can't be controlled then it's put down. Believe it or not, we're trying to save his life."

"Maybe so, but is torture necessary?"

Joe ran his eyes over the prisoner's grazed torso and, realising her meaning, chuckled lightly. "Ah, that's just Camilla being a red-blooded woman. I'm sure Matthew gets as much out of it as she does."

Violet's eyes dilated in unison with her gaping jaw. "She's *raping* him?"

"Rape is a strong word. I can't say that I approve as a brother, but urges must be satisfied – on both parts, I might add. Does the cycle of life not revolve around eating, sleeping and breeding?"

Violet sensed a meekness in Joe that she'd never encountered before.

"Camilla was turned by a pure blood, right? It must suck having a little sister who could kick your ass if she wanted to."

The muscles spasmed either side of Joe's jaw, the force that it must have taken to suppress such bitterness causing a satisfying delay in his response. "Are you aware that a large percentage of the ocean's deep-dwelling animals are bioluminous?"

"Bio-what?"

"It's the production of light from the enzymes of a living organism. Essentially, creatures that live thousands of metres deep are able to glow in the dark. Adaption and evolution are never-ending processes that largely revolve around one's environment."

"You're talking about the conversion from caveman to... *meta*-whatever we're called," Violet stated, rather than asked. "I can just about get my head around that, but it doesn't explain how I came into existence. Can you imagine how that feels? Having strangers dangling half-truths in front of you like kids at a petting zoo."

After a few moments, Joe broke gazes with her. He wandered back to the central room while lighting a cigarette that he'd had tucked behind his ear. With no option but to follow, Violet took a last look at Matt and then sombrely left.

Once Joe was sure that he had Violet's attention, he continued, "Imagine, for one incredulous second, that man never emerged from his cave. That this very building..." he opened his arms in gesticulation of the mill's grim interior, "is where you took your first and last breaths, and every breath in between. A life sentenced to darkness and seclusion, without advanced communication and only a basic understanding of what it is to survive. Would you not think differently, behave differently? Would your body mechanisms not be altered over time?"

"Are you saying that our history is nothing more than a fucked up science experiment?" Violet answered.

Joe smiled, although there was a deflation in his words. "As with most history, fact and myth are intertwined. In the days of religion and superstition, we were demons sent to do the devil's bidding. We were the products of witchcraft and curses, forced to dwell deep within the mountain caves as outcasts, feared by communities for centuries."

"And you believe that, like the earth, we evolved naturally over time?"

"Homo sapiens were thought to have interbred with many species of archaic human – Neanderthals, for example – and it's likely that they had no concept of incest. I don't doubt that a combination of such relations resulted in certain deformities that alienated us from everyone else. Even in the modern world, people are afraid of what they don't understand."

"So, our remaining senses had to compensate for lack of vision in the darkness," Violet theorised. "Skin thickened for protection and warmth; claws helped us to climb, increasing strength and muscle mass. What about food? Something tells me that we survived on more than bats and insects."

"In a superstitious world, it was a common belief that sacrifices would keep the devil at bay. Both animals and humans were offered freely, until common sense prevailed. By then we'd already developed a taste for it, so we began to venture out of the caves to hunt when the sun went down."

"What is it about a metasapien's blood that makes us so... contagious?"

"Although we're far from indestructible, our immune systems are more developed than most. We have impressive regenerative qualities, but the kicker is that old cells are destroyed by the new. I mentioned before that the transformation has a stressful impact on the body, which in turn raises adrenaline levels to such a degree that it acts as a trigger. It's as much neurological as it is blood-borne, similar to the contraction of rabies, whereby inflammation of the brain causes symptoms of aggression, confusion and even violence."

"Great," Violet mumbled. "Now I really do feel like a walking disease."

"Think of it as a defence mechanism, like the venom from a black widow. Of course, we couldn't always shift between human and meta on impulse. That luxury manifested further on in the evolution process."

"How so?"

Joe took a long drag on his cigarette while sauntering across to the other side of the mill, the smoke billowing around him like some kind of wraith. "During the fourteenth century, a group of nobleman decided that it was time to eliminate the mysterious cave dwellers once and for all. They poured gunpowder into the caves and sealed off all exits. Only when the howling ended did the cowards dare to walk amongst the ashes."

Violet said, "I'm guessing some of them survived and that these noblemen were linked to the Clan you spoke of?"

"Better they perished in those flames than endure what was to come." Joe flung the cigarette aimlessly to the ground, as if the nicotine wasn't enough to lull his animosity.

"They were held captive?"

"Experimentation, breeding, torture: they were subjected to all of it. More to the point, the artificial environments created by the Clan had similar effects on us as technology does to the modern man. Processed foods, laziness and other lifestyle habits have negative repercussions on the functioning of the human body. Even household pets have become domesticated to the point of being useless in the wild."

"So, what, we lost our edge and started to act more human?"

"There's no doubt that our abilities have been watered down over the years, not only by way of blood contamination. Humans and metasapiens are compatible mates, which is how you came to be. Of course, it has to happen through the process of artificial insemination and human females are unable to birth a meta child. The Clan's ultimate goal was to create a half-breed that possessed the qualities of both species."

"How did I end up on the other side of the fence? Others must have escaped or else none of us would be standing here now."

"That's where the story gets a little more complicated." Joe swivelled on his heels to face her again. "I told you before that there was a betrayer within the Clan. Trust me when I say that this person had no idea what they were letting loose until it was too late. How vital she'd become to the metasapien evolution."

"She..." It was Joe's drilling gaze that gave away his meaning. "*Me?*"

"Indeed, you."

"But, why?"

Violet wasn't sure if the delay was intended to torment her, yet she felt herself moving towards Joe as if she might beat the truth out of him. "Why am I so special to them?" she demanded.

"Before you, the metasapien only had one form. There was no such thing as a reversal process, the transitioning from beast to man and vice versa. If there is, indeed, some element of magic in relation to our existence then... well, my dear... you're it."

"Enter Moses, the one that got away." A jeering voice diverted their attention towards the mill's entrance. "Is that what she is to you, brother? A messenger of God sent to save her kin from damnation."

Camilla swaggered into the mill with Gypsy shadowing her. Kid was nowhere, much to Violet's relief. She had a suspicion that he was the most dangerous of them all.

"I was just giving Violet a lesson on the history of our origins," Joe informed her. "She's proven her dedication, and this is more her ancestry than ours."

Camilla folded her arms, looking to Violet while answering, "You're the last person that I'd expect to hear talking about miracles. Perhaps those twinkly eyes of hers have bewitched you, huh?"

"Well," Violet slung her bag over her shoulder so the strap crossed her front, "I think that's my cue to leave. I've got enough to process without having to deal with your jealousy on top."

"Jealousy?" Camilla scoffed, tilting her chin upwards so she could look down on Violet like lower class vermin. "Trust me, you've got nothing that I want."

"At least I don't have to chain a guy up to get him to screw me."

"What the fuck did you just –" Camilla would have walked right into Violet's path if it wasn't for Joe making a barrier with his arm.

"Leave it," he ordered.

"She thinks she's so much better than us. Bitch needs to take a look in the goddamn mirror!" Camilla barked, as Violet passed them. "You've been bleeding, haven't you?"

Violet turned to face her, intrigue postponing her escape. "Excuse me?"

"You know what I'm talking about. Your hormones are all out of whack, you get constant cramps and aches that you try to fuck away. Passion becomes lust, and lust becomes rage. Sometimes you'd rather have Dean on a plate than in your bed."

"You're seriously disturbed, do you know that?"

"And you're deluded if you think he'd stick by you if he ever discovered the truth. It's not just about sex; we're breeders. Procreation is a part of survival, and the truth of the matter is that you'd open your legs for anything with a ball sack."

"To hell with this!" Violet snarled her impatience before proceeding to the exit. "I need to get wasted – now."

"Want some company?" Gypsy was already heading for the doors.

"Not particularly."

As Violet emerged into the daylight, her eyes were more sensitive than usual and she squinted against the sunshine glancing through the trees. She promised herself that, one day soon, she'd clout the smirk off Camilla's face even if it meant removing her jaw completely. Right now, she was too wearied by events to make a fist.

"Hey, wait up!"

Hearing the trotting of booted feet behind her, Violet groaned inwardly.

***

Violet sipped the double vodka and coke, relishing the taste that she'd been deprived of for what seemed like a lifetime. In her other hand, she continued to scroll through the information that she'd Googled on her mobile phone. Joe's theory on testosterone affecting the human skeleton wasn't only subject to extensive study and research, but proven through the comparison of fossil shells from different eras of life.

'*Aggression of the caveman decreased upon the forming of communities, social tolerance, diet and activity. This led to a reduction in facial size with less robust features: thinner skulls, decreased brow ridges and rounder heads. High levels of testosterone also affect parts of the brain linked with emotion and social cognition, such as empathy.*'

"Well, bugger me." Violet sighed.

"S'up?"

Violet glanced at Gypsy across the table, having forgotten all about the young girl. "Nothing."

She was about to place the phone into her bag when it vibrated. She read the text message from Lucy: '*Missing you at work, hope you're okay. Call me x.*'

"Shit." Violet checked the time. It was coming up for midday and she hadn't even thought about ringing the office to explain her absence. Against her better judgment, she dropped the phone into her bag and zipped it – and her problems – away.

Irritated by Gypsy's probing stare, Violet said, "You haven't drunk your lemonade."

"I'm not a kid. Can't you get them to stick some rum in it?"

"You heard the barman. Get yourself some ID if you want serving."

"Ain't got the money, never mind the papers."

"How do you guys live? I know your requirements aren't exactly standard, but you still have phones, transport and so on."

"Five-finger discounts." Gypsy's chubby grin added to her youthfulness. "I'm kidding, Joe forbids that kind of thing. Whatever I need, he provides. I overheard him and Cammy arguing about some inheritance once. Joe has control and he's totally paranoid about leaving trails. Apparently he's got a load of cash hoarded away, but no one knows where it is."

"Are he and Camilla on the run or something?" Violet's interest verged on suspicion as she realised that she'd been so preoccupied with unveiling the secrets of her own esoteric past that she hadn't stopped to ponder anyone else's.

"We're all on the run," Gypsy stated. "The Clan is everywhere."

"Well, I'm sure Camilla has nothing to worry about. Five minutes of her bullshit and they'll be begging us to take her back – that's if they don't shoot her first." Violet took another swig of her drink.

"Hasn't it occurred to you that maybe the reason why you two clash is because you're so alike? Besides, watching your daddy kill your mum before blowing his own brains out is bound to screw with a person's –"

Violet spat the vodka and coke back into her glass, a surge of bubbles fizzing in her nostrils. "Wait – what?" She coughed.

"Didn't Joe tell you?"

"Their dad *killed* their mum?" Violet reiterated. "In front of them?"

"Uh-huh."

"Why?"

"Because..." Gypsy appeared hesitant, "she betrayed him."

"Must have been a pretty big betrayal for someone to –" The realisation cut through Violet's speech like a lightning bolt. "The mole... it was their mother all along. But that means Joe and Camilla's parents must have been part of the Clan."

"I thought you knew," said Gypsy.

"No." *And for good reason*, Violet thought, if the Clan really were behind Isabelle's murder.

As Gypsy went to lift her glass of lemonade, Violet's arm shot across the table to prevent her from doing so. The liquid sloshed over the brim, and Gypsy gave her a blank stare.

"Were Joe and Camilla part of this fucked up cult, too? Is that the real reason why they're in hiding?"

"They only tell me what I need to know," Gypsy answered simply.

Violet's hand was clenched so firmly around Gypsy's that the glass might shatter from the pressure. She forced herself to relax before the claws came out, and then slouched back into the chair. Gypsy slurped the lemonade, her eyes not leaving Violet's.

"Call me crazy, but maybe it's for the best," Violet reasoned. "None of us needs this getting out. Joe mentioned that the Clan are a bunch of rich bastards, so it doesn't surprise me that he and Camilla have money."

"What use is money when we could all be dead tomorrow?"

"I love your optimism." Violet pinched her eyes shut as her temples began to throb. Her head suddenly felt as light as the clouds.

"Violet..." Gypsy's voice sounded muffled, like her ears were stuffed with cotton wool. "Are you okay?"

"I'm fine – drinking on an empty stomach, that's all. I was supposed to be going sober but..."

"Wanna hunt?"

Violet grimaced at the notion, perhaps out of habit more than anything. She wondered if it would ever become as instinctual to her as it was for the others. "Please, can we just have one normal day and order something from the bar? I'll even get you that rum."

Gypsy's disappointment was replaced by an impish grin. "I haven't drunk alcohol since I was turned. Joe says that he doesn't want me losing control."

"I didn't have you down as the obedient type. Besides, I assume it passes through our bloodstream pretty quickly. Probably explains why I'm not dead from liver failure."

"Better make it a double, then."

With a playful roll of her eyes, Violet took her purse out of her bag. Gypsy was like the little sister she might have had if she and Isabelle had been blood relations. Violet remembered taking Isabelle out to celebrate her eighteenth birthday. By the end of the night, as usual, it was herself who'd needed escorting home. A tiny part of that feeling was rekindled as she saw in Gypsy what she'd lost three months ago. While her broken heart may never beat as it once did, perhaps it could one day be repaired.

CHAPTER TWELVE

The rhythm of the music pulsed through Violet as if it was a part of her life force, her blood. Every instrument came as its own distinct sound: bass, guitar, drums and electronics – things that she'd never bothered to explore beyond the lyrics. Listening through the music and clamour of those that flocked the rock club, she could make out snippets of nearby conversations.

"... that jerk, Phil, in marketing..."
"... can't afford it, mate..."
"... if she doesn't then I bloody will!"

Violet closed her eyes while trying to hone in on the juicier nuggets of gossip. The trick, she'd learned, was to let the sounds trickle in like goodies on a conveyor belt and pick out those of interest, rather than straining to hear everything. It was just as easy to block out sounds as it was to let them in, and she felt a thrill of excitement when she thought about the hours of fun she could have with a bit more practice.

Hands skimmed over her hips and settled loosely on her waist, synchronising with the swaying motion of Violet's body. She opened her eyes and smiled back at Camilla as they rocked together. Their bodies were close, thighs touching thighs, until Camilla's hands turned to her own body; gliding over her stomach and caressing her pert breasts, revelling in her bodily sensations while gyrating in time to the music. Everything felt surreal, the strobe-light effect on the dance floor playing with her vision so it looked as if everyone was moving in slow motion.

As the track reached its completion, Violet took a breath. Her vest was sticky with sweat, having ridden up over her belly to flaunt her navel bar. She straightened it out and tucked the edges under the waistband of her skinny jeans. Camilla was in her own world, diving straight into the next song as if there'd been no interval. 'Up for it,' had been one of the phrases slung her way by various men, and indeed she wasn't shy in her cropped T-shirt and shorts that barely hung below her butt cheeks. Little did they know that she'd eat them alive, quite literally.

Violet left Camilla on the dance floor where they'd been for what seemed like hours, but it was only three or four songs. At the bar area, Gypsy turned to her excitedly and thrust a bottle under her nose.

"Look, Vi, I got served!" she hollered, over the music. "Can you guess what's in it?"

The aroma of vodka and lemons was tainted by a sugary sweetness. "It's Smirnoff Ice, I'd know that anywhere," Violet remarked.

"Spot on! She's good at this, ain't she?"

Gypsy looked across to where Joe was propped against the bar, his eyes like laser beams targeted at Camilla. His face looked as though it might crack if he moved, it was that stern.

"I'm going for a piss." He drained his Disaronno from the tumbler and then stormed off into the hordes, barging past people as if they were skittles at a bowling alley.

"What's his problem?" Violet asked Gypsy.

"He doesn't like us mixing with humans, especially Camilla. She can be unpredictable, in case you hadn't noticed."

Violet gave an according nod while glancing back at Camilla. Her blonde layers thrashed lawlessly about her, licking the contours of her face. It wasn't so much beauty that she possessed, but something about her presence was magnetic – enticing almost. She was sexy without trying to be sexy and radiated a confidence that denoted the true meaning of a powerful woman.

"She's actually pretty fun once she ditches the attitude," Violet noted. "Besides, I never dragged anyone here. I just figured that we could try a bonding session that didn't involve running naked through the woods."

Gypsy was too engrossed in her drink to have heard, stopping every so often to lick her lips and appreciate the flavours. Violet had never known anyone to be so enthusiastic about an alcoholic beverage – then again, the girl hadn't stepped foot into a nightclub before tonight. It had become increasingly obvious that Gypsy had gone from streetwise teenager to metasapien without any experience of what it felt like to be an ordinary adult and, crucially, an ordinary woman. They'd spent most of the afternoon joking and chatting in the pub, eventually leaving at around 4 p.m. Gypsy scrubbed up pretty well after a makeover and some half-decent clothes donated from Violet's wardrobe. Joe and Camilla had met them later on in the evening.

"Tell me something, do you regret any of this?" Violet asked her friend. "I mean, if you could go back to your old self, would you?"

"Like hell I would! You'd have to be crazy to give up abilities like ours."

It was the kind of answer that Violet would expect from a naive young girl. "Did it hurt when Joe turned you?"

"No." Gypsy smiled, as if taking comfort in the reminiscence. "He told me to close my eyes, and that the pain would be over by the time I opened them. He was so gentle, I felt like I was losing my virginity or something." She giggled bashfully, tucking her neck into her shoulders.

Violet's pity for the girl flared up once more. She was supposed to be studying for a degree, going on dates and partying with people her own age: everything that Violet had taken for granted, and which Isabelle would never get to live out. She felt like saying all of these things but reminded herself, not for the first time, that Gypsy wasn't her responsibility. She was her own person with her own mind, and her own choices to make.

Gypsy went to finish her Smirnoff when Joe reappeared and swiped it from her hand. "Hey!" she bleated.

"You're on water from now on," Joe instructed.

"But –"

Joe guzzled the dregs and then slid the empty bottle back to her across the bar top. "Water or home, your choice."

Gypsy glowered at him with a duck-like pout to her lips. Without arguing, she stomped her foot and then flounced off towards Camilla on the dance floor.

Her observation switching to Joe, Violet said, "Why do you have to be such a party pooper? She's just a kid."

"A kid that's had to grow up fast," Joe shot back.

"Are we still talking about Gypsy?"

Joe looked back at her quizzically. Violet added, "You're not the only one who's had their life fucked up by their parents, you know."

"Ah," Joe gave a deceptive smile, "that the plan, was it? Ply the girl with drink and get her all loose-lipped so you could start digging into other people's business."

"Not at all – in fact, a part of me understands why you didn't reveal your connection to the Clan. I should have guessed with your extensive knowledge about our kind, but if our pasts are intertwined then that makes your business my business."

Joe had an absent look about him, as though he'd erected a mental wall around his emotions to keep them contained during the next few moments. "My father was a controlling, power-hungry man. I used to think of him as a James Bond villain, although to say that he craved world domination would be an overstatement. Rather, he wanted the means of obtaining it should the worst happen: outbreaks of war, famine or some natural disaster that left humanity on the brink of extinction. He saw *our* species as that means. Some might call him paranoid; others would see it as admirable."

"And your mum had a problem with these ambitions of his?"

"She disagreed with his methods, yes, but opposing him was her second mistake. The first was sparing you."

"Why would she give a crap about me?"

"She worked as a midwife, so it stands to reason that her skills were useful to the Clan. You were delivered as a premature stillborn – or so, that's what everyone thought. Somehow, perhaps due to your DNA, you managed to resuscitate yourself. I can't be sure, but we think that's why you remained unchanged for so long. Your body was in a state of repair and, along with the suppression of your abilities over the years, you never learned how to actively tune into them."

"Until Isabelle's death fucked me up," Violet concluded. "Aggression: that's the trigger, right? They killed her to flush me out."

"Emotions cause all sorts of chemical reactions in the brain. I only wish that it hadn't happened under such tragic circumstances."

"Stop treating me like some fragile little girl!" Violet bashed her palm against the bar top. "I've given you the benefit of the doubt more than enough times. If you'd rather I asked my mum then I'll head over to her place right now and give her the fright of her life."

"Calm yourself, Violet." Joe rested a hand on her shoulder. The gentle persuasion that she was becoming so accustomed to was beginning to sound practiced. "Intoxication makes one irrational and prone to outbursts – the very things that got you into this mess. Why do you think I'm so strict with Gypsy? She's young and she obviously idolises you."

Violet shrugged him away. "You're so patronising, do you know that? If anyone's making me irrational then it's *you*."

At that point, Camilla bounded up beside her, draping one arm around Violet's neck as if they were suddenly best buddies.

"Hey, guys, dinner has just walked in." She grinned.

The three of them turned simultaneously to the entrance where a group of people were filtering through. Violet stood on her tiptoes to see over the clubbers, and a face caked in garish blue eye shadow and cerise blusher headed their way.

"Oh, no!" Her cry stirred bemusement in her friends. Joe stretched his neck to get a better view of the sack of Play-Doh squeezed into a tube dress. Following her were more of Violet's work colleagues, but it wasn't until she saw Lucy that she pivoted so her back was to them.

"You know that walking heart disease?" Camilla joked. Violet assumed she meant Tina.

"That's a bunch of the office crew. I've been skiving work all day, if they see me then I'm toast."

Violet thought it best not to mention her relationship with Lucy, although they were probably familiar with her close acquaintances. Joe had made no secret about keeping Violet under surveillance in the previous weeks. She felt like a married woman having an affair, with two lives running parallel to one another. Combining them was out of the question.

"I, er... need to use the ladies'."

Keeping her head low, Violet scuttled off to the left of the bar and rounded a corner. She hid in one of the cubicles for ages, biting her nails and tapping her feet; listening to the sounds of people coming and going. The thumping music gushed in every time the main doors were opened, until silence offered her a few moments to think. It seemed that her best course of action was to duck out of the establishment and hope no one spotted her. Of all the frigging clubs in Derby!

Violet flushed for the sake of flushing and then unlocked the door. Lucy was standing by the sinks opposite, arms crossed, facing the cubicle that Violet appeared from.

"Oh, uh, hey..." Violet didn't force the surprise. Her constrained smile was more than enough.

"Are you trying to get yourself fired or what?" Lucy spoke waspishly.

"Huh?"

"What do you mean, *huh?*" Lucy unfolded her arms to place them on her hips. "Didn't you get any of my messages? I had to cover for you this morning – and you're welcome, by the way."

"Sorry, Mum. My battery must have died." Violet scrunched her eyes as she neared the brighter lights above the sink area, which created a glare on the mirrors that was like staring into the sun. Must have been the onset of a hangover – hardly surprising seeing as she'd been drinking all afternoon.

"What are you doing here anyway?" she asked Lucy.

"It's Tina's birthday, remember? We've just been for a meal at Frankie and Benny's."

"Boy, I'm glad I missed that." Violet combed her hair back off her face, realising how pasty she looked. Most of her makeup had sweated off on the dance floor, eyeliner smeared in rings under her eyes. As she used her fingers to wipe it away, Lucy caught her gaze in the mirror's reflection.

"I thought you were supposed to be laying off the partying? And who are those people that I saw you with?" she said.

"Friends." Violet was relieved that Lucy hadn't recognised Joe as his alter ego, Mr Screaming Orgasm.

"What friends?"

"I met them in therapy if you must know. I didn't think it was a crime to hang out with other people."

"You never mentioned that you'd started therapy."

"You never asked."

Lucy regarded her a moment, and when she spoke again, she'd lost the edge to her voice. "Violet, are you on something? No offence but you look like crap, and after that episode you had in the office the other day –"

"Since when did you become such a judgmental cow?" Violet spun around to face her directly. "However I deal with my issues and whoever I spend my time with are my choices. You can't help me. Dean can't help me. No one can help me except for *me.*"

Lucy appeared as though she'd been slapped in the face by a random stranger. There was no anger in her words, only bemusement. "What's wrong with you?"

Violet's response was hindered by the cramps in her stomach. She clutched a hand to her abdomen, unable to prevent herself from hunching over the sink.

"Are you all right, Vi?" Lucy reached out to steady her.

"I'm fine, it's just PMS."

"Does Dean know that you're here? Shall I call him for you?"

"There's no need."

"I'll just send a text –"

"No!"

Violet snatched Lucy's handbag as she delved through it for her mobile phone. The strap caught around her elbow, pulling her forwards as Violet began the tug of war. Lucy squealed as the chain ate into her flesh, then grabbed the bag with her free hand to keep hold if it.

"*Violet* – what the hell?" Lucy cried, but the words failed to penetrate the rage that swathed Violet's brain.

Spittle frothed through her teeth, blood dilating the capillaries beneath her flesh so the heat radiated from her. She could feel her muscles spasming, joints clicking as the beast inside tried to claw its way free; yet her humanity beat it back, prolonging the internal torture. Contents spilled from the bag until Lucy's phone found its way free. The screen cracked as it hit the floor, and Lucy bent to retrieve it.

"I said *no!*"

Violet rammed Lucy with her elbow, a force that was intended to keep her from reaching the phone that catapulted Lucy into the far wall. Thankfully she missed the hand dryer, but the thud of her back against the tiles was enough to quell Violet's temper. The shock of both women caused the atmosphere in the room to glaciate with them.

They heard the whoosh of the main door opening, followed by footsteps and then Camilla's voice. "There you are."

Violet looked around as if waking from a dream and not knowing how she'd ended up there. Lucy was braced against the wall, legs ready to buckle. The liquidity of her pale eyes as such that Violet could see no emotion in them; only horror.

"We're leaving. Are you ready to go?" said Camilla.

"Um, yeah," Violet uttered. What else was she going to do, scare away the rest of her colleagues until she didn't have a job left to go back to? There was no explanation that wouldn't be riddled with lies, no apologies that were deserving of forgiveness. With Camilla's scrutiny upon her, Violet dipped her head and shuffled towards the exit. As she passed Lucy, she heard the echoes of her heart punching against her ribcage. It was the first one that she'd been sharp enough to detect, and she wished she hadn't.

As they left the toilets, Violet tried to take solace in the fact that she was sparing Lucy from a world that was darker than a moonless night. That she was leading Camilla and the others away from her old life, even if it meant saying goodbye. Lucy and Dean were her strength, which also made them her weaknesses. Violet had to save them from such deviance and, more importantly, save them from herself.

CHAPTER THIRTEEN

"*Yeehaaaw!*" Camilla's caterwaul was carried off in the air as the Jeep flashed down the country roads at 20mph over the speed limit.

In the passenger seat, Violet had been watching the speedo glowing in the blackness, her panic rising as swiftly as the needle. Camilla was standing on the back seat, hanging out of the sunroof as if admiring the landscape from a balcony, but not a single bush or tree was visible in the thickness of the night.

"Joe – will you put the headlights on, for fuck's sake!" Violet was sunk back into the chair, one hand clutching her seatbelt and the other pressed to the dashboard; both feet braced against the footwell.

The car veered into the middle of the road, cat lights beneath the wheels making a *ker-dunk, ker-dunk* sound.

"Oh my god." As Violet shut her eyes, she heard Joe's deep guffaw from beside her.

"She's right, Joe. Cut it out." Gypsy was still sulking from her earlier drinks ban. Kid was sitting behind Violet with his head jutted out of the window, filling the Jeep with more wind turbulence.

"Where's your sense of adventure?" Joe spoke to both Violet and Gypsy. "Even if a collision did take place, we have at least a fifty percent higher survival rate than the average human."

Violet argued, "It's not us that I'm worried about, it's anyone else that happens to be on the road. I can't see a fucking thing!"

"A life without fear is a life without boundaries. Even if dangers and obstacles cannot be removed, they may still be worked around," Joe asserted.

"Is that another genius quote from your dad?" Violet regretted the quip when Joe pushed down harder on the gas pedal. Camilla came down from the roof, crouching with her head in between the front seats.

"Like picking at a scab, bringing up his daddy issues. Ain't that right, bro?" Camilla was brash enough to pinch the fat on his cheek like a pensioner cooing over a baby.

Joe jerked his head away from her biliously. "He was the one with issues, constantly expecting everyone to meet his ridiculous standards. So I never had the brains to be a scientist or the skills necessary to cut it as a hunter. If only he could see me now..." A malicious grin swept across his features, seemingly talking to himself. Reflecting on what was and relishing what is.

"I'm sorry, Joe. That was insensitive of me." Violet had one eye on the speedo as it crept back down to 50mph.

"I don't need your pity. My father overlooked my greatest quality of all: loyalty. I helped him to dispose of my mother's body and never told a soul, but it still wasn't enough for him."

"Dude, you're going to miss the turning!" Camilla pointed diagonally to the left of them.

Joe stepped off the gas, barely letting the speed drop before slamming his foot onto the brake pedal. Camilla was thrown forwards between the front seats, the screeching of wheels coalescing with Gypsy's screams from the back. If Violet hadn't been wearing her seatbelt then she'd have soared headfirst through the windshield.

The Jeep skidded for longer than Violet dared to calculate, stopping a few seconds before Gypsy's wailing ceased and they were left in a breathless silence. Camilla clambered off the handbrake where she'd fallen, her cackles indicating that she was unharmed. Joe shifted the gear stick into reverse, gave a brief over-the-shoulder check for oncoming vehicles and then glided smoothly backwards. After several metres, he spun the wheel to the left so the passengers swayed with the jarring motions of the car. Violet bashed her shoulder against the window as they rounded a corner into the car park, dirt and pebbles crackling beneath the tyres. It was little more than a clearing, with no other vehicles in the vicinity at so late an hour. Joe parked up with their nose pointed at the tree line, and Camilla pulled herself up through the sunroof so they could hear her boots clomping around on the metal above them. The others got out of the Jeep one by one, and items of clothing were shamelessly removed and flung onto the back seats.

Violet averted her gaze and focused on the clear-edged moon, illuminating the navy sky like a lighthouse amidst the ocean. It looked close enough to touch from their location on the mountains, and she found herself roaming in its direction. Joe must have noticed her admiring the glowing disc, for it wasn't until he spoke that she realised he was beside her. The angst of the last ten minutes ebbing as if he, too, was soothed by its beauty.

"Did you know that the word 'lunatic' orientated from the Latin word 'luna', which translates to moon?"

Violet eyed him peevishly. "Thanks, that's just what I wanted to hear while I'm stuck in the middle of nowhere with you lot."

Joe grinned, continuing in spite of the reproach. "Doctors used to believe that insanity was related to the phases of the moon, particularly in bipolar and sleep disorders due to the light's interruption with darkness. As the ruler of tides, it makes sense that the moon would control our emotions from an astrological or spiritual point of view. Rumour has it that most crimes are committed on nights when the moon is full."

"I thought you didn't believe in all that mystical bollocks?"

"I don't, but it's nights like these that cast my mind back to when I was forced to help my father bury Mother's body after he'd bludgeoned her to death – on our own land, of all places. Even as a grown man, I imagined that the moon's light was protecting me from her vengeful spirit. One has to wonder whether the night Goddess did have some effect on the brutality of Father's crime."

"Or he was still pissed at her for setting me free. Either way, it sure does explain Camilla's ill feelings towards me."

Joe shook his head as if to deny the conjecture. "Mother's secret remained so for many years after your birth. It was your father she turned to, begging him to take you in as his own. They were old childhood friends, although I suspect romance was involved somewhere down the line."

"How did your dad find out about me?" Violet wanted to know.

"Ten years ago, Beverly turned up at our family estate – not that I knew who she was at the time." Joe began to unbutton his shirt. "She was blind drunk: swearing, shouting and making all kinds of accusations. She cursed my mother for what she'd laid on their doorstep and demanded that she took back the 'spawn of Satan', as she called you."

"Ten years ago..." Violet frowned. "I was almost in my last year of high school. I know that she never recovered from losing my dad, but why drag it up after all that time?"

"Beverly made many mistakes, but we're all responsible for our own actions. She's no more to blame for the death of my mother than she is for firing that arrow through Isabelle's heart."

"But it's like you said, if she'd been straight with me from the beginning then I would have been more aware. I could have protected Isabelle, maybe even saved her life."

"I know what you're thinking," Joe regarded her solemnly, "but trust me when I say that you don't want to go there."

Violet wasn't sure she knew where 'there' was until Joe's warning confirmed it – the unintentional watering of a seed planted by her own despair. She glanced away as he pulled his arms free of his shirt sleeves, baring his smooth torso.

As if sensing this new blizzard of emotions, Joe added, "Camilla was dying, too. Sickle cell anaemia is a blood disorder that affects the shape of the cells carrying haemoglobin. You may be aware that patients have a shortened life expectancy, and when our father discovered the circumstances surrounding your birth, it gave him the perfect excuse to set up his own little experiment."

"So, that's why he never came after me. He didn't want to draw attention in case the Clan waded in and spoiled his fun."

Joe nodded while slinging the shirt over his shoulder. "Our blood has proven to be effective against many bacteria and viruses of the autoimmune nature, including the common cold and even AIDS. The first drawback is that patients are often in too weak a state to survive the transformation; secondly, even if it is successful, losing one's humanity was an unavoidable consequence... until you came along."

"How did he get a hold of my blood?"

"It's likely that Mother had samples frozen periodically over the years. It wouldn't be as effective as fresh blood, but ours has a longer shelf life than human cells. Our mother was no scientist, but it would have been foolish not to have a contingency plan in place should the worst happen."

"You mean the Clan would need to find a way of killing me if I turned out to be a psychopath?"

Joe undid his belt buckle as if to evade the accusation in her eyes. "No one knew who or what you'd become. My point is that there's no way of guaranteeing that Isabelle would still be alive had you substituted her blood with yours. Camilla got lucky, but it wasn't without cost."

They both looked to the half woman-half beast creature on the roof of the Jeep, squatting with her hands flat against the metal, head tilted to one side. Violet knew that she was listening; preying like the formidable jaguar, but a hundred times more deadly. She couldn't imagine such a specimen being anything less, and to think of her growing up, plagued with sickness and the torture imposed by her father, Violet had to wonder if this was salvation or damnation.

"Father insisted that it was her best chance of survival," Joe explained. "I'd like to believe that his intentions were pure, and there's no denying that he performed a miracle in what he achieved. Unfortunately, my mother couldn't see past Camilla's suffering and threatened to confess everything to the Clan. There was no way that Father was going to share the revelation of a metasapien being able to switch back to its human form. I should have stepped in – I wanted to – but it was already too late." Joe whipped off his belt, the tail of it almost thrashing Violet.

"What about the police?" she questioned. "Someone must have reported her missing: friends, work colleagues..."

"The cover story was that she'd walked out on us. Even if the Clan had suspicions, they've always kept themselves to themselves. If the government bodies got wind of their organisation without having any knowledge about the nature of our kind, they'd have an epidemic on their hands before they knew what had hit them. That's why Camilla and I have been able to stay off the radar for so long. We put all of our assets on the market and left before the Clan could properly dig into Father's suicide."

Violet felt a flush of awkwardness as Joe tugged his trousers over his hips. She turned her body sideways in time to see Camilla's muscular legs extend to their full lengths, jetting her skywards at a startling velocity. After a dramatic leap towards the tree line, she took off in her bra and shorts like a drunken streaker. Gypsy was straight after her, and they both became one with the forest.

"It doesn't make sense. Why would your dad end his life after making such a huge breakthrough?" Violet peeked back at Joe, waiting for an explanation, but she stood alone.

"Joe...?" She rotated on the spot, scanning the Jeep and the encompassing shadows, but her questions remained unanswered. "Christ, not again."

Violet strolled over to the vehicle, which had been left unlocked with the key still in the ignition. There was no one around to pinch it, and it was well after midnight so there was little chance of any naturists turning up. With their superhuman hearing, any potential thieves would be lucky to make it out of the car park before having their spines ripped out of their backs.

Violet removed the key anyway and hid it in the glove compartment, then slipped off her boots so she could wriggle out of her jeans. She left them on the passenger seat alongside her coat and made sure that her bag was tucked out of sight. Although it was a mild night, her body hairs prickled up as they were exposed to the night air, like billions of tiny antennae. Her flesh was tacky with dried sweat and her underarms didn't smell too fresh either. She left her vest on, not feeling totally comfortable with exploring the eerie forest in her underwear, and then she stepped back into her boots to protect her feet.

After closing the passenger door, she turned towards the same route that Camilla and Gypsy had taken. "Holy shit!"

Violet sprang back against the car, gasping as the silhouette by the trees became more distinctive. Kid stared at her, running his tongue back and forth over his lips and then sniggering to himself. Violet crossed an arm pointlessly over her chest, using her other hand to obstruct his view of her knickers.

"Don't even think about it, freak," she warned.

Kid's unpredictable nature never failed to set Violet on edge, even more so than the way he looked at her. The guy hadn't uttered a syllable in her presence since the day they'd met, but he made it unequivocally clear that he understood everything that was being said to him.

Joe's voice beckoning from the forest came just at the right time. "What are you waiting for? Try to keep up this time."

Violet gazed around as the echoes of laughter retreated – along with Kid, much to her relief. She took a final glance over her shoulder to check for passing traffic, but the road was deserted. Once in the shelter of the trees, a place that appeared so daunting on the surface seemed to welcome her. Tree boughs reaching out to embrace her, the essence of Mother Nature growing in familiarity until it felt like she was returning home after years of being marooned on a desert island. Violet's strides became longer, fleeter; feet lifting higher, arms pumping as she broke into a sprint. She didn't know whether it was the sense of freedom or fresh air provided generously by the plant life, but it felt as though her cells were rejuvenating themselves; shedding old layers of skin and flushing the toxins from her blood. Her joints were like springs, the soles of her boots skimming the ground to minimise sound, and the darkness didn't stop her progress. The adjustments to her eyesight didn't register until that point, a silver-grey hue enhanced by the cloudless sky; although most of it was obscured by the trees. There was nothing in the way of colour, but dozens of shades and tones to distinguish one object from another.

As Violet weaved between the tree trunks, hurdling over patches of thicket and ditches in the ground, a shape flitted out in front of her. She lurched to a halt and anchored her footing. It was barely a foot in height, four stumpy legs carrying it across her path. The remarkable white stripes on its face were the signature of a badger, but it scurried into the wilderness after little more than a glimpse. The vigorous drumming of a heartbeat remained, although Violet wasn't skilled enough to differentiate between animal and human. Filtering out other sounds was an intricate task, but it seemed to be getting closer even though the badger was long gone.

The pong of unwashed clothes and body odour reached Violet a second before she heard a branch being trodden on. She turned in the same direction from which the badger had appeared just in time to dodge the object that came swinging at her neck. She guessed it was metal from the reflective glint – one that she might not have seen without the improved visibility. She threw back her torso, bending at the waist with a flexibility that she didn't know she possessed. The head of the axe sliced through the air above her face as it slanted towards the sky, and she caught a magnificent view of the stars through a gap in the trees. By the time she'd straightened, there was a jarring pressure to the side of her abdomen. She knew what had happened, though it wasn't until she looked down and saw the axe embedded in her flesh that the pain swiftly took hold, increasing like acid burning deeper and deeper through layers of tissue.

Violet waited until the attacker had forcibly yanked the steel from her body before placing a hand over the savage gash. Thick, syrupy liquid oozed through her fingers without surrender, so much that she expected her torso to separate from the rest of her body and leave her legs standing pathetically on their own. Guttural sounds spluttered from her as shock and pain collided and her eyes met with the attacker's. She could tell that it was a man, but his face was bleary through the concoction of tears, darkness and her senses fading out as wooziness took over. His rapid breaths were synchronous with his heart palpitations, while the sudden lull in his assault evinced a sense of reluctance.

It didn't last for long. The man flung the axe over his shoulder and took a downwards swing at her. Violet managed to twist to the side, causing the laceration to gape even wider, and she couldn't suppress a sharp cry of agony. The assailant stumbled forwards, almost following the momentum of the strike all the way to the ground.

"S-stop…" Violet hardly had enough breath to gasp a sentence, and in the back of her mind she had no clue how she was conscious enough to try.

When the man came at her a third time, she had no choice but to lift her hand from the wound to catch the handle of the axe. She could feel his frantic efforts to pull it back, little whimpers suggesting that he was just as fearful of her as she was of him; but nevertheless determined to finish what he'd started.

"You psycho, what the fuck is wrong with –" A fist hammered Violet's temple, stunning her into silence. Her battered form hit the ground, dragging the man down with her as they both remained affixed to the axe. The energy was leaking out of her as fluently as her blood, yet even as they scuffled for control of the weapon, and despite the nauseating sting, she could feel muscle tissue and flesh trying to knit themselves together. It was a peculiar sensation, like a tingle or itch that she couldn't scratch away.

"P-please," Violet grunted. "I don't want to… hurt you."

The man changed strategies, gripping the axe at each end and trying to drive the handle into her throat as if to choke her. He growled as all of the muscles in his arms worked to overpower her, saliva bubbling over his lips and flecking her face. Violet felt her own arms trembling and thought they were ready to give up; but when that same tremor ran the length of her body, she realised it was the primitive force inside her being ignited. It was the same feeling she'd had during her first training session at the Peak District, and again with Lucy in the club toilets. The extra blood pumping through her heart rushed to those areas that needed it most, where it coagulated to form a plug in her side.

With a miraculous surge of strength, Violet pushed up with her arms to elevate the axe and create some space between herself and the man. She managed to squeeze a leg up in between their bodies, gritting her teeth at the pain, and kicked out at his abdomen with her last reserves of might. He careened backwards, both of them losing their hold on the axe as it was cast uselessly into the dirt. Before he could rise, with restored vitality pulsing through her, Violet scrambled up and threw herself on top of him.

"Fucker!" She ploughed her forehead into his nose, like smashing an egg with a football. Blood spurted onto her face, and the man's shrill cry trembled through the forest.

"You're with *them*, aren't you?" Violet boomed. "They sent you to kill me, just like they killed my sister!"

His hair was too short to grip, so she lifted his head and then slammed it back into the ground. She worried that she'd killed him when his body went flaccid, but the half-dazed whimpers reassured her that it wasn't over yet.

"Please... they g-give me no choice." Even murmured, Violet detected the man's European accent. "They say I must k-kill you before you kill me, then I be free."

"Was it the Clan? Did they put you up to this?" Violet slapped his face to keep him conscious. "Answer me!"

"I'm sorry."

Thankfully, the man's reflexes were sloppy and Violet caught the movement of his arm in her peripheral vision. He swiped at her with a three-inch blade that must have been concealed in one of his pockets. Her instinct to protect her skull was excruciatingly successful as the blade split open her forearm. Just as soon as the wetness began to trickle down her arm, the knife was stabbed into her shoulder at half of its length. Violet let out her first scream and, securing the man's hand in hers, she snapped her jaw shut around his wrist. Ivory spikes bit several millimetres into flesh, nicking a vein so the coppery-tasting fluid emptied into her mouth. The pangs of hunger that had been niggling at her all day became crippling, like a crack addict due their next hit. The man's howling rasped on Violet's sensitive ears as much as it did her nerves, and the more agitated she became, the deeper that craving burrowed into her psyche. An ache that flowed through her body, lending fluidity to her muscles and bones. She felt them beginning to shift, like ethereal hands bending and twisting them. As her natural instincts were unleashed, her emotions melded together like thunderclouds over a sullen sky.

The next thing Violet knew, she was gnawing into the man's shoulder. As she ripped back her head, shreds of tattered flesh and muscle sinews dangled from between razor-tipped teeth. She used her tongue to roll the chunk to the back of her mouth and then gulped it whole, as if her throat had widened to make room for it. She hadn't been aware of the man's dwindling cries, each inhalation coming shorter than the last. He shivered beneath her, despite the copious sweat that he'd broken out in. Although his heart rate alone was enough to convince Violet that he was going into shock.

As her adrenaline levels began to drop and that wrathful haze ebbed to its resting place, she was brought back to reality with a wince-inducing sting. She looked down to the blood weeping over her hip and realised that she'd reopened her side wound during the tussle. The main issue, however, was the knife lodged in her shoulder. Violet clasped her blood-slick fingers around the handle and pulled, yowling as it came loose with a splattering of red. She would have buried it in the man's face had a vision of Camilla's mugger not flashed in her mind's eye. Violet remembered that night in the park as if it was yesterday, for it had haunted her ever since. Inspecting the weapon in her hand, her thumb found the hinge that locked the blade into its handle. Just as the truth began to dawn on her, it was obtruded by the arrival of four figures from between the trees.

They stood before her in a row, semi-dressed and human in form, though the ravenous glints in their eyes would have been patent to anyone. Violet could sense their ferocity in the air. She breathed it in and it became a part of her, circulating in her lungs and rotting her from the inside. From there, it infected her mind and soul like an army raiding new land. Her blood ran through every one of them, making the bond as tangible as it was metaphysical.

"It's a set up," Violet mumbled, the blood in her mouth still warm as it dribbled free. The nibs of her teeth grazed her lips, making speaking difficult at first. "This isn't the first time that someone's come at me with a penknife. You took it from that thief, then gave it to this guy and sent him to attack me."

"What use is a soldier without experience in the field?" There was nothing defensive about Joe's manner, only the insouciance that was expected from them all.

"You bastard, he's fucking dying!" Violet looked helplessly around her, at the puddles of blood soaking into the earth and the delirious victim. Knowing that even if he wasn't beyond saving, there was no way the others would allow her to call the emergency services.

"Don't let the guilt screw with your mind," Camilla reassured her. "We're not dealing with a few cases of petty theft here. Doctor Slimeball fancies himself as somewhat of a fantasist: pigtails, pop socks and little girls wearing little skirts, to be specific. Always keeps them above the age of consent, but that didn't stop him from abusing the trust of his patients. If you ask me, it was only a matter of time before driving past the local school at PE time became a little *too* tempting."

"Doctor..." Violet studied her assailant's crumpled face. Her blood loss didn't aid her faltering vision, but his skin appeared swarthier than the average Caucasian. Her speculations were confirmed by the black stubble that matched his unkempt clothing, and Violet let the knife drop from her fingers as his identity became clear. "Otis... Otis Yans."

"You read the papers, then," Joe assumed.

"He was a client of the company that I work for. He's under investigation for sexual harassment." Violet wasn't sure that she'd have recognised him from the grinning bald man that she'd seen in the local newspaper. Moreover, it was Tina's ramblings of him that had connected the dots.

"Your company recruited this sick pervert?" Camilla didn't bother to suppress her amusement, and even Kid indulged them with a demented snort. "Small world, eh?"

"If he's sick then what does that make you?" Violet shot back. "This wasn't training, it was you manipulating me into murdering a human!"

"If you're unable to take a human life, then why are you here?" Joe's austerity was dampened by the view of him standing in his underpants, but

Violet was too aggrieved by the betrayal to care. "A metasapien's biggest advantage is neither speed nor strength, but the way in which we process pain: physically, mentally and even emotionally. It's that which gives us our edge, and it's also what will make life without Isabelle all the more bearable."

"No," Violet shook her head, "you can't justify what you do because some chemical imbalance in the brain masks the guilt. Once you kill someone, there's no going back."

"It's understandable that your emotions may get in the way, more so than ours. You've had years to bond with the metasapien in a way that no one else has. Our rage is like a tornado ripping through all sense of logic and reasoning; yours is more of a wave, gradually building before crashing onto the shore. Either way, what you did tonight was an act of self-defence – just like it was with Matthew."

"Self-defence, manslaughter – what's the difference? And what happens when someone turns out to be innocent?"

"We're never wrong." Gypsy stepped forwards, perhaps more anxious than the others to elucidate their scheming. "We're not mind readers, but the human body doesn't lie. Heart rate, temperature, mannerisms: it's just a case of learning how to read people. That's why we'll never be anything but truthful with each other."

"Like when you told me that you weren't cannibals?" Violet snapped. "I trusted you... *all* of you... but no one said anything about eating people!"

"Technically, we're not human so the term 'cannibalism' isn't –"

"Fuck your technicalities!"

Gypsy gulped while shrinking back into the group. Disappointment at the girl's treachery sank far deeper than the superficial trauma left by the others, but the brunt of Violet's anger was targeted at herself for being so easily fooled. For allowing grief to skew her judgment and see things in people that were never there in the first place.

"Come on, Violet, you knew the score from the beginning." Camilla spoke up. "It was your thirst for revenge that spurred you into joining us, so it's a bit late to start developing a conscience now."

"Revenge." Violet dragged her glare across to Camilla. "I guess we're not so different after all."

"How so?"

"From what I hear, Daddy subjected you to all manner of torture in his mission to tame the beast. Who knows, maybe Doctor Yans wasn't the only one with a kink for naughty girls."

She and Camilla swapped expressions as if they'd had their faces transplanted onto one another's skulls.

"Say that again," Camilla dared her.

Violet shuffled onto her feet and rose painfully, using her hand as a compress to slow the bleeding from her abdomen. She was too weak for any more conflict, and her injuries were taking longer and longer to heal. Even her skeletal framework had reverted to its human bearing, yet she knew that her only chance was to keep the adrenaline pumping.

"We might not be the best of friends, but I know you well enough. Living out your days as a dog in a cage seems unlikely, so maybe blowing your dad's head off was the best option."

Camilla opened her mouth, retort brewing, when Joe broke in to prevent further quarrel. "You're not entirely wrong, Violet. There wasn't a lot that our father feared. The Clan was a part of his lineage; it was everything he stood for and his purpose in life. Five years ago, I decided that enough was enough and it was time to set Camilla free. The only reason I went along with it for so long was because of the teaching that Father had to offer. I had a lot to learn about what Camilla had become – what I was destined to become if I stood any chance of protecting her."

Violet replied, "I'm starting to wonder if that was such a good idea. If I was your dad then I wouldn't want a psycho like her getting out either."

"The only psychopath in our family was him, threatening to murder his own daughter. For that reason, I came up with a counter offer: either we turned him into the one thing he feared or..."

"Or he killed himself," Violet surmised.

"As far as my father was concerned, there was no other option. Becoming a meta was a fate worse than death, even if it was the only chance of saving what remained of our family. He put that shotgun in his mouth out of cowardice, not by force."

"Well, maybe if you'd stayed away then none of this would have happened. Maybe the link to Isabelle wouldn't have been made."

"Her death was the reason that we risked exposure by coming back,"

Camilla told Violet. "We've spent the last five years trying to make some kind of life for ourselves. Honing our abilities on the off-chance that a war should break out – which is more than likely, thanks to your pisshead of a mother and her big mouth."

"You don't know that," Violet argued. "I don't believe for a second that she'd risk putting Isabelle in danger."

"Why not? She's done it once before. Plus, she's the only person with that kind of information outside of our circle – everyone else is dead. We should have cut her tongue out when we had the chance."

Violet covered the ground between them in a couple of limps, all concern for the unconscious victim forgotten. Though equal in height, Camilla's strength showed in her build. Violet didn't doubt that her comrade had an edge as far as skills went, both in combat and sensory faculties; yet the fact that she made no first moves intimated that perhaps Violet had the advantage of mystery. The scope of her latent abilities wasn't known to a single living person.

"Ladies, please." Joe attempted to defuse them both. "Let's leave the past where it belongs. There've been faults on both sides."

"I don't know what her problem is," Camilla said. "We all know that she can't stand the sight of Beverly. She'd bump her off in a heartbeat if only she had the balls to do it."

"Talking of heartbeats..." Joe circled around them towards the doctor, "I think six just became five."

"What?" Violet spun around, locking her senses onto the inert form but unable to hear anything over Camilla's cackling. "No... h-he can't be."

"You know it's for the best," Joe insisted. "This was only ever going to end one way."

"We can still save him. We just have to stop the bleeding and –"

Gypsy prevented her from rushing to the doctor's aid, even though she knew that it was too little, too late. Unable to contain his excitement, Kid bulldozed past them and dropped onto all fours. He crawled around the corpse, prodding and poking it as if testing for reflexes; lips glistening with saliva as he tugged at the shabby clothing. It hit Violet that not only was she responsible for a man's death, but they were going to dispose of the evidence in the most gruesome way possible, whether she chose to partake or not.

"What about his family? Friends..." Violet's voice came as a shudder, her throat aching with buried sobs. "Oh, God, what if he has kids? If I don't end up in prison then I'm definitely going to hell."

"There are an estimated two hundred and fifty thousand missing person cases in Britain every year, and we never stay in one place." Joe spoke casually as ever. "If you were a detective, which would you prioritise: the scumbag on trial for multiple sexual assaults or the vulnerable teenager with their whole life ahead of them? Human nature can be a powerful ally."

"That doesn't alter the fact that you're a bunch of conniving bastards. You tricked me into this, and now I have to find a way of living with myself."

"Don't think of it as taking lives; think of it as saving them," Camilla reasoned. "A couple of years ago, Joe and I stumbled across a youth stealing motorbikes. We followed him home, and it was a good job, too. We heard an argument break out between him and his mum, and she started battering him over something unrelated to the bikes. If it wasn't for the two kids crying at the bottom of the stairs then we'd have left them to it. Instead, we barged in just as the youth was about to stick a kitchen knife into his mother's gut."

"And then what, you all baked a cake together and everything was hunky-dory?" Violet shook her head cynically. "You truly are a psychotic bitch."

"Let's just say that it wasn't the first time those kids bore witness to such violence, but it'll definitely be the last."

Camilla was overcome by a smugness that reminded Violet they were in this business for the pleasure as much as anything else. She wrenched herself from Gypsy's arms and started to back away from the scene, shambling through loose soil and branches that further hindered her balance.

"I'm done with this shit," she spat. "I can't do it anymore. I *won't!*"

"Enjoy the walk home," Camilla jeered, as Violet turned and half ran, half hobbled through the forest. "And to think, I was just beginning to like her..."

Gusts of laughter followed Violet on her way back to the Jeep, which didn't take more than a few minutes now that she was more acquainted with the layout of the woodlands. She kept expecting to hear four pairs of footsteps behind her, but as time went on, it dawned on her that they'd never coerced her into anything. She might have been free from Joe and his minions, but no matter how far or how fast she ran, there was no escaping the monster inside her. The guilt at what she'd done and the shame of having to lie to those she loved snowballed into a weight that felt material. Just putting one foot in front of the other seemed to take double the effort, and by the time she emerged into the car park, she was dripping with as much sweat as she was blood.

Violet fell against the side of the Jeep a second before her legs gave in. "Jesus Christ." She panted, amazed that she'd fended off the faintness for so long. As she leaned over to catch her breath, she noticed the streaks of blood down her left leg. She put a hand to her side and it came away wet. It seemed that the slightest movement agitated the cavernous gash.

Violet opened the back door and rifled through the abandoned clothing for something with sleeves. The first thing that came to hand was Joe's shirt, which she wrapped around her waist, making sure the lesion was covered and then knotting it as tightly as she was comfortable with. The puncture in her shoulder was still sore, but it seemed to have dried up so wasn't too much of a concern. With no time to waste, she scooped the remaining garments out of the car and dumped them in a pile for when the group returned – all but Camilla's, for which Violet felt a thrill of satisfaction.

After struggling into her jeans, she lumbered around to the front of the car and eased herself into the driver's seat. She wiped an arm across her sopping forehead and then retrieved the key from the glove compartment. Ramming it into the ignition, she fired up the engine before fumbling to activate the headlights. Their beams illuminated the tree line – still no signs of the others. Nevertheless, if they'd heard the engine rumbling then they'd already be heading her way.

"Come on, Violet!" She flicked the gearstick into reverse and stomped erratically on the pedals while trying to remember what Dean had taught her on their driving lessons. Fortunately it was an automatic gearbox, but that didn't stop the car from lurching backwards into a wall of bushes.

Spinning the wheel into full lock, Violet shifted the transmission into the 'drive' position and swung the Jeep towards the car park's exit. She pulled into the road without any indication and a cursory scan for headlights in either direction. After swerving into lane and getting to grips with the handling of the car, she hit the gas in a jolting acceleration. The road was straight for a good twenty miles and Violet tried to keep below the 60 mph speed limit, but panic prompted her to keep checking the rear-view mirror.

While confident that she was at a safe enough distance from her companions to be unable to catch up with her, all it took was for a police officer to pull her over and she'd be done for driving a stolen car without a license – and, worse, well over the legal alcohol limit.

Violet chuckled at her musings, for they were rather trivial in comparison to what lay back in the woods. "What am I doing?" She slapped the steering wheel. "What the *fuck* am I doing?"

Headlights approached fast from up ahead, and another vehicle zoomed past her in the neighbouring lane. There wasn't much traffic in these parts, being the early hours of the morning, but once she was off the country lanes it would be denser. She wasn't even sure of the route back into Derby – or more importantly, what she'd do once she got home.

If she arrived in one piece.

CHAPTER FOURTEEN

After taking the stairs to her flat two at a time, Violet fumbled to get her key in the door and then jerked the lock so hard that she was surprised the metal didn't snap in half. So eager to get inside was she that she forgot to lock the door, dropping her bag down in the hallway and dashing into the bathroom. She whacked the light switch and left the key on the side of the sink while she opened both taps to their fullest. She splashed her face with water, scrubbing her jaw and neck with her fingers and watching it gurgle down the plughole with a reddish tinge.

Violet rolled up her sleeve to examine the slash mark on her forearm, but she was soon to learn that the lack of sensation was due to the fact that there was no injury. Yet the blood and dirt that crusted her arm assured her that it hadn't been imaginary. Once it was all rinsed away, she cocked her head and stuck her mouth under the stream gushing from the cold tap, slurping and spitting while using her tongue to loosen the bits of flesh out from around her canines.

Fastening her hands around the rim of the sink, Violet leaned over it with her head hung down. "Shit," she hissed. "*Shit, shit!*"

She clamped her eyelids together, but it only amplified visions of the nefarious events that had befallen that night. Every act that had been committed against her and, more importantly, those she'd dealt upon the doctor in return. She heard a creaking from the sink and opened her eyes to find a fissure developing in the sealant between the basin and the tiles. She let go of it before unwittingly tearing it away from the wall, and then unzipped her jacket so she could remove Joe's shirt from around her waist. The axe had left an oblong rip in her vest, but all she felt was an ache deep beneath the skin that was similar to the dreaded side stitch.

Violet rolled up her top to feel for irregularities, but the blood was daubed on like plaster and kept crumbling away. She chucked more water at it, puddles drenching the floor and saturating her jeans. By the time it was clean, the only evidence of the attack was the pink, bumpy line of a fresh scar – not nearly as severe as it had been an hour ago. Maybe it would be a permanent reminder of her sins, or her body hadn't finished healing and needed that all important sustenance to help it along.

It was with reluctance that Violet looked into the mirror in front of her – now a hundred tiny mirrors after she'd smashed it the other week. Her face was as colourless as her lips, pupils reduced to pinheads in the artificial lighting. Strands of hair were matted together with blood; she even plucked a leaf out of the back of it. Though her physical features were all as they should have been, Violet could still feel the beast circling like a shark beneath the ocean's surface, ready to breach at any second. She felt it more every day, and part of her wanted to give in to the transformation so she could see it in front of her; to prove to herself that it wasn't some fucked up delusion. She wasn't even sure that she'd grasped the complexity of the shift and believed that, sooner or later, it would exceed her control and she'd be stuck like that permanently.

"No." Violet shook her head at her ghastly reflection. "I'm not doing this. I won't let it control me!"

She picked up her door key and held her left arm over the sink. "I hear that you don't like pain." She spoke to the force inside her as if it was another entity, a demon festering in her subconscious.

Grating her teeth together, Violet pressed the tip of the key into the centre of her inner wrist, grunting as the steel disappeared into her flesh. Blood oozed up from the slit, dappling the sink as she carved a line up towards her elbow. The outpouring of rage could have been a physical substance, and the relevance of the crimson liquid made her chuckle. It didn't matter how deep she went or which vein she nicked, for it was the mental scars that would never heal. With each millimetre the incision grew, as did her relief.

"Violet!" A voice boomed from the bathroom doorway. Dean was upon her before she could turn around, snatching the key out of her hand and throwing it across the room as if it had been dipped in a deadly toxin. As the key rings clattered against the tiles, he grabbed a hand towel and folded it over her wrist, keeping it there despite her attempts to withdraw from him.

"Why did you do that? What the hell is wrong with you?" The panic fractured his voice, a distressed sheen to his bulbous eyes. But that was nothing in comparison to the horror of seeing Violet's blood-soaked vest for the first time, and the colour evaporated from his face completely.

"Did someone attack you?" Dean looked so fragile that she was afraid the slightest draught would sweep him off his feet.

"I-it's not what it looks like." Violet was grateful for her jacket cloaking the rest of her maimed body. "I'm fine, I promise."

"Fine? I just walked in on you hacking into your own arm! Tell me what happened or else I'm calling an ambulance."

"You don't understand. You should leave before I hurt you, too." Violet tried to wrest her arm from his grasp, but the sting thwarted her more so than Dean's strength.

"Then, make me understand," he urged. "Were you trying to kill yourself or what?"

"No, I..." Violet looked into his eyes and saw his soul-deep affection for her. Affection that she'd never felt from anyone else in her life, apart from the one person that was no longer with them. The tears began to pour as she stopped resisting him, too fatigued to argue any longer.

"I'm a monster!" Violet wailed. "She always said it, and she was right."

"Who?"

"Beverly."

"Your mum?"

"Yes – only, she isn't. I was adopted, Dean. I don't know who or what I am. Just that there's an evil inside me that I'll never be rid of."

"Oh, Christ..." Dean sighed, as though whatever he'd expected to hear would be far worse. *Nothing could be worse than the truth,* Violet thought.

"I'm sorry, that's the last thing you need on top of everything else. Is that where you've been, with Beverly? Did you guys have a fight or..."

"She has every right to hate me." Violet sniffed. "It should have been me they took, not Isabelle. Why couldn't they have killed me and got it over with?"

As if the mental strain of the last couple of weeks had accumulated into a dark mass inside her head, a tumour, she collapsed into Dean's arms. He sank with her to the floor, cradling her into his body as though to shield her from everything bad in the world. Little did he know that the real threat was right in front of him.

Dean pressed his lips to her forehead, kissing her long and softly. Letting her cry because the grief required an outlet, and because it was all he could do. Violet clutched onto his T-shirt, rumpling the material that was already sodden with tears. After many minutes, the salty dryness left her eyes red and sore. Once she'd stopped shuddering, Dean peeled back the towel to expose the laceration in her wrist. As predicted, the blood had already clotted and it looked a lot shallower than it had done when fresh.

"Doesn't look like it'll need stitches." Dean seemed none the wiser. "Maybe you should get it checked over tomorrow, go for a tetanus jab or something."

"It's just a scratch." Violet laid her head against his chest, listening to his robust heartbeat. She noticed that he had jog pants on without socks or shoes and wondered what he was doing there in the first place.

"Did you arrange to come over tonight? I can't even recall waking up this morning."

"You gave me a key, remember? I was waiting up for you and must have crashed out on the sofa. I didn't think you'd appreciate me hounding you with text messages."

"I'm sorry, you shouldn't have had to see me like this. I guess I just lost myself for a moment, but I swear that I'll never do anything as stupid as that again." She referred to her self-injury.

"I believe you, but you have to tell me how you ended up in this state. I know you've been drinking, I can smell it on you."

"It was my own fault, really. After finding out the truth about my parents, I did what I always do and ran straight to the nearest pub." Violet closed her eyes, trying to blacken visions of the woodland slaughter. "I thought the walk home might help to clear my head, but I stumbled into the road and..." the images were ingrained in her mind, so she squeezed her eyes tighter, "... he came at me."

"He?" said Dean.

"The driver, I mean. The next thing I knew, I was on the ground with a bunch of people hovering over me."

"You were hit by a frigging car? Shit, Vi, you should be in hospital."

"It's just a few scrapes and bruises, not as bad as it looks. In fact I can hardly feel a thing anymore."

For a while, Dean was nonplussed to the point of speechlessness. "Look, I don't know what went on between you and Beverly, but if there's one person that understands what you're going through then it's her. Maybe some good can come out of this and you guys can, dare I say it, start building bridges."

Violet arched back her head so she could see his face, and she was surprised by the seriousness of it. "While we're on the cliché train, I think that ship sailed a long time ago," she managed blithely. "There's so much you don't know about her, Dean – things even I don't know. Right now, I wouldn't trust her with a bag of toenail clippings."

"Well, you can't go on like this and you refuse to see a counsellor. You need support that I'm not sure I can give you, and that tears me up inside."

Violet pushed herself upright, keeping her awesome gaze on him. "Why am I so special to you? You've given me everything, and I've given you nothing but grief."

"You know why."

The words carried a heaviness brought on by the weight of burden. Dean was tired – she could hear it as well as she could see it. Perhaps he was even tired of feeling the things that he felt for her, only to have them persistently rejected. Violet brought a hand up to his bristly cheek and gently caressed it.

"I care about you so much that it scares me. Everyone I care about ends up in the ground or hating me, and right now I'm not strong enough to take any more risks."

"I know, Vi." Dean placed a hand over hers, drawing it from his face and kissing her palm. "But I'm not going anywhere."

"Good." Violet smiled at him. "All I really need now is a shower and some time to sober up. Have you, er, spoken to Lucy at all?"

"Not for a couple of days, why?"

"No reason."

Dean nodded, absorbing her lies as he always did, whether he believed them or not. "I'll give you some privacy and make us some coffees. Take as long as you need."

He eventually left her alone to clean up, and Violet spent ages lathering up her body and hair to remove all evidence of the woods. But no matter how vigorously she scrubbed, the filth seemed to have seeped into her pores and invaded her very nucleus.

After wrapping herself in a towel, she spent the best part of ten minutes perched on the edge of the bathtub with her hair dangling over her shoulders in dripping tails. While it was too early for self-forgiveness, she kept repeating Joe's words out loud in the hope to convince herself that it had, indeed, been an act of self-defence. Violet had never believed in religion or even contemplated the existence of heaven and hell, but recent events had kindled a new perspective on the afterlife.

Her damp skin began to attract the cold, and she felt herself shivering. She crossed to the bathroom door and, before it was opened fully, the sound of muted speech entered her ears. Violet stuck her head out into the hallway and traced the voice to her bedroom opposite, but the door obstructed most of what was being said. None of her senses had been as keen since the attack, and it seemed as though her recuperation was sapping the rest of her abilities. Instead, she tried to lock the voice into her mind and amplify those parts that she could make out.

"I know, but how can I after this?... Of course I do... I've tried that... You know what she's like."

It dawned on Violet that the missing parts of conversation were due to Dean being on the phone. She couldn't hear the person on the receiving end, but there was only one name that came to mind.

"That's all she'd say... I can't leave, not now."

Leave... Violet didn't have time to recover from the stab to her heart as the conversation reached a swift conclusion. Footsteps approached from the other side of the bedroom door. She ducked back into the bathroom and pushed the door to, leaving one had propped against it.

"You okay in there?"

Violet startled at the rapping on the wood, tensing her limbs in an endeavour to prevent the fluidity of emotions from overcoming her.

"Violet?"

She sniffed back the tears and opened the door. The moment she saw Dean's fraudulent smile, her hurt burned away into cinders.

"Dean, I... I think you should go now."

The smile was gone, as if it had never been present. "What?"

"This isn't fair on either of us. You said it yourself: you can't give me the help that I need, just like I can't devote myself to this relationship."

"Is this a joke? After everything we've just spoken about – everything we've been through. Now you want to throw it all away?"

"*We?*" Violet glared up at him through tear-fogged eyes, thankful that she couldn't see the despondency that had risen to his voice. "You met Izzy twice at most. I was the one who lost her, not you."

"Christ, when are you going to stop feeling sorry for yourself?" Dean's candour stunned Violet into silence. "You think I don't know you, but it's obvious that Isabelle is just another reason to punish yourself for things that are beyond your control: your volatile childhood, being abandoned by Beverly – even your dad's cancer."

"Who else is there to blame? Beverly was a selfish cow, but I didn't make life enjoyable for her. My dad didn't find out about his cancer until it had already spread and he had six months left to live, likely because he was too busy worrying about me."

Dean pulled a face. "How is that relevant? You were just a kid."

"I-I'm just saying that things were full on at home," Violet answered evasively. "Mum had just given birth to Isabelle and –"

"Exactly, there are all sorts of reasons why he might not have recognised the symptoms – that's if there even were any. Why don't you tell me what you pushing me away is really about?"

"I'm trying to but, as usual, you're too busy patronising me. I can't stand it anymore, I feel like I'm being suffocated!"

Dean resorted to shaking his head, furrowed brows peaking in the middle to give him a look of childish desperation. "This is because of what I said earlier, isn't it? You don't think that you deserve to be loved."

"Shut up, *shut up!*" Violet jammed her hands into his chest. Even with her diminished strength, it caught Dean off guard and his arms flailed to steady himself.

"You're a fucking liar, plotting with Lucy behind my back when I specifically told you not to. Good old Dean, always wanting to play the hero, even if it means sacrificing his own happiness. Well, I don't need your help – either of you. I'm not some damsel in distress, and believe me when I say that I can fight my own battles."

Violet didn't need superpowers to sense the emotions churning inside

Dean. He stood before her as a well-formed man with the soul of a child that had been snatched from its bed and dumped in another continent. Feeling her bottom lip begin to quiver, Violet swallowed her guilt and looked away.

"You were right when you said that I don't deserve to be loved," she admitted. "What I needed after Izzy died was something that any man could have given me. I used you, and I'm sorry for that."

"No." Dean's response brought her gaze to him once more. "It's my fault for taking advantage. I should never have let it get this far – not until you were in your right mind."

Seriously? Violet thought, laughing quietly to herself. "Just go, Dean. I'm not your problem anymore."

"How do I know that you're not going to do something stupid as soon as I walk out of the door?"

"I told you, if I was going to top myself then I'd have done it already. Just get your stuff together and leave. If there's anything left behind then I'll pass it on to Lucy at work. Please, don't make me throw you out."

As if believing that she would, Dean retreated into the bedroom without argument. He returned a short while later wearing a fleece and trainers, van keys clutched in one hand. The look of detachment on his face was even more agonising than tears and despair, and Violet almost wanted him to look back before leaving. She was glad he didn't, for that was all it would have taken to succumb to her feelings. Even if she could retract what had been said, deep down, she knew that she couldn't lose what she'd never had. Their relationship was as much a lie as her whole life prior to Joe walking into it.

Once the door had closed, Violet exhaled the breath that she'd been holding in and went to pick up her bag that she'd dropped upon arriving home. She took it into the living area and rummaged for her mobile phone. It occurred to her while dialling Joe's number that most of their belongings had been left in the Jeep that she'd stolen – or borrowed, for a better term. Perhaps it was best all around if contact was permanently lost, but there was little time for reassessments when Joe's placid voice intercepted the ringing.

"Violet, I was wondering how long it'd take."

Violet's gulp was audible to herself, so she had no doubt that Joe would have heard it, too. "I'm sorry, okay? I freaked out, but can you blame me? I wasn't ready for... *that*."

"Then, the mistake was mine." Violet waited for a 'but', which never came.

"Sorry about the Jeep, too – not that I made it very far. I left it on a lay-by just outside of –"

"You think I don't have insurances in place? The Jeep is tracked, we picked it up not too long ago."

"Of course it is," Violet mumbled to herself.

"You're not usually one for apologies, Violet. What is it that you want?"

Violet inhaled while leaning back into the sofa. "You know what."

"Yes, but I'm not sure that *you* know it. This isn't a game, and the justice that you seek doesn't end with one human life; it ends when the Clan has been eradicated from this earth. You do understand the consequences of retaliation?"

"I understand that it means pissing off a lot of people."

"Then, why the sudden change of heart?"

"Like you keep saying, what have I got left to lose? Besides, someone made me realise that the reason I blame myself for Isabelle's death is because there's no one else to hold accountable."

Violet heard a sigh from the other end of the line. "Revenge isn't a cure, but it will offer some relief. Not only from the pain, but from the anger that you've been carrying around for so long. The key to our survival is learning how to control the metasapien, rather than letting it control us. That's why we do the things that we do. A clear mind is a rational mind."

"Right now, I'll do whatever it takes to find even a second of peace. If that means more bloodshed then... well, they started this war. All we can do is finish it."

It didn't take long for Joe to consider his reply, and there was a pleasantry about it that bordered on smugness. "As you wish. Take some time to heal and I'll be in touch."

The line cut out.

CHAPTER FIFTEEN

"You're sure she's the one?" Violet looked earnestly at Joe in the driver's seat. The house at the opposite end of the street was one of six in the cul-de-sac, set back from the road by a drive and solid wooden gates. A wall fenced the courtyard and grounds, but the parts of the house that were visible suggested an Edwardian detached property. There didn't appear to be any lights on in the upstairs rooms, and even as the Jeep had passed, Violet could hear no sounds from the TV over the purring engine – or any signs that someone was home. She began to question whether her abilities were up to the calibre necessary to tackle just one member of the Clan, never mind the entire organisation.

"As head of security, Jenna Lance is the one giving the orders," Joe declared, "which means that she's also held accountable for them. Something of such a delicate nature as this, along with the potential for a major fuck up, would have to be on her head." He glanced across to Violet with one arm draped over the steering wheel. "Besides, if I know Jenna then she wouldn't think twice about wiping out a city if it meant capturing just one stray meta."

"What if her husband comes home? You've got my back, right?" Violet resumed chewing her bottom lip. Its soreness was the only distraction from her sickening nerves.

"Gypsy will send an alert if necessary," Joe reassured her. "I told you that we've been keeping tabs on the Clan's committee members since we got back into town. Jenna's husband spends four evenings a week at their base of operations. The quicker you get it over with, the less chance there is of drawing attention to yourself. We don't want the police sniffing around any more than the Clan do."

"I know, it's just..." Violet gave the house another sidelong viewing, her neck muscles too tensed up to move. "Christ knows what'll be waiting for me beyond those doors."

"It's not the frigging mafia," Camilla poked fun at her from the back seat.

"*Hunter* is an old-fashioned term carried over from the days when the metasapien was considered a public threat. Now it's just a word they use to freak us out. It's a deterrent to the metas, not that they understand much in the way of language. They're not like you and me, but that doesn't mean to say they can't learn."

Violet threw a frustrated scowl over her shoulder. "If you're so sure of yourself then why haven't you wiped the bastards out already?"

Joe clarified, "She just means to say that with everything being contained for so many centuries, their main role is security. Even during training, the artificial conditions mean that they're not used to being under any genuine threat. Like an army recruit, nothing can prepare someone for the pressures of battle apart from battle itself."

"The same could be said for us," Violet pointed out. "We might have strength and resilience, but what good are they with an arrow in the gut? You said the hunters use weapons that are difficult to remove in order to prevent healing."

"The trick is not to get shot in the first place." Camilla spoke shrewdly. "Naturally, they'll go for weak points like the heart or the head, but that's only if they have the advantage of distance. Close combat is where their skills are lacking; without a weapon, they're no match for us."

"Which is why they'll do whatever they can to debilitate us." Joe reinforced the perilous nature of Violet's task. "Remember what I taught you back in the woods?"

Violet nodded. "The best form of defence is attack."

"Good. Don't think, just act. Your conscience has almost got you killed once before."

"How could I forget?" Violet winced at memories of the axe hacking into her abdomen.

"Of course," Joe added, "we don't have to do this tonight. If you feel that you need additional training then Camilla will –"

"No," Violet cut in, "if I don't handle it now then I never will. And if I'm as powerful as you say then I've got nothing to worry about."

"Our biggest advantage right now is that the Clan have never faced anything like us before. Depending on how much Beverly told them, Jenna may not have the first clue as to what you are."

Violet witnessed a sly grin pass between Joe and Camilla in the rear-view mirror. "If I play this wrong then pretty soon the whole goddamn organisation will know," she said.

"Perhaps that wouldn't be such a bad thing. While the hunters are out scouring the streets for us, it leaves their HQ unguarded – a perfect opportunity to cut out the heart of the beast. For all we know, your biological parents might still be alive, cooped up as prisoners and guinea pigs..." Joe leaned closer to her, bringing the utmost lucidity to his seriousness. "The Clan took from you the most precious thing in your little world. Return the gesture and not only will they fall, but you'll gain the family that you never had. We can bring civilisation to our kind if only they had a leader."

Joe's words stoked a fire within Violet which, if left to burn, she feared would devour the nation in one great inferno. "Anyone would think that you wanted this war."

Joe retracted into his seat with his usual poise. "The difference between us is that Camilla and I have grown up around these people. Our father may have been a maniac, but at least he was an honest one. How long do you think it'll be before the metasapien becomes a weapon of biological warfare? Power is power, and the Clan are tyrants."

"I understand." Violet gave a staunch nod. "Whatever happens, I'm ready."

"Good. All you have to do is walk in there," Joe pointed to the house twenty yards from them, "take one look into that bitch's eyes and you'll see the wickedness in them for yourself. If she can't beat you by force then she'll resort to manipulation: lies mixed with half-truths and false reasoning. Just remember what brought you here in the first place."

Violet nodded again, apprehension billowing in her stomach until it felt like it was pushing against her lungs and bladder. "Okay." She exhaled. "I guess that leaves me with one question: how do I get past the gate?"

Joe grinned. "You jump, my dear."

"Jump. Gottit."

Another half a minute passed before Violet climbed out of the Jeep and started down the street, keeping close to the verge of the pavement where the shadows from hedges and walls cloaked her. She drew up her hood while scanning for any twitching curtains or night-time meanderers. She'd spent the last few months fantasising about all the methods of torture that she'd wreak upon Isabelle's killer, yet now she was in the moment and the house loomed closer, all she wanted to do was run in the opposite direction. *No going back now*, she told herself, as Joe edged the Jeep around the corner so it was out of view.

Towards the end of the pavement, Violet broke into a trot regardless of the six-foot gate. Her pumps kicked off the wooden structure, bounding up it vertically until she was high enough to vault over the top of it. She landed stealthily on the other side, but movement triggered the front yard security light. Violet dashed in a half-crouch around the parked Audi Estate, her black sweater and jeans aiding her nocturnal disguise. She heard noise from the television as she ducked past the bay window towards the front door. Her hands were sweating inside the gloves that she wore, but the risk of her DNA ending up in a police database would be a potential shit expolison for everyone involved.

Violet's knock on the oak began as a meek tapping, so next time she made sure that her knuckles felt the impact. Everything below the knees turned to mush, but her icky stomach didn't have much to shed due to the anticipation that had supplanted her appetite all day. The whole setup felt surreal, like she should have been sneaking through windows or waiting until Jenna was asleep. However, Joe had warned her that they'd have security measures in place, particularly in case of retaliation after Isabelle's assassination: cameras, alarms, floodlights and so on. Besides, slitting a woman's throat in the middle of the night would make her no better than the people she despised.

Violet heard a key scraping in the lock, before the door opened with the chain still attached. A face that matched the photo that Joe had shown her on his phone appeared in the crevice: middle-aged, brunette – nothing to distinguish her from any ordinary woman in any ordinary neighbourhood. However, most conspicuous – in fact the only conspicuous feature – was the void in her eyes. There was no hint of a smile or a frown. No welcome, yet no intrigue either. Perhaps Violet had recognised the expression because she, too, shared it: the look of knowing.

Violet's instincts took charge in a vehement fight-flight response, spurring her to strike before she was stricken. She blasted the door with her foot, the chain pinging into a dozen pieces and the woman – Jenna – bounding backwards before her face was smashed into her skull. The reason for her composure became even more apparent when Violet charged into the house and a cattle prod was jabbed into her stomach, just below the ribcage. Her clothing gave minimal padding to the electrodes as sparks of pain zapped through her body, muscles clenching into a temporary paralysis. A smell of charred flesh accompanied the recurrent bolts of electricity, and Jenna's dark, wild eyes looked as if they might engulf her face when Violet's clawed fingers grasped the barrel of the cattle prod.

Shrugging aside the declining agonies, she swiped it from Jenna and swung it like a bat at her opponent. Jenna's reflexes were on point, and no sooner had she ducked than Violet felt a smarting on her jaw line. She spotted the dagger that Jenna brandished, its point splashed with blood; the serrated edge, however, wasn't intended for a clean cut. The hunters went for nothing less than maximum damage, which would have been the case if the blade had pierced her a few centimetres lower.

"You nasty bitch!" Violet snarled, lobbing the cattle prod down the hallway so it was far out of reach. Jenna could have turned into stone for the inability to fathom what she was seeing: that was, the same monster she'd fed and caged all of these years interacting in a way that, before now, had been impossible. She looked as if her dog had just told her to pick up its own shit.

As soon as Violet advanced, Jenna made erratic swishing motions with the knife in her first display of panic. It flashed through the air, once from right to left and then back again. Having predicted a repeat manoeuvre, Violet brought her arm up in between them to block the attack without breaking any more skin. Her other fist snapped forwards, knuckles bursting both of Jenna's lips. The second blow hit her in the centre of the chest, and she dropped the knife while toppling backwards and groping for the stair banister. Despite Joe's instructions to go straight for the kill, Violet's desire to dole out as much suffering as Isabelle had felt escalated with every second that she spent in the house.

Jenna bolted through a door opposite the stairs, and Violet stormed after her. As she entered the kitchen, an object skimmed through the air just milimetres from her face. The needle-like tip lodged itself in the door behind her, and attached to it was a thin silver tube. By the time she'd located Jenna, the woman had loaded a second dart into the tranquiliser pistol and re-aimed it at Violet. With a timely half-turn, she swerved back behind the door to shield herself from another projectile.

"Fuck," she hissed, a swell of dread catching in her breath. She'd foolishly believed that strict firearms regulations would be enough to deter the Clan from using illegal weapons outside of their establishment. To take such a public risk told Violet one of two things: either they were more fearful of an uprising than she thought, or they were desperate to take her back to whatever hellhole that she'd spawned from.

Unhooking a framed painting from the wall in the hallway, not bothering to admire the poncy artwork, Violet stepped out from behind the door and tossed it like a Frisbee at the gun that Jenna held. The woman cried out when one of the corners shaved her hand and left her stumbling sideways. Violet saw her opportunity and charged forth, clutching the sleeves of Jenna's jumper and heaving her upwards over one of the kitchen worktops. Violet could have sniggered when her legs slid out of view like a human slug. She hadn't banked on the experience being so goddamn exhilarating, and her mind was unfettered of past doubts.

Apples and oranges rolled across the floor from the fruit bowl that had been knocked off the side, and Violet's eyes traced a particularly rebellious one towards the adjoined conservatory. Beyond this, she could see a swimming pool that was illuminated by the rear garden's security light.

"Another rich twat," Violet noted, at the same time wondering how many partners their organisation had.

"We're just trophies to you, aren't we?" She strolled around the central workspace to where Jenna was scrabbling away on all fours. "A way of making yourselves feel high and mighty."

Violet spotted the tranquiliser gun on the floor and scooped it up, assessing the bodywork and stroking the metal. She aimed it at Jenna's pumpkin-shaped arse and squinted one eye for effect. The woman was soon upright, nursing the elbow of her right arm while limping from the kitchen. Violet set the gun onto the worktop before pursuing her. In the hallway, Jenna was nearing the front door which remained ajar from Violet's earlier break in. She noticed a mini screen on the wall beside it, which was a receiver for the front of house security camera, and realised that she'd been at a disadvantage since knocking on the door.

Jenna was one foot out into the night when Violet latched onto her hair with both hands and manhandled her towards the living room, ignoring the elbows battering her sides. She wasn't too cautious about noise considering the sporadic housing – if anything it was her ears that suffered Jenna's despairing wails. Violet used her victim to barge open the door and released her so the impetus sent her cannoning into the drinks cabinet. The glass doors shattered on impact. Neatly arranged tumblers and flutes flipped from their shelves, while an assortment of bottles toppled over the edge of the counter. Violet grabbed Jenna's cowering form again and threw her into the scattering of objects, enjoying the crisp, tinkly sounds of exploding glass. Jenna whimpered as the lethal shards bit into her hands and knees, blood streaking the carpet as she wriggled away on her side like the maggot she was. Violet stalked after her in a deliberate gait, glass crunching beneath her pumps.

"I thought you were supposed to be the big bad hunter?" She scoffed. "Even Doctor Paedo was more of a challenge than you."

"Please!" Jenna gave a fretful screech while staring up at Violet, rivulets of blood mapping her jaw. One arm was curled around her stomach, and the other dragged her along awkwardly.

Violet saw the TV remote on the coffee table by the sofa and leaned across to pick it up. She tapped the volume button until the voices behind the screen were clamorous enough to compete with Jenna's pleas.

"Stop this, I beg you!" she bawled.

"At least you have a chance to beg for your life. That was more than my sister ever got." Violet gave her a vengeful glare. "You remember her, *don't you?*"

"Y-you're Violet Kendal..." Jenna faltered, as though short of breath. "I read about your sister's murder in the papers. Isabelle, wasn't it?"

"Like you didn't already know that."

"I didn't, I swear – not until after it happened."

"I'm not here for a discussion." Violet cast the remote onto the sofa. "I came here for justice."

She drew back her hand, nails bursting through the tips of her gloves, pointing down towards her prey.

"I'm pregnant!" Jenna became still, eyes frozen wide in terror – an emotion that hadn't existed within her until now. Her hand was fanned protectively over her belly, which was shrouded by the loose jumper that she wore.

Before Violet could spurn the words of a desperate lie, she'd already tuned into the rapid thumping behind Jenna's breast. She was no expert in the detection of untruths. As of yet, Joe had advised her to listen for inconsistencies rather than the specific blips and ticks. Jenna was so overwrought with emotions that there was no telling what was normal and what wasn't. The one thing that Violet became positively aware of, however, was the second heartbeat. One that she'd almost confused with her own, but it was much too faint.

"Whatever you've heard about me or my organisation, we had no involvement in this." Jenna spoke tentatively, as though afraid to tip Violet over that murderous verge. "The manner in which your sister was killed stood out as being odd, but it wasn't until several weeks later that we got an anonymous tip-off about a stray meta. We started investigating and –"

"Shut up!" Violet closed her eyes while trying to keep focused on the mission at hand. The television filled her head with more voices, which she couldn't differentiate between her own thoughts. "There's too much noise... I can't think straight. Joe said that you'd do this, you manipulative bitch."

"Joe... Joe *Carter*?"

Violet opened her eyes to meet Jenna's. The mention of Joe's name seemed to have stirred resentment into her panic. "I should have known that he'd be behind this."

"Don't try to bullshit me," Violet warned. "You can't lie to me any more than he can. You'd know that if you treated us like people rather than target practice."

"Joe doesn't have to lie to get what he wants, I know that better than anyone. The biggest mistake that he and Camilla made was going AWOL as it increased our suspicions that they were up to no good. We looked into your family and tried to find a link between you and the Carters. Our records showed that their mother, Rochelle, delivered a stillborn in 1992, which coincidentally matched your age. Taking into account their father's suicide and Rochelle's disappearance –"

Jenna was cut off by Violet's helpless laughter. "Their mum isn't missing, she's dead. Murdered by her husband for rebelling against the sickness and cruelty that you people are filled with."

"Dead..." Jenna's face blanched a second, before concern for her own life took precedence once more. "Look, I don't know how any of this came to be or what you are, but if I can't lie to you then why would I try? What is it, respiration rate or... *heartbeats*." Jenna answered her own question. "That's why you didn't kill me when I told you that I was pregnant. You can hear the baby."

The woman's accuracy unnerved Violet. Her type learned fast, and the more knowledge the Clan had, the more dangerous they became.

"You obviously have a conscience, Violet – that's what sets you apart from all the others."Jenna wiggled closer to the sofa, using it to heave herself upright. "We don't have to be enemies. We can help each other."

"Help each other..." Violet began to pace forwards. "Is that before or after you stick me with whatever weapon you've got hidden back there?"

Jenna's arm had already slithered around the back of the sofa. Before she could reach any further, Violet stomped a foot down onto her ankle. Her yowl was choked by the hand that clamped her throat, and Violet leaned in so their faces were closer. "You almost had me fooled for a second, but all you've done is prove that I'm not the real monster here. I do have a conscience, which is more than I can say for you and yours. Maybe Joe got it wrong and you didn't fire that lethal shot, but someone took the order. Either way, your head in the post is a message that no one will forget in a hurry."

"Th-think about it..." Jenna spluttered. "A public place in the middle of the day, do you honestly think we'd risk that kind of exposure?"

"A public place surrounded by woodlands to scuttle off into," Violet stressed. "Isabelle was there all afternoon. You waited until dusk when it started to quieten down, and then you took your shot. Better than doing it in the middle of the street, right?"

"I'm not the one with built-in night vision!"

Violet had no answer. No comeback, nor a single thought that she didn't immediately chase away. "You're not even capable of being honest with yourself, let alone anyone else," she said, letting her hand fall from Jenna's throat.

"We do what we feel is necessary for the greater good, just like you coming here tonight. The only difference is that I'm trained to kill metas, not humans."

"There was a time when I believed that I wasn't capable of murder, but desperation can drive people to unspeakable lengths. You can't pretend that there's nothing you wouldn't do to protect that baby from growing up in a world where the bogeyman is real."

"No, you've got it all wrong! We can work this out if you'll just –"

"Unless you can resurrect the dead, there's nothing to work out. Bye bye, bitch."

Jenna scrabbled back on her hands and feet, shaking her head in helpless horror. A storm of laughter vibrated from the television speakers, and Jenna's screams were lost amongst them.

***

Violet's breath fogged in the air, which felt a lot brisker than it had done before entering the house at the end of the street. Either her body was still learning to acclimatise to the weather or she was being haunted by the restless souls of her victims, human and animal alike. The thought made her shudder as she rounded a corner and dived into the waiting Jeep.

Violet threw back her hood and met the stares of Joe and Camilla from the front seats. "It's done," she said, panting. "Jenna's gone. I can't fucking believe it!"

She let her head fall back while emitting a satiated chuckle. The sound of her heart slamming against her ribs would have made Joe's response inaudible if it wasn't for the same note of panic that resided in his circular eyes.

"You took your bloody time – in and out, I said. What the hell happened back there?"

Violet noticed Camilla beside him looking unusually tense and answered, "Sadistic fuck was everything you described. You didn't honestly think that I'd grant her the mercy of a quick death, did you?"

"I expect you to do as you're told. For all we knew, she could have had you in a cage or worse. Only fools take unnecessary risks."

"What's your problem?" Violet argued. "I thought you'd be congratulating me. You wanted her out of the way, and now she is."

"She's right, Joe." Camilla surprised them both by jumping to Violet's defence. "We should get out of here while we still can. This place gives me the creeps."

The mobile on Joe's lap buzzed before he could pursue the issue. He picked it up and swiped a finger across the screen, illuminating the darkness inside the vehicle. "It's Gypsy. She says that Jenna's husband is on the move."

"Already?" Camilla turned back to Violet. "You're sure that you finished her off? My dad kept me prisoner for long enough, and if your fuck up results in any of us going down the same route then no cage will be able to stop me from ripping your heart out."

"If you don't believe me then go and check, but I'm not sticking around to save your backsides when the cavalry shows up. This is their territory, and I'm not dying tonight."

Violet reached for the door handle, but Joe triggered the automatic locks before she could tug it open. "No one will die as long as we stick together," he stated. "Trust is more important than ever at this point."

"Agreed," said Violet. "What happens now?"

"We lay low for a couple of days, and you make whatever arrangements you need to before we move on to bigger and better things. It's best if you stay with us at the mill for now."

"You mean leave? I can't just take off, I have responsibilities. My life is here."

"A poxy office job that you never show up to, an ex-boyfriend and a mum who isn't your mum?" Camilla almost took enjoyment in her situation. "Even if you do patch things up with your little BFF, her life will be a lot safer without you in it."

"So, we run away? Let them chase us out of town with their pitchforks?" Violet said.

Joe replied, "What would you rather do, hang around waiting to be picked off one by one? It won't be forever. We're not ready to take on the organisation yet, if it comes to that."

"Even so, I need time to mull this over. Unlock the door, please. I think

I'd rather walk home." Violet began yanking at the handle.

"What part of 'sticking together' don't you understand?" Joe spoke impatiently.

"If you don't let me out then I'll put the bastard window through, I'm serious!"

At that instant, the lock clicked open and the door swung outwards with Violet's excessive force behind it. She hopped down onto the road, slammed it shut and then started to walk away from the Jeep. Joe wound down the window and called to her, "It's a long way home. Let's hope that you make it back in one piece."

"Walking helps me to think," Violet replied, without stopping. "Besides, it's like Camilla said: if I drop dead then there's no one to miss me."

"No one but us."

"Not if Jenna's husband gets to you first. I'll call you tomorrow."

Violet felt two pairs of eyes on her back before the engine kicked in, and the Jeep passed her a few seconds later. As it turned a corner up ahead, she accelerated in the same direction.

CHAPTER SIXTEEN

It sounded like gunfire at first. The Clan's army blasting the door off its hinges, ready to exact the same destruction upon her head. Violet snatched the damp flannel off her face, what had initially been a cooling agent now lukewarm. The banging on the front door was unrelenting and, groaning, she hauled herself out of the sofa like a ninety-year-old. Her limbs were stiff and achy, joints cracking as if still recovering from the exertion of the past few nights.

"All right, I'm coming!" The trek down the hallway was more of a zigzag than a straight line, occasionally using the wall for support. Violet unlocked the front door, but it wasn't until opening it that the resonance ended.

"Christ, did you just crawl out of a morgue or what? I thought you were dead in there." Lucy surveyed her from top to bottom, face wrinkled in a fusion of concern and distaste.

Violet went to speak but found that her mouth was too dehydrated. She swallowed while rubbing her eyes as if to stimulate their puffy lids into opening fully.

"You stink, Violet," Lucy snapped, while shouldering past her.

"Come in, why don't you?" murmured Violet, closing the door and shuffling after her.

In the living area, Lucy gazed from the spirit bottles and takeaway containers posted on the coffee table to the mountain of dirty pots in the sink. "Well, this explains the last two days of silence. How are you still breathing?"

"Did you just come here to pick faults or was there a point to your visit?" Violet skirted around her and flumped back onto the sofa, where her backside had started to leave a depression.

"You're lucky that I'm here at all after the crap you pulled with Dean, not to mention at the club the other night. I didn't tell him about it but I wish I had now."

"Oh, shit, it completely slipped my mind. Don't worry, I'll pay for the damage to your phone –"

"This isn't about the phone! You really freaked me out, Violet. Dean's hardly spoken a word to me since you guys split up. Neither of us knows where we stand with you anymore."

"What's the big deal? I know he was planning on leaving me anyway. I overheard you and him talking on the phone."

"Leaving you?" Lucy scowled at her. "Then, you heard wrong. The only place he was going was up north for a job that he'd been assigned to."

"Oh... well, it's probably for the best." Violet retrieved the flannel and draped it over her face so that it muffled her voice. "I might not be around for much longer."

"What does that mean?"

"It means the only thing left for me in this town is bad memories. You and Dean are better off without me."

"Look, I'm not here as his cousin; I'm here as your friend. You haven't been the same since that business with Matt. I know there's something you're not telling me."

"Matt tried to rape me. Maybe I deserved it, maybe I didn't. It's done now."

Violet's eyes snapped open when the towel was yanked from her face and Lucy towered over her. "You idiot, why didn't you say anything? I could have helped."

"How, exactly?"

"By supporting you, by going with you to report it to the police. Unless..." Lucy took a precarious step away from her. "Please, don't tell me that you've done something stupid. Is that why you were so cagey when they started sniffing around?"

Violet sat up, wishing she'd never opened her mouth. "It's not like I murdered him and then dumped his body in a lake. He was fine when he left. He'll turn up, you'll see."

"If you want me to trust you then tell me about these so-called friends of yours. What are they?"

What... It was spoken deliberately rather than by accident. The women regarded each other with the same chary inquisitiveness, Lucy not wanting an answer any more than Violet wanted to offer one. Before she could say anything, the silence was fragmented by Lucy's absent chuckle.

"I've been over that night in my head so many times." She backed into an armchair opposite the sofa, retreating within herself to where harrowing memories festered. "I was tipsy from celebrating Tina's birthday, exhausted after a day in the office. Not to mention all of the stress and worry that you've been causing me. Even insanity seemed more logical than the alternative."

"Lucy, what are you talking about?" Violet pressed.

"Your eyes..." Lucy was present once more as she focused on Violet. "After we argued and you pushed me, they changed. It was only a second, maybe less. But I can see it now, even after convincing myself that it's not possible."

"See what?"

"The darkness. It's the reason I stayed away for so long. I thought that not being around you would help me to forget it, but here I am."

"I... don't know what to say."

"Say that it's not true. Tell me I imagined it. Call me a crazy bitch if you want."

"You're a crazy bitch."

Somehow, they both managed a light-hearted chuckle, which seemed to force the tears from Lucy's eyes. She flicked them away almost apologetically, yet they shared a silent understanding that came from their intimacy as friends.

"Those people... I knew there was something not right about them. I felt it like... like someone walked over my grave." Lucy sniffed while embracing herself as if she was cold. "I won't pretend to understand what the hell you've got yourself into, but if I can help then just tell me how. I'm sorry that you've felt so alone in all of this."

"Don't apologise." Violet shook her head in emphasis. "Neither you nor Dean are to blame for my fucked up circumstances. This isn't me pushing you away, it's –"

"Protecting us," Lucy finished. "That's about the only thing that does ring clear."

"Good. Then, you'll walk out of here and not look back."

"I'm not sure that I can."

"You know in your heart that the truth scares you even more than I do.

If you want to help me, then save yourself. You're as much a sister to me as Isabelle was, and I can't go through that again."

Their eyes locked in a short but emotive gaze, before Lucy got out of the chair. Without saying anything, no premature farewells or grand gestures, she kissed Violet's crown and then made for the hallway.

"Luce..." Violet said. "Thank Dean for me."

Lucy stopped. "What for?"

"He made me realise something the other day. Something that I need to do, but I've been avoiding it for too long."

Lucy smiled at her, and then she left. Violet opened her mobile phone and was relieved not to find any messages or missed calls from Joe. He'd already called once the previous day and a second time that morning – there wouldn't be a third time. Next, he'd show up on her doorstep with his minions in tow. Before then, it was time Violet paid someone a visit.

***

Chaddesden, one of Derby's residential suburbs most known for being dominated by council housing. The block of flats on Waterford Drive was as drab as Violet remembered it. She thought back to the evening of Isabelle's wake, when she'd last been in the area. It was a small gathering: a couple of aunts and uncles, the odd cousin and some close friends of Beverly's. Violet had turned up solo to spare Dean and Lucy the misfortune of meeting her family – or what she'd believed to be her family at the time, not that it made a difference either way. They were nowhere to be seen all the times that Violet had been thrown into foster care. It was only Isabelle's begging that had allowed her to keep returning home.

Violet passed through the barred gate that ran the perimeter of the flats and followed the path to number twenty-two. Base music thudded from the upper tier, causing her to grimace at memories of lying in bed trying to sleep, too frightened to ask the residents to keep the noise down. *Inconsiderate fucks wouldn't have any ears left to listen to the crap if I knocked on their door now,* Violet thought morbidly.

She rang the doorbell and heard its familiar chiming from within the flat. It hadn't always been home. They used to live in a cosy little terraced house not far away, until her dad died and Beverly decided to blow their benefit money on booze, fags and marijuana rather than rent and food. In fact, Violet was shocked when Beverly answered the door without a white stick dangling from her lips, although the dressing gown was standard. Her bleached barnet and gold-plated earrings reminded Violet of a character from Coronation Street, but she was looking well all things considered.

"Hello, Mother." Violet kicked off the false pleasantries.

An uncertain silence passed between them, before Beverly left the door open and plodded down the tiny hall with her gown floating behind her like ethereal wings. Violet knew at that point that her visit had been expected. She stepped into the flat, closing the front door and accompanying Beverly in the living room. The stench of tobacco had pervaded the walls and furnishings, and it was so long since Violet had encountered the staleness that she wanted to gag. Beverly perched herself onto a worn leather chair that was almost as old as Violet. A mental spectre of her dad dozing in it on Sunday afternoons made her smile inside – even though there was no blood relation, their bond had been real at the time.

"Drink?" The woman's husky voice brought Violet back to the present.

"Going off your usual selection of beverages, I think I'll pass," Violet said.

"You look like you've had enough of those already," came Beverly's rejoinder. Although Violet, having been the instigator of the exchange, held her tongue.

"Besides, you won't find any of that poison in here. This is an alcohol-free zone now."

"You've gone teetotal? Next I'll be hearing that you've joined a convent."

Beverly overlooked the remark and picked up a pack of Marlboro from the arm of the chair, ruby nails flicking back the lid.

"Don't," Violet said.

Beverly paused, contemplating her a long while before agreeably setting down the pack. She crossed her legs in an exaggerated manner, tugging her gown over her thighs where it had fallen open. The room, too, was a grand facade: tidy, vacuumed and minimal with everything in its place. It made Violet want to trash the flat.

"Why didn't you tell me the truth about where I came from?" Violet couldn't keep the words locked inside her a moment longer. She'd prepared herself for a row and felt almost disappointed when Beverly failed to grant her one.

"How could I?" the woman answered. "Our lives were complicated enough. One minute you were a child that had lost her dad, and the next you were a wayward teenager. The longer this... evil... was suppressed, the better as far as I was concerned."

"Christ, that's so rehearsed that it almost sounds believable. Then again, I suppose you have had twenty-five years to come up with an excuse."

"Think of me what you wish. I can't change the past."

Violet reddened at Beverly's self-possession. "What about Izzy? You must have been concerned for her safety as much as your own. Is that why you sent me away all those times?"

"I watched you love and protect Isabelle for as long as she was alive. As much as I wanted to split you up, what good would it have done? That's the one thing I did get right."

"You just wanted someone to look after her while you were out drinking yourself into stranger's beds."

Beverly chuckled. "Sometimes I forget that we don't share the same genes, for all of our similarities. How did you find out anyway?"

"It doesn't matter how. I came here for one reason: answers. You will tell me what I want to know."

Beverly's pencilled eyebrows inched their ways upwards, as though mildly intrigued by Violet's audacity. "You needn't bother threatening me. I vowed after Isabelle's funeral that I'd make my peace with life before the day it's taken from me. I've put right a lot of wrongs, and you're the last piece. After that, we're done."

"Don't worry, there's a good chance I won't be around to cast a shadow over your perfect life for much longer."

"What have you done, Violet?" It was an accusation, not a question. The same mistrust that Violet had received from this woman all her life.

Violet scanned over the photographs on the mantelpiece. One of her parents from the late eighties; a double frame with a baby portrait of Isabelle on the left, and one from her first year at high school on the right. There was a sparkly-eyed vitality in both pictures that warmed Violet as much as her physical presence had done. Even their old pet Beagle was on display but, of course, Violet's face wasn't amongst the family memorabilia.

She drifted over to them, if only to be closer to Isabelle, while answering Beverly, "Remember how I had a tendency to get sucked into the wrong crowds as a teenager? Let's just say that I never did learn from my mistakes."

"Others like you?" Beverly's interest peaked for the first time since Violet's arrival.

"Metasapiens – you can say it." Violet broke eye contact with Isabelle to look at her. "They had me convinced that a hunter from the Clan was behind Izzy's murder. The confrontation didn't exactly go according to plan."

The dread seeped through Beverly's features, and she shrank back into the chair as though the weight of her enemies was bearing down on her.

"I could have killed her – almost did," Violet went on. "When my so-called friends find out that I spared her, I'm going to be in deep shit. Neither of us wants me here any longer than I have to be, so the sooner you fill in the blanks, the sooner we can be out of each other's lives."

"I-I didn't tell them everything, I swear." Beverly gulped. "A woman showed up here a few weeks ago claiming to be from a child bereavement charity. She seemed more interested in you than Isabelle, wanting to know where you lived and how old you were. She said that she had a daughter of the same age and joked about us being on the same maternity ward. When she enquired about your birthday, I started to get suspicious and asked to see some ID."

"And then what? She pulled out the torture kit or...?"

"On the contrary, she reminded me about the prosecution I'd face for making a fraudulent birth certificate – not to mention kidnapping. I've never been good at thinking on my feet, and this *cult*... whatever they call themselves... have had me paranoid for as long as I can remember."

"My birth certificate isn't legal?" Violet shook her head, knowing that she couldn't change the situation. "Fact is that she played you, Mum. Jenna would never have involved the police. I'm too valuable to the Clan."

"Jenna?"

"She's the one that I was supposed to kill. It was her you spoke to, and you've just confirmed everything she told me."

"Why didn't they come for you sooner? I know I should have warned you but..." Beverly's head drooped. "I was a coward."

"They were biding their time. They didn't know what I was, what kind of backup I had. Up until the other night, I was led to believe that they were a group of power-hungry sadists. Maybe they are, but if you didn't tip them off then someone else did. Why?"

"To brainwash you into doing their dirty work," Beverly presumed. "How well do you know these friends of yours?"

"Probably as well as you knew their mother, Rochelle Carter."

Beverly's mouth fell open long before words escaped her. "Oh, tell me you're joking? Shit, Violet, open your fucking eyes!"

Violet was too taken aback to dodge the cigarette packet that came flying at her, although it bounced off her thigh with minimal sensation.

"Those kids had every reason to hate me after the shit I caused between Rochelle and her husband. I'm not proud of what I did, but it can't be a coincidence that they should track you down after all this time. They still hold a grudge, and you've been running around with them doing God knows what."

"My whole life has been turned upside down twice in the space of a year. I had no one to turn to except for them. Besides, there must be some element of truth in what they say because we have what you might call a mutual understanding. They're metas now, just like me."

"Not like you. They can't be." Beverly saw the bemusement in Violet's frown and explained, "Your mother was a descendant of the original metas; the sources. Every generation before her was bred, not created. No watering of the bloodlines, test tubes or whatever experimentation they get up to. The only linkage to humans comes from your biological father. I bet your *friends* never told you that, did they?"

"What difference does it make? I always knew that I was stronger than them. I'm lucky to have gotten it under control before even more people were hurt."

"Why do you think I went to the Carters in the first place? A time came when I couldn't hold myself together any longer. I suffered a breakdown, and it's no surprise when I was forced to raise something like you for seventeen years."

"At last, the real Beverly!" Violet clapped in mock applause. "I was wondering how long you'd keep up this ridiculous show. You could have shot

Isabelle point-blank in the face and still found a way to blame everyone but yourself."

"I do blame myself, all right?" Beverly rose from the chair while being careful not to invade the space between them. "I blame myself for not drowning you the second Kevin brought you into our home. I prayed every day that Isabelle would never find out what you were. I might not have been able to separate you in the past, but I'll die before I let you near her again."

"How can I get close to someone who no longer exists?"

Beverly was quiet, lips sealed as if by glue. Her jaw looked like a plaster cast, incapable of any type of movement. She turned from Violet, hugging herself tightly.

"Isabelle *is* dead, I saw it," Violet confirmed.

"Of course she is," grunted Beverly.

"What are you hiding from me? I said I came here for answers, and I'm not leaving until I get them. You owe me that much."

"I-I just meant that with your... abilities... it makes sense that you'd try to bring her back."

"I won't deny that it crossed my mind, but I can hardly resurrect ashes."

Beverly remained with her back to Violet. She kneaded her upper arms with their opposite hands, fingers pinching into flesh through her dressing gown sleeves.

"Mum?"

"Don't call me that. I think it's about time we said our goodbyes. I've cooperated, and what you decide to do next is your business. I just want to move on with my life."

Violet wasted no more time and spun Beverly around by her shoulder. As the woman sucked in a nervous breath, the quiet allowed Violet to concentrate on the drum inside her chest.

"I know you're lying," Violet snapped. "Don't make me force the truth out of you."

"Go ahead. Beat me, torture me – it won't make any difference!"

With a hefty shove, Beverly descended butt-first into the leather chair. Violet's fists were coiled so tightly that she could feel her growing nails eating into the flesh of her palms.

"You don't have to say a word. Your heart will do the talking for you."

Beverly whimpered when Violet stooped over her, gripping her jaw and tilting her face so their eyes met. "I saw Isabelle's body. You and I both said our goodbyes at the funeral. After the cremation, I took her ashes and –"

Beverly blinked in unison with the irregularity in her chest, almost as if there was a triple pump rather than a double. Violet unfurled her fingers so her hand slipped from Beverly's face.

"They weren't Isabelle's ashes," she told herself. "Dad used to work at the crem, and I know you were screwing that apprentice a while back. You could have pulled strings and had me believe anything. She's in a cemetery somewhere, isn't she?"

"Stop it!" Beverly's arms thrashed at Violet in the attempt to squirm out of the chair. Her sleeves rolled back in the struggle, and as Violet caught her hands, she spotted the faded red scars across both wrists. The dots from the stitches were still visible, almost white now. Violet felt a stab of pity that was vehement enough to make her release Beverly. The woman tugged down her sleeves while keeping her eyes dipped in shame.

"If such a miracle was possible then it'd be partly down to my lineage." Violet injected a note of softness into her tone. "That's why Joe never went into details about my biological mother. The longer Izzy is left to rot in the earth, the less chance there is of her coming back. He must have been at the funeral, and he was set on turning me against you from the beginning."

"You're as much a mystery to me as you are to anyone else," Beverly replied. "All I've had to go off are second-hand theories. The people that can help you to prove those theories are the people you're running from. Your dad... Kev... was the only person that Rochelle trusted with the truth."

"Why him?"

Beverly shrugged, still sitting tenaciously in the chair. "She and your dad were best friends growing up. I suppose I was jealous in a way. I knew that turning up on the Carter's doorstep would wreck their marriage at the very least. Rochelle was more afraid of her husband than the Clan put together. I figured that she was overreacting, seeking your father's attention. I knew upon meeting the man himself that I'd made a mistake that would come back to bite me. I just never expected it to be through Isabelle."

"It didn't have to end like this. If you'd put your hatred towards me aside for one second then I could have saved her. Joe tried to convince me that it would have been a bad idea, but he's proven himself not to be the most reliable of sources."

"You don't think that I'd give anything to have her back in my arms? I had every intention of seeing the cremation through, but it just seemed so... final. I couldn't bear the thought of her not being part of this world in some fashion."

"There's nothing more final than death. A lifeless body doesn't change that." *Or did it?*

"Either way, it's done now." Beverly looked as though she'd been eavesdropping on Violet's musing. "Izzy is at peace, and we have no place interfering with that. I've accepted it and, deep down, you know it's the right thing to do."

"Yeah. But since when did I ever do the right thing?"

Violet turned before Beverly's eyes had reached their full expansion, not wanting to dampen the new emotion that mounted inside her. A dreamy hope which, although without promise, devoured everything including her grief – the one thing that had been a constant through all of this.

"Violet!" She heard Beverly's footfalls chasing her to the front door but didn't stop for them. "Please, don't go looking for her."

Violet was already outside, making determined strides towards the pavement. As if remembering that she was barefooted and in her dressing gown, Beverly came to a standstill in the doorway, bawling Violet's name over and over and cursing without regard for the occupants of the surrounding flats.

"You evil bitch, I'll kill you for this! You're going straight to hell!"

"I'm already there," Violet thought aloud.

It wasn't until the bus ride back to town that she'd received an urgent call from Gypsy. The possible deceptions of her allies had returned to the forefront of her mind and she almost let it go to voicemail, but it was more intuition rather than a conscious decision that had led her to pick up. Apparently Matt was on the loose again, but whether the story had been invented to lure her back to the mill was incidental at that point. Violet had another incentive for showing up at the party. Beverly had conveyed the same contempt for the Carters as Jenna had done, and Violet realised that perhaps she hadn't been asking the right questions. She'd just accepted whatever was said to her because it was all she could do. The trust between them had always been thin as glass, ready to be shattered by the first curveball that was thrown.

CHAPTER SEVENTEEN

"Hello?" Violet gazed from one side of the mill to the other and up at the floor above. The sun was already setting, but the twilight inside the building was easily penetrated by her newfound abilities.

"Don't be screwing with me, I'm not in the mood!"

The silence was unbroken, save for the wheezy breaths coming from Matt's cell. Assuming Gypsy and the others had managed to get him back in the shackles, Violet wondered if she'd be better able to commune with him now she'd forged the connection to her inner self; that she could somehow tune into the darkness that she'd infected him with.

The stench of human excrement hit her as though she'd walked face first into a door and rebounded off it. How she hadn't picked up on it sooner, she could only attribute to the stifling dust and damp that had long contaminated the building.

"Jesus." Violet cupped a hand over her nose and mouth while peering into the room. A bucket lay on the ground, which she would have kicked or tripped over if she hadn't stopped. The surrounding concrete was darkened with half-evaporated urine and a few more solid forms of waste that she didn't care to look at for too long. Matt was sprawled on his back, the film of grime and bruising so extensive that he was almost camouflaged in the gloomy lighting. The chain was beside him, disconnected from the wall fitting. Claw marks scored the brickwork as if someone had come to blows during a game of noughts and crosses.

"Oh, God." Violet hopped over the bucket and rushed to Matt, dropping to her knees. "Matt, can you hear me?"

She shook his head in her hands. Most of the blood on his face was dry and crusted, as though he'd been in this state for hours rather than the time between now and the call from Gypsy. His eyes were so swollen that she couldn't tell whether they were open or closed, and he only had a pair of boxer shorts to protect him from the encroaching cold. Although there didn't appear to be any grievous wounds, the collage of black and blue around his abdomen must have been deep enough to cause internal damage.

With a raspy gasp, Matt began to stir, head flopping from side to side.

"Matt, what happened?" Violet whispered. "Did they do this to you? Talk to me."

He lifted an arm, the effort wrenching a groan from his chest. His bloodied fingertips followed her hair up to her face. Most of the nails were cracked and a couple missing completely. Violet matched this to the scratches on the wall, and her guilt presented itself in the form of teardrops that blobbed onto Matt's forehead.

"It's Violet. Stay calm, you're going to be okay. No one is going to hurt you again."

"Vi-olet," he croaked.

"Yes, that's it." She clasped his hand, squeezing hopefully. "We met in a bar a couple of weeks ago. You remember my friend, Lucy? She liked you – we both did."

Still, it was difficult to know if Matt could see anything at all through his puffed up lids. Each breath he took seemed to rattle, so deep and drawn-out. Violet was no medical expert, but the discolouration around his ribs hinted at a punctured lung.

"K-kill..."

"What?" She lowered her head to hear him, ear to his mouth.

"Kill me... Violet."

"No, I'm going to help you through this. I promised you, didn't I?"

Matt's arm went limp, so she laid it by his side. As he moaned, she saw the gaps in his teeth from where they'd been knocked out of his jaw. Violet scanned the room for a weapon, something heavy or sharp enough to do the job while being as pain-free as possible. But such a thing didn't exist in the immediate vicinity.

"I can't," she whispered. "I just can't."

"*Pleeease.*"

Violet dried her eyes with the back of her sleeve, chin quivering feverishly. Ever so slowly, she placed her right hand over Matt's mouth, using her other to cover his nose. At first, her reluctance prevented her from pressing down too hard. With no resistance from below, she added a little body weight, ensuring there were no cracks between her fingers. She closed her eyes and prayed for it to be over – even believed that he was nearing the end – until his body jolted back into function. As Matt's oxygen supply depleted and he flushed from blue to red, his head began to twist, legs kicking feebly. A hand closed around hers, but it didn't pull. He kept Violet in position, perhaps to reassure her or even assist her. Despair racked her body and she grunted with the strain, sure that any second his skull would be crushed like a meringue, but still he suffered. Still he lived.

"I'm sorry," Violet cried. "Forgive me!"

As quickly as the idea had come to her, she reached for the chain and coiled its length around Matt's neck. With the ends traversed over each other, she pulled as hard as her biceps would permit. The rings grated together and his face turned a dark purple. She wished that she could shut her ears to the gurgles in his throat, but after more shudders, Matt's eyes turned upwards and his body became still. Violet sustained the pressure on his throat a few more seconds, convinced that he'd spring up the moment she loosened the chain. However, she heard in no uncertain terms the closing beat of his heart. After that, there was nothing apart from the presence that had emerged in the doorway, impeding what scant light there was.

"You did the right t'ing," came Gypsy's distinctive accent. "I'd have taken care of him myself but…"

"But they told you not to," Violet mumbled dismally.

"I'm sorry, Violet. I know you two had… history, shall we say… but everyone is entitled to a mercy kill. His body was too damaged to repair itself. He was too weak."

"Right, I forgot that you'd rather watch a man slowly die than risk taking him to a hospital. Too bad I ate Doctor Yans, huh?" Violet projected a thunderous look at the girl. "Were you in on their other little games as well?"

"What games?"

"Setting me up to kill Jenna when the Clan had nothing to do with Isabelle's death."

The rumples spread across Gypsy's face until her slitted eyes were almost lost within them. "That's ridiculous! Why are you trying to turn me against them? Joe warned me about this."

"Funny, that's exactly what he told me about Jenna." Violet used her arms to push herself up, her body still trembling from the shock of what she'd done. "They kept the truth from you so that you wouldn't have to lie to me. Because they knew you'd remind me of Isabelle, and that was the easiest way of manipulating me. You're just a pawn in all of this, Gypsy."

"No..." Gypsy backed out of the room, as if to escape the lies. "They love me. We're a family."

"You saw what you wanted to see, just like I did. It's fucking genius when you think about it." Violet pursued her into the main atrium of the mill. "What do you think beating Matt half to death was all about? They were letting me know that they call the shots. They decide who lives and who dies."

"You don't know what you're talking about. If they didn't trust me then why did they instruct me to keep you distracted while –" Gypsy broke off even before Violet had eliminated the distance between them in a relentless charge.

"While what?" she demanded.

Gypsy's face started twitching as though she might burst into tears. Violet snatched the front of her jacket, yanking her closer. "Where are they?"

"Y-your friend, Lucy... Camilla thinks she knows about us," Gypsy stammered.

"Why?"

"It was after she walked in on you and Lucy arguing in the club toilets. She said that you'd transformed right in front of her."

"Lucy doesn't know shit! Even if she did, what are they going to do about it? If they touch her then I kill them, simple."

"They just want to talk to her. If anyone's a danger to your friends, then it's you with your constant betrayals."

"*My* betrayals?" Violet echoed, with disbelief.

"We know about your secret meetings with Beverly. Did you think we'd never find out that you two are in league with the Clan?"

"What are you talking about?" The irritation spread to Violet's scowl. "I spoke to her once this afternoon, and I made sure that I wasn't being followed. How many spies do you people have?"

"Joe had your phone tracked."

Violet remembered how Joe had done the same to his Jeep when she'd stolen it. With so much of her memory running like a blank tape over the last few weeks, she didn't need to question how or when Joe had got a hold of her mobile and applied whatever program necessary to keep tabs on her location. The notion was almost as disconcerting as the thought of Dean and Lucy being left unprotected.

"I suggest you get hold of Joe right now and explain very clearly what's going to happen if they mess with my friends," Violet cautioned.

"I-I can't... Joe left his phone here."

Violet sniffed back the anger and spoke gruffly through her teeth. "How could you do this to me? I thought we were friends. I cared about you."

"Was it me that you cared about, or was it the illusion of Isabelle?"

"My sister would never have been such a gullible idiot. If anything, it's my younger self that I see in you. It's the only reason why you're not dead already."

Gypsy quailed as Violet released her, as though predicting the same fist would punch through her trunk and squeeze her heart until it burst like a runny-centred chocolate.

"If anything happens to them, then it's on *you*." Violet stubbed a finger into the girl's shoulder. "Wake the fuck up, and get yourself out of this mess while you still have a chance."

She made briskly for the mill's entrance before her temper took control of the reins, knowing that a minute longer would result in two deaths that day. The temptation was close to irresistible when Gypsy bleated after her, "Where am I supposed to go? I don't want to be alone again."

"Then, stay. But if you see me coming back here, be sure to run."

It was the last sentence to leave Violet's mouth before she departed the building into the emerging night, praying to whoever was listening that she didn't have to return.

***

Violet crashed through the bus doors before they'd fully opened and almost greeted the driver with the ungovernable butting of skulls.

"Town centre, please." She panted.

The man gave her a blank look as she tossed a scattering of change onto the metallic tray. After he'd processed the ticket, she scooted down the central isle towards the back of the bus, squinting her eyes against the lights and paying no attention to the handful of passengers. Once seated, she tried ringing Lucy's mobile but, as with all the times before that, it went straight to voicemail.

"Come on, Luce, don't be ignoring me," Violet muttered.

She searched for Lucy's home number in her contacts and tapped her foot frenziedly as it rang out. When Mrs Smith's voice answered, Violet groaned a long-awaited sigh.

"Hi, is Lucy there?" She spoke in the most self-possessed manner that she could assume.

"She's out at the minute. Is that you, Violet?"

"Yeah – sorry, I'm kind of in a rush and I can't reach Lucy on her mobile. Do you know where she went?"

"I think she mentioned something about going to see Dean."

"When was this?"

"About half an hour ago. Is everything all right?" And so began the inevitable prying. "I'm sorry to hear about you and Dean breaking up –"

"Gotta go, thanks!"

Violet hung up and called Dean instead, but half a minute passed and the dialling went on. The lack of responses caused an escalating sense of foreboding. If their silence was going to be everlasting then she'd rather it was out of hatred or even spite than they were lying dead somewhere.

"No," she protested out loud, "they're going to be fine. It's all a misunderstanding."

Keeping a rational mind was the only thing preventing Violet from kicking the driver out of his seat and taking over the wheel. The bus would pick up and drop off passengers at every other stop, thus delaying the journey even more. She contemplated calling the police and have officers sent over to Dean's place as a precaution, but subsequent thoughts of spooking anyone thwarted her from doing so. The last thing she needed was for one of the psycho siblings to panic and take someone hostage – or worse. On the other side of the battlefield, by involving the law, she risked pissing off the Clan, too.

An agonising twenty minutes later, the bus pulled into Derby station and Violet raced to the nearest taxi rank. The drive would normally be another quarter of an hour, but she offered to pay double if they got there in half of that time. Fortunately, rush hour was over and the experienced driver was familiar with all of the local shortcuts, although every second felt like a day had passed.

After arriving at Dean's housing estate, and with Violet navigating the network of streets, she littered pound notes into the driver's lap and almost tripped over the curb as she blundered out of the back door. The row of new builds looked like what Violet referred to as Lego houses because they were all uniform in shape and size. She didn't stop to heed any warnings from her senses, but the closed living room curtains were the first sign that something was amiss. It was one of Violet's pet hates to sit there with the lights on so every pleb that walked past could see into the house. For once, she wished they were open so she could prepare herself for whatever was beyond number twelve.

Violet's legs felt so brittle that she ran as if floundering through water, the cold stinging her cheeks and adding to the tears that were already brimming. Her body seemed to have a preconceived idea of what was coming, a sixth sense that rippled through her gut and brought every nerve ending to attention. Her shoulder thwacked the front door with greater force than necessary, the latch giving way without breaking. It rebounded off the adjacent wall so the handle dented the plaster, and Violet wasn't sure if it was the smell of blood or instinct that brought her stumbling into the boxy living room. The first thing she saw was the television's plastic framing lying amongst a blanket of diamonds next to Dean's body.

"No!"

Violet's upper half plunged forwards, forgetting that she needed to move her legs. As if she was buried ankle-deep in sand, she hit the ground and crawled obliviously through the glass.

"Dean!" She gave his shoulders an aggressive shake, even though the hopes of rousing him were already extinct. His once tanned complexion had a greyish hue, and his lips looked cold and blue. Violet lifted his head onto her lap and cradled it in her arms, feeling the viscid matter that had smeared her hands. The same fluid soaked her jeans and she realised that she was kneeling in a pool of blood. She crunched her teeth together, a prominent scowl constricting her vision.

"You shouldn't be touching him."

Violet's head shot around to the sofa that was tucked behind the living room door, her inner flame extinguished before it presented itself in a more deadly fashion. Lucy was sitting in a round-shouldered slouch, her face damp and blotchy from crying, although it seemed that her tears had run short.

"The police are on their way. You're interfering with a crime scene." Her friend spoke robotically, as if she'd wept out all of her emotions and become hollow inside.

"Lucy... I... I'm so sorry." Violet wanted to console her, to pull her close and share in their heartache, but her yearning to protect Dean was compelling as it was futile.

"I saw them," Lucy murmured. "I saw what they are. What you are..."

The shame and trauma curdled in Violet's gut. "This is all my fault. I never imagined that they'd go this far."

It could have taken all of Lucy's strength to drag her head towards Violet, the loathing in her eyes like a torch cutting through mist. Not loathing – blame.

"They must have followed me here," she presumed. "'Two birds with one stone', as they put it. It was supposed to be a warning. I kept telling them that you and I had agreed to have nothing to do with each other. I begged Dean to let it go, but he wouldn't. He didn't understand like I did."

"It was an accident," said Violet. "Are you sure?"

"That guy, Joe, he was taunting Dean. Saying that you were his now. Dean struck out and... the other one stepped in."

"Camilla." Violet's eyes were on Dean again. "She did this."

"One push, that's all it took. That... *thing* was no woman. With any luck, once the police get a hold of it, they'll put a bullet in its brain like it deserves."

"No, Lucy." Violet abandoned the body, shuffling over to Lucy on her knees and clasping her hands. So cool, they were, as if the shock had slowed her circulation almost to the nonexistent rate of Dean's. "You can't tell the police about Joe and Camilla, it'll dredge up a whole load of shit that they aren't ready for. Besides, what the hell would they think?"

"That I'm crazy, probably. But they won't need my convincing once they catch those monsters."

"They can't be caught, they can only be killed. Don't you get it?" Violet spoke with desperation. "Even if the police did manage to apprehend them, they aren't going to expose themselves in front of the masses. Custody won't hold them for long, and then it won't just be you and me that they come for. No, first we get the luxury of watching everyone we love die in ways that you don't want to imagine."

Terror flashed through Lucy's face, enough to blunt the virulence in her eyes, albeit for a second or two. "Y-you're just trying to scare me. Don't want to put yourself in the frame, is that it?"

"It's you that I'm trying to protect, not me. These people have no concept of remorse."

"Protect me? Last time you said that, I believed you. A few hours later, my cousin is lying dead in his living room and I could just as well be lying next to him!"

"I underestimated them, yes, but they also underestimated me. The kind of power I have running through my veins is... beyond comprehension."

"Like raising the dead?" Lucy balanced her voice, unnaturally so for the words that she formed. It was the kind of 'nothing to lose' demeanour that overrided everything else. A mindset that created a recklessness which, until seeing in Lucy, Violet had been oblivious to within herself. Beverly had every right to want to protect Isabelle from that.

"You're not thinking straight." Violet felt like a hypocrite for even thinking it. "Whatever they told you –"

Lucy snatched her hands out of Violet's grasp, now sticky with blood. "It doesn't matter what they did or didn't say. I'm not stupid, Vi. I've seen you transform from a living, breathing corpse to whatever the fuck you are now. I know this thing spreads, and I'm willing to bet that you passed it on to Matt. Tell me I'm wrong."

"Matt's dead, okay? I thought I could control him, but in the end he begged me to put him out of his misery. Do you really want to watch Dean die all over again?".

"Matt was a prick – a rapist, more or less. I've known Dean all my life, and I've never seen him harm so much as an insect."

"I can't!" Violet jumped to her feet, not daring to turn around for the risk of seeing the body and doing exactly what she promised herself that she wouldn't. "Hate me all you want – it's exactly what Joe intended – but one day you'll thank me. Maybe Dean isn't beyond healing, but the world doesn't need any more freaks. This was always going to end in bloodshed, and trust me when I say it'll be theirs."

No sooner was she heading for the living room door than a hand on her wrist forestalled her departure. Violet looked down to her friend's fraught features.

"Even if I agreed to keep quiet, others won't," Lucy said. "One of the neighbours heard all the commotion and came to check on things after Joe and the woman had left. That's who went to call the police."

"Then, I'd better get to them before anyone else does."

"Violet..." Lucy's fingers dug deeper into Violet's arm. "Please, stay with me."

"But I thought... isn't this what you want?"

"I don't know what I want, but I need to be with someone that understands. Whoever's fault this is doesn't matter right now."

Violet regarded Lucy pitifully as fresh tears glistened over her cheeks, and she had to curb her own with a tightened throat and concrete jaw. She settled beside Lucy, lifting an arm so her friend could huddle up close. As Lucy laid her head on Violet's bosom, she embraced her shoulders in a motherly fashion.

"What are we going to tell the police when they show up?" Lucy mumbled.

"Tell them the truth: two thugs barged their ways in as you showed up to visit Dean. They had their faces covered and started raiding the living room for Dean's van keys. He's an electrician so it'll be full of tools to sell off for quick cash."

Lucy looked half amazed, half bemused by Violet's assuredness. She went on, "Naturally, Dean would try his luck at getting the upper hand. He's a man protecting his property. Did they hurt you at all?"

Lucy shook her head. "Well, they grabbed me. It'll probably bruise a little."

"Even more reason for Dean to take a swipe. They got in a lucky push and... you know the rest."

Violet forced her gaze back to her lover, seeing nothing but a shell that was barren of all the things she'd once cared for. She knew in that moment that there was no putting him back together. The twinkle in his eyes would be replaced with darkness, smiles with anger; love with hate. The metasapien had never been a choice for Violet, and she'd be damned if she was going to impose that hell on another human being.

"I'm frightened, Vi." Lucy's voice chased away her musings quicker than the sirens that Violet heard approaching from the south. "They could be anywhere right now. Christ, my parents –"

"Trust me, they'll be laying low while the heat is up. They're bullies, picking on anything smaller or weaker than them. When it comes to someone who can handle themselves... well, I guarantee that they'll be shitting diarrhea all over the walls right about now."

"You can't take them all on. What happens to the rest of us if... I mean, too many people have suffered without adding you to the list."

"You're right, and it all began with Izzy. They took her from me, Luce. I fell into their trap and I dragged you guys down with me."

Lucy emitted a deflated sob, the final expulsion of her strength. "I'm sorry," she whispered.

"You did the right thing by stopping me from leaving. They wanted to cut me off from everyone and everything that keeps me grounded – that's what tonight was all about. Working through this pain is the best way to stop it from fucking with my head. If I go wading in there now then they'll be expecting me."

"I just hope you know what you're doing."

"I do. This is the first time I've thought clearly in... *forever*."

CHAPTER EIGHTEEN

"Will you stop pacing?" Camilla shot across to the other side of the mill. "I swear, if you don't sit down then I'm going to break those twiggy little legs of yours."

"When will Joe be back?" Gypsy whined. "Why are we still hanging 'round here like walking bullseyes?"

"Aww, are you afraid the psycho killer is going to burst in with her machete?" Camilla spoke in mock sympathy.

A coarse chuckle echoed from above them. Kid sat with his legs dangling over the crumbled edge of the upper floor, where half of it had broken away in the previous years.

"How can you joke about this?" Gypsy despaired. "You killed her ex and she's bound to be on the warpath. She already said that I was as good as dead if we ever crossed paths again."

"I told you, Dean was an accident," Camilla stated. "Besides, there's one of her and three of us – that's if she has the guts to show her face. Probably too busy babysitting that Barbie doll friend of hers."

"So, why not just pack up and leave? Violet isn't like us, this was never going to work out. It was a mistake coming here."

"Oh, you're on her side now?" Camilla rose from where she'd been slouched against the wall, several empty beer bottles lined up beside her, and flounced over to Gypsy. "We took Violet in, gave her everything she wanted and she shit all over us."

"I know, I-I'm just saying –"

Camilla silenced her with a playful shove. "I'm kidding, quit being paranoid. Joe will be back as soon as he's finished tying up loose ends. We've always taken care of you, haven't we?"

"Course, but you didn't see Violet last time she was here. I think taking Matt's life changed her. It wasn't like the doc, she was in control and... I dunno... detached."

"Yeah? Well, bring it on." Camilla swivelled on her heels and wandered back to her former position just as Kid made the ten-foot drop from above.

"One thing's for sure: if you're right about her conspiring with the Clan then we're all fucked," Gypsy finished.

"Look, you're starting to piss me off now," snapped Camilla. "Jenna's dead, which means the hunters don't have a leader. We'll be long gone before they come looking, and Violet will have a bigger bounty on her head than any of us."

"But I thought she'd made a deal with the Clan? That's why she went to see Beverly, ain't it? You said –"

"Drop it, okay?" Camilla plucked a bottle of Coors from a box on the floor and threw it to Gypsy, who caught it last second. "Drink up and try to relax. You'll keep more of a clear head with something to take the edge off, rather than standing there as tight as a nun's –"

Their attention jumped to the mill's entrance when Kid pulled open one of the heavy doors, and a torrent of wind blew in a scattering of damp leaves.

"Hey, where the fuck are you going?" Camilla barked. Kid half-turned in the doorway, groping his crotch in the cup of his hand as though making a crude gesture.

"Can't you piss in a bottle or something?" said Gypsy. "Joe told us to stick together."

Kid snorted and then left the mill.

"Don't take too long or else you just might lose it!" Camilla referenced his manhood.

The door clanged shut as he ventured into the blustery night, bouncing a little and remaining ajar on its hinges. Kid kept close to the perimeter of the mill, hair whipping about him like the male version of Medusa. A few metres away from the entrance, he unzipped his flies and flopped his member out of his jeans, aiming the stream of urine at the dirt-encrusted brickwork.

Just out of throwing distance, Violet was shrouded by a leafy sky and branches that swayed with the capricious gusts of wind. All day she'd waited, watching the group's activities and listening to the conversations within the mill. One by one, her associates had snuck out to relieve themselves, making sure the area was clear before baring their most delicate parts. One of the wooden boards in a side window had a corner chipped away where, presumably, some vandal had attempted to prise it off with a crowbar or other tool. It had provided a convenient spy hole, especially with the howling wind reducing any chances of being detected by senses as supreme as theirs.

Now, further out of range, the cloudy sky gave an ominous depth to the night. Violet had felt the humidity in the air a while before the first raindrop wet her cheek. A storm was imminent, and every time a tree branch creaked, she expected Kid to spin around and alert the others to her hiding place.

Joe, the mastermind of their operations, had left in the Jeep half an hour ago with a package concealed inside a bin bag. Hardly likely to have been the trash from a spring clean, and because no one had roamed more than a few yards away from the mill over the course of the day, Violet came to the unpleasant conclusion that their stomachs were filled and it was whatever remained of Matt that Joe was transporting.

Gypsy, strong of heart but weak of mind, would be the easiest to dispatch should it come to that; but not before getting through the brawn that was Camilla. With her skill and experience, Violet would have been a fool not to fear her, but now she had the motivation to conquer that fear. That left one hurdle in her road to the ultimate destination: freedom.

As soon as Kid had emerged, Violet had used her thumb nail to open the vein in her wrist. The thick rivulet of blood rushed down her hand and fingers, splashing the leaf-ridden ground. Kid finished his business, zipped up, and then turned back to the main doors.

He paused.

With his back to Violet, she just saw his head tilt back like a cat that had caught a whiff of cream. The coppery goodness was so dispersed by the multidirectional winds that Violet was certain that Kid, the most animalistic of the pack, would sniff her out like a police dog to a bag of cannabis.

Several seconds elapsed before he turned around, his eyes tracing the tree line until he found Violet. She shushed him by putting a finger to her lips. Without so much as a twitch, he watched her unzip her leather jacket until it fell open. Intrigue crept into the voids that were Kid's eyes when she gathered her locks and flicked them back over her shoulders. She brushed her fingers sensually over her breasts before letting her arms drop by her sides. Her top was snug as a second skin, slashed jeans flaunting glimpses of thigh. Kid moistened his lips with his tongue, chest swelling with each breath.

With uncertainty no longer inhibiting his movement, he veered towards the woodland in a trance-like state. Then all too abruptly he swept in, large hands almost covering the full girth of Violet's waist. He twirled her around so she came face to face with the trunk of a nearby tree. Violet endured him pawing at her butt, cringing as he nuzzled the back of her neck, rancid sweat making her want to puke. She clung to the ridged bark of the tree to stop herself from tearing his hand away from her breast, fingers rough and eager.

At last Kid turned to himself, rubbing his crotch through his trousers, grunting and panting until dropping his flies and reaching inside for his erection. Before he could start tugging at her belt, Violet slammed her elbow back into his gut to separate them. Next she aimed higher, clouting him in the bridge of his nose. He reeled back, more dazed than she'd anticipated. With a flick of her wrists, Violet's claws extended and she hooked them into Kid's shirt before ripping it straight down the middle. Then she thrust forwards her arm at such a velocity that all five of her fingers punctured his gut. They gouged deep into his abdominal cavity, lubricated by his own bodily fluids. For a moment Kid simply gazed at her, mouth agape in voiceless agony. It was the first time Violet had perceived up close what was secreted behind that veil of hair: the sharp hook of his nose and cleft chin. Her hand squelched through the barrier of stomach muscle and fat until closing around the tubular-shaped intestines. Only when she ripped them from his body did a spluttering moan pass his lips, and Violet let the entrails spill forth like afterbirth. She gathered his locks in the same bloody hand and wrapped their lengths around his neck in order to stifle his whines. Kid clawed at her arms, too enfeebled to struggle free.

Violet saw his eyes begin to blacken like some biological defence mechanism and yanked more fiercely on the ponytail noose. Inch by inch he subsided, intestines hanging like jellyfish tentacles. Violet straddled his front, flickers of feeling like dying sparks; embers reminiscent of the conscience that they'd all been so desperate for her to lose.

"Know that I take no joy in this." Her voice was low and toneless. "I'm only doing what you didn't get a chance to do to me first."

As if to counter, Kid retracted his lips in a show of lengthy teeth. Violet gripped his head like a vice and, with one jolting twist, she ended his suffering. The cracking of his spinal cord seemed to reverberate in her mind.

She shut her eyes to refocus, and to avert his deathly stare. After checking over her shoulder to ensure the others hadn't formed a search party, Violet decided to take precautions and severed Kid's intestine as if she was pulling off a clothes tag. No reviving him now.

Leaving the jaws of the woodlands, Violet wiped her hands on her jeans to remove the glutinous blood and chunks. The rain was spattering her in gusts now, mud sucking at her feet – she hadn't realised how heavy it was coming down. Into the mill she stormed, throwing the doors open as though it was a police raid. Gypsy shrieked at the resounding bang and squashed herself against a wall so she was almost flush with it. Her eyes swivelled between Violet and Camilla, waiting to see what would play out.

Across the far side of the mill, the blonde stood concrete-footed, locking Violet in an unswerving glare. The lantern's brilliance flowed around her petite but sturdy form, creating a willowy, almost alien-looking shadow.

"One down, three to go, right?" Her words were seasoned with a well-matured hate.

Keeping a vigilant eye on Camilla, Violet said, "Have you forgotten about our last conversation, Gypsy?"

The girl's pulse doubled in speed, shallow breaths distorting her speech so she babbled out unrelated syllables.

"Think you're some kind of badass now, do you, with a few measly kills on your chalk board?" Camilla broke in. "A couple of humans and one mutant that was already dog food by the time you got to him."

"I didn't kill Matt, I liberated him," Violet answered. "Joe once said to me that killing an unarmed man in cold blood was a coward's game. It's one of the reasons why I never suspected him – or any of you – to have taken that shot at Isabelle. That and you gave me enough reason to believe the Clan was behind it."

"So, what's your point?"

"The answer was right there all along. Joe *is* a coward and he knows it. He used you to give him the power that he so desperately craved. He used your dad's own fears to shoot himself into an early grave. He tricked me into assassinating Jenna and would have done the same to Beverly by chipping away at the rift between us."

The smugness returned to Camilla's voice, albeit muted. "We merely stated that Beverly was the catalyst to this unfortunate turn of events; after all, it didn't begin with Isabelle. It began the second my dad found out about Mum's deceit."

"You're not denying that it was you who tipped off the Clan, then?" Violet scoffed at the expected response – or lack of. She glanced back to Gypsy, who hadn't shifted an inch, and said, "I've got a better idea: why don't *you* ask her what happened to Isabelle? Open up those ears and listen real hard."

"She doesn't need to," Camilla snapped, before Gypsy could summon her voice. "That's the thing about loyalty. Each of us knows that whatever Joe does, it's for the benefit of our kind – *your* kind."

"I-it's not true..." Gypsy's voice quavered. "Tell her, Cammy. You wouldn't hurt an innocent girl. Isabelle could just have easily been me."

"I didn't hurt anyone. Now, do yourself a favour and get out of here. Things are about to get messy."

"But –"

"Leave!"

Gypsy hopped into the air with a fright, and then she followed the wall to skirt around Violet. After scuttling out of the entrance doors, the sound of her footsteps was dispersed by the choppy winds.

"The next person to leave this place will be the last." Camilla linked her hands, turning them outwards and cracking her knuckles as Violet stalked closer. "You know that you don't have the skills to beat me, right? Kid had his uses, but he wasn't a fighter. Neither are you."

No sooner had the words left her mouth than her fist deviated from her side, swatting Violet's cheek like a warning shot from a cat when its arch-enemy, the dog, gets too close. Enough to bruise human flesh, but Violet felt no more discomfort than if she'd taken the battering through the padding of a cushion.

"You know," she smirked, "sometimes I get the feeling that you and Joe are a little *too* close, if you get what I'm saying?"

The second right hook carried a sting in spite of Violet's anticipation. Her head jerked to the side and she tasted blood in her mouth. She circled her jaw until it clicked, and then brought her head back to the centre until her eyes rested on Camilla.

"You'd honestly risk your life to protect Joe, knowing that he wouldn't return the gesture? He ran away like a little girl who'd had her pigtails chopped off and left you to clean up his mess. You're nothing but a guard dog."

"Your mind games might work on Gypsy, but I'd save your breath with me. You're going to need it."

Camilla twizzled in a fleet roundhouse kick that struck Violet in the side of the head and rendered her deaf for a second. Her arms windmilled as she fell, her shoulder crashing into the wall before she reached her knees. Camilla gave her no time to recuperate before setting upon her once more.

A fist came swooping in from the left, and Violet used her arm to shield her skull from further damage. She countered with a sneaky punch of her own, which glanced off Camilla's jaw, almost falling short from her stooped angle. The biggest mistake she made, however, was leaving her trunk open to the swinging uppercut; her underdeveloped abs doing little to cushion the ferocious impact. The earlier boot to her head had left a ringing in her left ear, which was so high-pitched that it blocked out external sounds.

Violet coughed as Camilla grabbed her by the throat and slammed her back into a wall. By now, the woman's blonde ponytail was the only vestige of her human self. It was a contrast to the black ovals that glared their enmity at Violet, the over-prominent angles of her cheeks and forehead a reflection of the primitive soul that had consumed her over the years.

"I told Joe from the beginning that you were a waste of talent," Camilla growled. "Yet again, you've proven yourself to be a disappointment."

"On the contrary," Violet puffed, "I'm just biding my time. A bit of foreplay makes the climax all the sweeter."

Spittle was ejected through Camilla's teeth in a throaty snarl. She yanked Violet away from the wall and thrust her in a downwards motion. Violet's palms were first to smack the concrete as she threw them in front of her face, followed by her knees that were already poking through the rips in her jeans. Skin was shaved off, leaving them raw and bloody, though the soreness was short-lived.

As she began to slither away, a hand caught her boot. Violet twisted around and stamped her other foot into Camilla's crotch. The woman's knees turned in towards each other and, for a second, her hideously puckered features opened up to pain-filled shock. Violet shook her leg free and continued to scrabble away on her front. It was as she rose to her knees that four nails raked across her back, tearing through the leather jacket. Although the material offered some protection, she felt a fiery sting that caused her to scream out.

Camilla's arm locked around her throat, strangling her voice. Violet squeezed her chin into her neck to create some wiggle room and then rolled her shoulders forwards, using Camilla's own weight and grip against her. Unprepared for the manoeuvre, the woman plunged headfirst over Violet's body and tumbled onto her back. Violet grimaced at the weeping claw marks beneath her jacket, unused to the sensations, however temporary they may be. Camilla flipped onto all fours, remaining crouched so that each assailant mirrored the other in a standoff.

"I see that you have learned something after all." The blonde grinned. "Maybe you're not as pathetic as you look. But I don't tire easily, and you can't keep healing yourself forever. There's only so much pain that a living creature can take."

"You're forgetting," Violet retorted, "I've already faced the worst of it. Mentally, may be, but eventually it spreads to the physical. First your brain starts to ache, then your stomach twists itself up. Muscles become tenser and stiffer until your whole body is fatigued and you can't get out of bed in the morning. I *know* pain, I live side by side with it every day!"

With a wrathful charge, Violet dived at Camilla. They locked arms in a tussle, collapsing together as they wrestled to overpower one another. More than once, Violet had to push through the dizziness while her injuries took precedence over mustering the strength to beat Camilla. Yet as the woman's desperation soared, her blows rained down mercilessly on whichever part of Violet's body that she could reach. Violet didn't know if it was the booze or adrenaline that made Camilla so ungainly; all she could do was slap and scratch in retaliation, blood droplets speckling her face, of which she hadn't a clue who they belonged to. At one point, a punch aimed at Violet's jaw turned out to be counterproductive when Camilla's knuckles were lacerated by one of her canines. Almost in annoyance, she dragged Violet up by the collar of her jacket and then rammed a knee into the side of her ribcage. Several of them fractured and Violet slumped back down, air vacating her lungs in a defeated howl. That's when a discarded bottle caught her eye, one of several that had been bowled over in their scuffle. She extended her arm, but the fingers entwined in her hair prohibited her reach.

"As impressed as I am by your tenacity," hissed Camilla, "I was also prepared for it. I don't blame you for seeking revenge; I admire you for it. Sibling to sibling, I'd do exactly the same. That's why I have to say goodbye."

With a groan, Violet stretched her body to grab the bottle, her scalp lifting from her skull as though it might tear off like a strip of Velcro. Camilla pulled her head back further, exposing the full thickness of her neck. On the ground, Violet saw the shadow of an arm rising up behind her with magnified talons that made her wonder if Nosferatu was creeping up on her. That thought alone triggered an adrenaline spike that loaned her enough power to edge forwards those last few but crucial inches. She used the tips of her fingers to drag the bottle over and smashed it against the ground so just the neck projected from her clenched fist. Then she thrust her arm upwards so the jagged rim pierced the underside of Camilla's jaw. Violet couldn't even guess the depth of the lesion, but the fluid that cascaded over her hand and down her sleeve was a gruesome indication. As the pinching sensation eased from her scalp, she elbowed away her assailant. Camilla was too busy gurgling on the blood that filled her mouth to find her voice, and there was a loud squelch as she yanked out the bottle. Violet clambered to her feet before wiping away the blood that was about to dribble into her eye.

"You know what your problem is, Camilla?" She rocked a little before steeling her footing, words spraying out like a drunkard. "Too fucking complacent!"

Violet lunged forwards, one hand closing around Camilla's shoulder and the other gripping her dishevelled ponytail. Then she launched the woman at the nearest wall as though she was a sack of fruit, her feet leaving the ground in a mid-air hurtle and the momentum far too powerful to reverse or even halt. A cracking thump sent vibrations through the structure that would have been imperceptible to the average human. Camilla's teeth scraped against the brickwork as she descended and flopped against it in a half-conscious daze.

In that moment, Violet finally felt it: the supremacy, the fearlessness of a predator incapacitating its prey and the invisible barrier between perception and emotion. As Camilla's limbs turned flaccid and she rolled onto her back, the deformity that used to be a face didn't cause so much as a reflux in Violet's stomach. One eye looked as if it had either exploded or been crushed by her own skull. Violet thought she could see bits of throbbing brain matter through the imposing chasm, but it was hard to tell amongst the crimson pulp that daubed her face.

It wasn't until the convulsions began that Violet ceased her advance, what she originally thought was a reaction to the pain turning out to be something much more sinister. Camilla's chest rose off the ground and her head arched back, fingers curling like the edges of autumn leaves; legs giving short, jerky kicks. Violet wondered if the fitting was down to choking on her own blood rather than the head trauma. With the briskness of a speeding arrow, it occurred to her that there was still time to flip Camilla over and slap her back like a child that had swallowed a button. Whatever good it would do, she never got to find out.

Violet was too riveted by the spectacle to have heard the clicking of the trigger. She felt a sharp prick in the side of her neck and spun towards the mill's entrance. Even more alarming than Joe's presence was the pistol pointed her way, which bore a close resemblance to the one in Jenna's house.

Violet plucked the dart out of her neck and examined the blood-tipped needle. "You bastard," she spat.

A step forwards saw her right foot dragging along the concrete. The second step was like trying to budge a dead weight. The paralysis spread from her limbs to her core, and she came tumbling down like a game of Jenga. Joe lowered the pistol as his gaze moved over to Camilla, the severity of his countenance masking whatever dread that might have filled his black heart. With wheezy laughter, Violet summoned her voice before the ability to converse was stripped from her as well.

"If anything was an incentive for you to grow some balls, then this should have been it. Are you so afraid to fight me like a man that you have to render me helpless first? No wonder your dad favoured Camilla: she was everything you should have been, and what you *wanted* to be."

Whether it was the cutting remark that galvanised Joe into action or the reality of what he was witnessing, Violet couldn't be sure. She made a grab for his leg as he passed her, nails scraping his trousers before the rest of her body descended limply onto the concrete. She shook her head – the only part of her that could still move – while her vision began to seesaw. Joe crouched beside Camilla, his body at such an angle that Violet couldn't see his face. He smoothed the backs of his fingers over the unmarred side of her forehead and down her cheek. Then he cocked his head, almost in contemplation. As he stood, his head dropped towards Violet.

Finally: "The concoction in that dart is enough to kill a human; fortunately, our system is designed to flush out foreign substances at a much faster rate. Think on that before you slip into dreamland. Remember the feeling of powerlessness left by Isabelle's murder and know that, in a matter of hours, you're about to feel it... all... over... again."

Violet's cheek met the ground, sounds wafting away into the oblivion that was fast becoming her mind; aches and pains dissolving with the fluid numbness. That was the worst part of all, for soon there was nothing to distract her from the sedation that overwhelmed her consciousness with unstoppable effect.

CHAPTER NINETEEN

The bang rattled the pane of glass in the skylight window, wind moaning through the crevice until it blew back to its closed position. Violet had woken to the sounds of Mother Nature, as if they'd been made specifically for that purpose. While her senses shot from nought to a hundred, she was still lost in the fog of events that had led up to that point.

Violet circled her eyes around the room that she found herself in. Though wide, the sloping ceiling and mellow lamplight gave an illusion of confinement. There wasn't much in the way of furniture from what she could see: a chest of drawers ahead, a chair in the far corner with her jacket folded on top of it and a cabinet next to the bed on which she lay. Everything smelled old and dusty; uninhibited, as though it had been starved of heat and bodies for some time.

A little further out of reaching distance was a bucket filled with discoloured water and a bloodstained cloth draped over the rim. The feeling had returned to her body, tender as it was – notably the left side of her ribcage, which twinged with every breath she took. Glancing down at herself, Violet realised that she was topless apart from her bra. Her flesh had been cleansed of glutinous bodily fluids, and her wrists were bound together with chains identical to the ones that secured her ankles. She was going nowhere, and exhausting what little energy she had on an unfeasible escape was the last thing on her mind.

Violet heard the sound of a toilet flushing and cast her gaze to the far left wall. She hadn't noticed the door that matched the surrounding wood until it opened inwards and Joe emerged from the other side. She glimpsed part of a snug-looking bathroom and, immediately, she felt like she'd been shrunken and placed inside a doll's house. Joe waltzed out of the room while rolling down the sleeves of his shirt, eyes focused on hers before they met his.

"Ah, the sleeping beauty finally awakes. It seems that your abundance of injuries caused you to be more susceptible to the tranquiliser than I anticipated." Joe spoke as though she was a patient that had just come around from anaesthesia after major surgery. "I guess your body needed time to recover. I've never seen you looking so vulnerable... so helpless."

"Where are we?" Violet asked him.

"This used to be one of my parents' properties before Camilla and I sold up and left. We rented it out to our gamekeeper and his handicapped stepdaughter, although she died some years ago. George was a very loyal and discrete man, shall we say."

"Was?"

Joe turned down his lips in a sort of passionless regret. "Everything in this world has an expiry date. I signed the cottage over to George as a goodwill gesture, and to ensure his silence. Going underground made it difficult to oversee the transactions and procedures that would secure our finances. He was my eyes – my middle man, so to speak."

"Until you didn't need him anymore. You never stop finding ways to become more and more depraved." Violet flexed her biceps, almost forgetting about the restraints. She began to twist her wrists, but the friction of the metal pinching her skin caused even greater discomfort.

"With the Clan on our backs, I couldn't afford to take any risks," Joe tried to justify himself. "Besides, we needed somewhere to lay low while I figure out where to go from here."

"What's with all of this 'we' crap?" Violet spat. "Unless you're planning on keeping me leashed and muzzled for the rest of my life, then I'd advise you to end this now. I won't rest until one of us is dead. You killed my fucking sister."

"And you killed mine. Does that not make us even?" Joe planted himself on the bed and leaned over her, one arm bearing his weight. "The anguish that I've caused you has intoxicated your mind, devoured your soul. My reasons were selfish, I'm not going to pretend otherwise. But I can offer you peace of mind in the sense that you don't have to blame yourself anymore. You always believed that Isabelle was in the wrong place at the wrong time – a place she never would have been if you hadn't suggested it. The truth is, we'd have got to her one way or another and the end result would be the same."

"They were all expendable to you, weren't they? Kid, Gypsy – even your own sister. You were willing to sacrifice her for... *this*. The worst thing is that you don't even care."

"I'm in control of my emotions; they don't control me. I saw with my own eyes that there was nothing left of Camilla in that vegetable you created. She would have been useless and, given the chance, she'd have begged me to finish her off. That's what I have to focus on because the future of our kind depends upon it. Depends upon you..."

Violet felt the sharps of Joe's nails grazing up her thigh, continuing over her hip. She wriggled when they reached her midriff, as if trying to shake off a bug. "Are you going to start spouting poetry next? That really would be torture."

"I'm not so naive as to think that I can seduce you into anything, but our fates were sealed the day my mother spared your life. We're the same, you and I, wandering this earth without purpose or direction; abandoned by those who are supposed to love us. We're the creators of a new generation. Your blood and my seed, can you imagine the possibilities?"

"If you really believe that I'm so magnificent, then why didn't you use my blood to save Camilla? Why not try to bring her back?"

"My job was to protect her, not to turn her into a guinea pig all over again. Without a comprehensive analysis of your DNA, I can only assume that, as with the turning of a human, your blood acts as a boost – a transfusion of sorts. After that, the body must work to stabilise and repair itself. Fresh blood cells are created and, eventually, those substituted are flushed out of the system. Just because someone receives a dose of your blood doesn't make them immortal, as neither are you. But it may well be the closest thing to immortal that exists in a world that's evolving at such a rate that mankind will never be able to keep up."

"Wow, that's a sweet little fairytale. Daddy's bedtime story, was it?"

"Hope is a powerful thing, Violet. You may not see it today, tomorrow or even a year from now, but I'm a patient man and we have all the time in the world to start building a better future."

Violet acknowledged the fantasy with a bitter laugh. "This isn't about us, it's about you and your alpha male complex. Jenna told me all about your failures: years of studying for a law degree and fuck all to show for it, how your first encounter with a meta left you with sodden undies and a thrashing off Daddy. Yeah, we had quite a laugh about that one."

Joe flicked a hand over his shoulder as if to silence her with a nipping backhander, but the impact never came. His eyes glazed in mental deliberation, and then his arm returned to his side.

"I'm not my father, despite what you might think." Joe spoke dolefully. "I'm not denying that the Clan are insects waiting to be stomped out by a species more deserving. There was a time not too long ago when I'd have given my heart just to watch them fall, but now... now I have other priorities."

"You're actually serious about this, aren't you?" It was a question that, deep down, Violet already knew the answer to.

"Why do you think I was so desperate to give you everything you desired? Revenge for Isabelle, the potential to reunite with your biological mother; harmony between the light that shines bright in your eyes, and the darkness that dwells behind them. To gain your trust, respect – even love."

Joe's hand rose again, this time to pick a strand of hair off her cheek. Violet responded to his tenderness by spitting a projectile of saliva into his face.

"Do what you want with me," she dared him. "Rape me, beat me; force me to pop out your mutant kids. One day I *will* kill you, if it's the last thing I ever do."

Joe straightened while wiping the drool from his cheek. Then he got up off the bed, saying, "I don't want to hurt you anymore than I have done already, but maybe we can come up with a truce of sorts. I guarantee that Lucy and Beverly will come to no harm by my hands; all I ask in return is a chance to prove my worth to you. If your feelings towards me don't change... well, there isn't room for both of us on this planet. Before you make a decision, remember that while you're incapacitated here, the people closest to you are wandering around out there like cattle."

Violet smirked. "Cattle, maybe. But not alone."

Joe stopped walking, one foot in front of the other. He twisted his head fractionally over his shoulder in a stare that didn't quite reach her.

"You honestly didn't expect me to have a contingency plan in place?" Violet went on. "It turns out that Jenna isn't quite the mega bitch that you made her out to be. I'm not in the habit of making deals with the enemy, and I trust the Clan no more than I trust you. Right now, I'm more valuable to them on the outside – especially Jenna. She told me about the affair that you two had. You know what they say about a woman scorned, right?"

Joe allowed his head to droop almost to his chest and then, with a defeated chortle, he turned to face her. "I'll be damned, that bitch is still alive. I have to admit, I never saw that one coming. You're a lot of things, Violet, but *calculating* requires a patience that I never knew you had in you."

"Well, I learned from the best, didn't I?" Violet replied. "I was so worked up that night that maintaining an erratic heartbeat wasn't difficult. Getting you away from Jenna was my first priority. Whose idea do you think it was to call her husband and get him to come home? I knew you'd be too chicken to stick around, just like you leaving the mill tonight."

"You did what you thought was necessary, just as we all do. The Clan has a duty to protect humans, but they'll never see the metasapien species as equals. Once this favour has been repaid, you'll be in their crosshairs all over again; therefore, the best place for you is beside me. Together."

In perfect harmony, both of their heads circled around to the bedroom door. Violet silenced her breaths, as did Joe. She projected her hearing beyond the walls of the house, cutting through the rain that spattered the brickwork and window in gales.

"Expecting visitors?" Violet taunted. "It sounds to me like this party is about to get a whole lot bigger."

"You have no idea what you've done." Joe was too flustered to be angry. He walked back to the bathroom and swerved behind the door. Violet's eyes doubled in size when he returned with a shotgun grasped in both hands.

"There's no situation that Father didn't prepare us for. Camilla and I were playing target practice on our private land long before high school. You'd better hope it's me that walks back through that door, or else you really will be wishing you were dead."

Joe disappeared into the darkness beyond the door, and his dull footsteps were the only means of tracking him until they became one with the creaking of the old house. Immediately, Violet sat up and wiggled her hands and feet to work loose the chains, at the very least hoping that either the blood or sweat would act as lubrication. On further inspection, she noticed that they were held in place by mini padlocks, neither of which were penetrable without tools.

A scraping sound brought her gaze to the skylight window above the bed. The lamplight glinted off the drizzle-splattered glass so it looked like some kind of meteor shower. The successive clunk was more intrusive and similar to the one that had roused her, but this time the window swung outwards on its hinges. A damp blast of air poured in, and then Gypsy's face appeared against the backdrop of the sky. Violet breathed a lengthy sigh and shuffled aside as Gypsy eased herself through the window and dropped onto the bed. Her clothes were sopping wet and her Dr. Martens left muddy prints over the floral quilting.

"What the hell are you doing?" Violet whispered coarsely. "Did you follow us here?"

"I've been an eejit. I saw everything that went on at the mill and then hid in the boot of the Jeep." Gypsy kept her voice hushed while tugging at the chains around Violet's ankles. "Joe buried Camilla in the land to the back of the property. I tried to sneak in then but you were out cold. If I got caught, there was no way I could take him on by myself."

"It was you that left the window open," Violet realised. "Shit, you need to get out of here. Forget about me, I'm not going anywhere with these things hindering my every move." Violet nodded at the chains.

"It's amazing what you pick up on the streets when you're starving and penniless," was all Gypsy said.

As if to demonstrate her point, she plucked a couple of instruments out of her cargo jacket pocket: two pieces of wire that resembled unbent paperclips, which she inserted into the padlock.

"Well, you'd better be quick," Violet urged. "The Clan are already here."

Gypsy glanced her perturbation at Violet. "How...?"

"It doesn't matter. With any luck, they'll keep him occupied long enough for you to set me free and then I can finish him off once and for all."

"But how are we going to escape if this place is surrounded by hunters?"

"Trust me, okay? You can do this, just concentrate."

It was an incentive for Gypsy to pick up the slack and work the tools with nimble fingers. Wiggling the end of one wire inside the locking mechanism and holding steady the other, trying so diligently to curb her tremor that she could have been performing heart surgery. When the metal hoop clicked open, they both gave an exhalation of relief. Violet shook her legs free of the chain while Gypsy started on the second padlock that secured her hands.

There was a thud from somewhere downstairs. Both girls solidified. The footfalls were distant at first; but the heavier they became, the swifter they approached. Gypsy waggled the lock pick, determination fixed into her forehead. Violet contracted her jaw muscles until breathing was impossible.

Creaks on the stairs leading to the attic... footsteps echoing in what sounded like a wooden passageway...

"Almost there." Gypsy glanced frequently between the padlock and the door, moisture raining down her face. Whether it was residue from the elements or sweat, Violet could only guess.

"There's no time, you have to distract them." Violet nudged Gypsy off the bed as the footsteps slowed beyond the door.

Gypsy gawped at her, fear snatching away her voice. Violet pointed at the door, mouthing the words 'trust me'. Gypsy stuffed the lock pick back into her pocket and tiptoed across the room. She pressed her back against the wall by the side of the door, her blanched face set with dread. Violet reclined into her original position with the chain over her ankles to give the appearance that she was still shackled. The doorknob turned and Joe strolled obliviously into the room, shotgun over his shoulder.

"Nice try, but it was nothing but the wind." He paused at the foot of the bed. "Even if that wench did manage to track us down, you're all the leverage I need. You don't know how these people work –"

Violet discerned the flaring of Joe's nostrils a second before he whirled around, swinging the shotgun into position with its barrel aimed at Gypsy's chest. His finger curled around the trigger, and Violet braced herself for the deafening boom and spraying of body parts.

"Well, if it isn't my little pup." Joe grinned, absorbing the girl's trepidation. "You wouldn't turn against your master, would you?"

While Gypsy stumbled over her words, Violet rose furtively to her knees before launching herself across the bed. She hooked her arms around Joe's neck, using the chain to crush his windpipe from the front. The shock of the attack caused his finger to squeeze the trigger, but not before Gypsy had dived to safety. The resounding blast filled the attic as a cavity was blown into the bedroom door, splinters of wood showering the carpet.

Violet went deaf for a second, and was still coming back to her senses when Gypsy grabbed the end of the shotgun and forced it upwards so that any more shots would hit the ceiling rather than either of them. A combination of Joe losing his footing, the manhandling from Gypsy and Violet's chokehold caused them all to collapse onto the mattress like dominos. To stop Joe from squirming free, Violet wrapped her legs around his waist while Gypsy tried to wrest the gun from him. Gagging against the chain, he kicked out with his right leg and Gypsy went rocketing into the far wall. The weapon clattered onto the carpet during the tussle, inclining Violet to pull back tighter with her arms so the chain embedded itself into his throat. Joe wrenched at her hands while stabbing the elbow of his other arm relentlessly into her side. The bruising from her earlier battering off Camilla had sunk bone deep and, without any sustenance to rejuvenate herself, her ribs felt like old, creaky floorboards.

Violet couldn't refrain from hunching up, and Joe took the chance to hurl himself sideways off the bed. He used his body weight rather than strength, knowing that her eight-stone frame would plummet to the ground with him. Violet felt the chain come loose and figured that Gypsy must have picked the lock without either of them realising. Landing on all fours, Joe flung Violet from his back with a jolting twist. She fell against the side of the bed, propped up by the hand around her throat. Joe pinned her to the mattress, claws puncturing her neck to the point of drawing blood. Violet glared up at his mutated face, aching and winded from the strikes to her abdomen.

"Don't move!" screeched Gypsy.

Violet peered around Joe to see straight down the barrel of the shotgun. Against the girl's miniature stature, it looked almost surreal, but her tremulous hold was by no means difficulty wielding the firearm. The dread in her humungous eyes gave enough assurance that there was slim chance of her pulling the trigger without significant hesitation, if at all. While Joe's attention was elsewhere, Violet thrust her knee up into his groin so he hunched forwards, and then she slashed her claws across his neck.

Blood squirted out like ejaculate onto Violet and the bed, and Joe clamped his hands instinctively over the gashes. Violet scrambled around him to get to Gypsy and seized the weapon from her flimsy grasp.

"You murderous piece of scum!" She tucked the stock into her shoulder, securing the barrel and bracing herself for the recoil. Having never handled a firearm, she didn't know how many rounds were left or whether it'd be enough to finish him off; but a blast to the skull would leave no room for doubt.

Joe remained on his knees, blood cascading through his fingers and down his chest. Even that didn't prevent his now human face from wearing that smug expression.

"I'll fucking kill you," Violet hissed. Nightmares of Isabelle's death trickled to the forefront of her mind until they became visions and she was back in that park all over again.

"N-no, you won't. You're not... like us." Joe coughed out a breath, as if every word brought with it more discomfort. "You never had a choice with the doctor. It's why I set you up to assassinate Jenna in circumstances that would force you into an act of self-defence. Killing me would first and foremost be vengeance... and vengeance isn't justice."

Violet was close to crushing the barrel with her fingers, chest bobbing in exaggerated motions. Controlling her heart rate was impossible, and she knew that Joe was listening. Reading her like a book that he'd written because he'd been calculating her reactions ever since that night in Cherry's Bar.

"Do it, Violet." Gypsy's voice in her ear was as small as the girl herself. "He's just trying to get inside your head, buy some time while he heals."

"All I ever w-wanted was to unite us against a common cause." Joe looked from Gypsy to Violet again. "To end the suffering of our kin and make some kind of peace with the world that we inhabit."

"It's too late now." Violet spoke resignedly. "One way or another, you're going to die tonight. I don't care what happens to me, as long as I'm here to witness it."

Joe gave a spluttered laugh while removing his blood-drenched hand from his neck. The lacerations continued to spill out fluid, albeit less of a spray now. Joe was stooped over, holding himself up on his arms while coughing crimson sputum onto the carpet. Violet guessed that she'd nicked his trachea and blood was seeping into his airway.

"Ironic, isn't it?" He rasped. "How you're the least human of us all biologically; yet emotionally, you're a fucking saint in comparison. I almost want you to pull the trigger. At least I'll die in the knowledge that my efforts weren't all in vein. That deep down, we're exactly the same."

"No, she isn't."

Violet was just as surprised as the others to find Jenna poised in the doorway to the bedroom, having been too engrossed in the ruckus to detect anything outside of the attic. The tranquiliser pistol was readied at her side like an Old West gunslinger, hair gelled back into a ponytail that pinched back the skin of her face to emphasise the harsh angles and slanted eyes. The cuts on her lips still looked sore from their last skirmish, and Violet was hoping to avoid a rematch.

"Joe." It was spoken in cold acknowledgment. "I'm almost disappointed after hearing so much about your recent endeavours. I geared myself up for Satan himself, but it appears you're still the snivelling wreck that you were growing up."

"Don't go b-breaking my heart, now." Joe's response was just as unfeeling.

Violet interrupted their reacquaintance, aware that time was short. "Is Lucy okay?"

"She's safe. We thought you were dead."

Gypsy made a step towards the hunter with her lips curled back over her teeth, delicate features monstrous and twisted.

"It's okay," Violet assured her. "They tracked my phone. I linked it with Lucy's mobile and left it in my jacket pocket, told her to contact Jenna if she didn't hear from me by midnight." She glanced back to Joe with a vague smirk. "Guess I learned a few things from you after all."

Joe forced a chortle from his ripped throat, glowering at them from the side of his eyes. "You women are all the same, too fucking wet to do what needs to be done. If I were you, Violet, I'd save that bullet for myself because you're no good to them dead."

"Listen to me..." Violet felt Jenna's gloved hand on her arm. "There's another hunter in the house and two snipers outside, front and back. You can still make it out if I create a distraction."

"We'll be walking straight into an ambush," Gypsy intervened. "They hunt in pairs for stealth, but more will be waiting. Unless we take *her* hostage."

"Shut up!" Violet levelled the gun at Joe, hands damp and twitchy. "No one is taking anyone hostage. We had a deal, and I'm not a fucking traitor."

"Then, what are we waiting for?" Gypsy again. "End this and let's get the hell outta here!"

Violet's finger locked onto the trigger, squeezing the stock so tight into her shoulder that it began to ache. "I-I..." She ate into her bottom lip. "I can't do it."

She looked to Jenna. "I thought I could, but if I do then I'll never fucking stop. I know it."

Jenna slipped the tranquiliser gun into a harness strapped around her thigh and opened a hand to Violet. "Give me the weapon."

As she edged forwards, Violet caught the handle of her boot knife jutting from its sheath and pivoted the gun at her, more of a knee-jerk reaction than in defence.

"Give it to me," Jenna repeated, "and don't turn back."

"You'd let us go?" said Violet.

"I owe you one, but after tonight we're quits. I'll take care of *him* for free."

Violet doubted the woman's integrity no more than she doubted her own hunger for revenge, and if ever there was a time to bury her conscience then it was now. Gargling laughter left Joe's jaw streaked with blood, his slit windpipe having not yet sealed itself. His pasty complexion was glossy with perspiration.

"Would a man on the verge of bankruptcy walk away from a bathtub full of cash?" He spoke as if with a throat full of mucus. "That's all you are to them: a prize. Let your guard down and you'll be locked in a cage by morning."

"We don't have much time..." Jenna's voice in her ear.

"Come on!" Gypsy skirted around Joe and hopped onto the bed, aligning herself with the skylight. "Vi, let's go!"

Violet gave them all a passing glance, anxiety rising quicker than her pulse, mind torn in each direction. She felt like closing her eyes to concentrate solely on her intuition; after all, the spectrum of emotions that had been slowly devouring her like maggots to a corpse left nothing but. All that remained of her was framework, sturdy but not indestructible; enough to exist but not to live. A limbo that she wasn't sure was worth the last dregs of tenacity required to make it out alive.

Joe's guttural voice reached them from below. "Maybe Camilla was right about you all along. You're just as pathetic as your bitch little sister. I should have made you watch as I –"

In a tactless fit of temper, Violet took a lunging stride forwards and jammed her foot into the centre of Joe's face. His arms and legs splayed out so he thudded onto his front. Violet raised the shotgun in preparation to club him over the back of the head, but a firm hand clutched her wrist. She met Jenna's admonishing stare, saw the grotesque reflection in her eyes as they captured the lamplight. A divine, opportune symbolism that made her see what she'd become for the very first time.

"Go. Now," Jenna ordered.

The next time Violet's eyes fell to Joe, astonishingly, her anger had dissipated. "Dying is just an inconvenience to you. Dying at the hands of a hunter is something else entirely. I won't give you the satisfaction of tarnishing either myself or Isabelle's memory with any more bloodshed."

Violet crammed the gun into Jenna's hands with a permissive nod. Another punt to Joe's gut flung him onto his side, and he curled up with a moan. She made a detour around him to grab her jacket from the chair and shrugged it on over her unclad torso. Gypsy's legs were already disappearing through the window when Violet reached the bed. She jumped up, latching onto the frame and hauling herself up through the opening.

Once she'd clambered onto the roof, Gypsy was sliding precariously over the tiles on her butt and hands, several of them dislodging under her weight. Little avalanches of grit and dirt clattered down the slope into the gutter. As Violet was scanning the land ahead of them, a thunderous boom vibrated the roof beneath their feet. Her lungs seized up with the rest of her body; in fact the night itself could have been put on pause. The trees with their broken whispers, not a flutter from nocturnal birds or inhabitants of whatever woodland that encompassed them.

Finally, the air began to creep around her, stimulating her perceptions to life. A silhouette darted across the front of the house from behind Joe's Jeep, too large for an animal and, she ascertained once her eyes had fine-tuned themselves, it was another hunter about to crash through the front door to assist their squad members.

Violet turned her head back towards the window as if expecting a battalion of arrow-firing ninjas to come pouring out of it, but all she got were intermittent wafts of blood. Perhaps those emanating from an exploded head that left its mess splattered over the ceiling and walls of the attic room. She heard Jenna calling out to whoever it was charging up the stairs, and even without being in close enough proximity to listen for heartbeats, Violet knew that Joe had perished. It was without the accompaniment of joy or relief. More than anything it was purposelessness that she felt, for she'd been fixated on revenge for so long that it had almost become a distraction. Perhaps it had been preventing her from seeing Joe for what he was all along.

"*Psst...*" A whisper brought her attention back to Gypsy's position on the verge of the roof. "Are you coming or what?"

"Go. I'll be right behind you." It was a demand, not a request.

Gypsy didn't need to be told again and plummeted from view. Violet headed after her, surprisingly fleet-footed across the slippery tiles until there was nothing but air beneath her. The descent looked far higher than it was, yet the nearer she got to land, the swifter she seemed to fall. She bent her knees in preparation for the alight so that her calves and thighs would absorb most of the impact. The rush of fearlessness came with a sort of innate knowledge, and before she knew it, her feet thudded onto the grass. Gypsy's childlike figure raced through the night as if she was bound for a destination that was calling out to her. Without checking for enemies, Violet sprinted after her, away from the nightmares of the past and into whatever uncertainties lay ahead.

She didn't know which was more daunting.

CHAPTER TWENTY

The digger piled the last mound of soil onto the gravesite, a barren-looking dome amid the expanse of dewy grass. Row upon row of headstones were so unique in their individual structures and epitaphs but, together, all of those memories blended as one. It was a shame, Violet thought, how insignificant it all seemed; but what counted were the memories that would be with her long after walking out of the cemetery gates.

The workman that had been operating the machinery was now laying a colourful melange of bouquets onto the dismal grave. Standing a little further back so as not to crowd him, Violet's withered heart began to bloom. One wreath spelled out the word 'Son', its dazzling white chrysanthemums as pure as the soul buried several feet beneath them. Violet was grateful for the presence that drew up beside her, almost as ghostly as the surrounding residents in its amble.

"I'm glad you came." Her graveside companion stared ahead with Violet, neither offering the other any gestures of compassion. The ambiance between them was enough.

"Sorry I didn't show my face at the funeral," replied Violet. "I heard everything. It was perfect."

"As perfect as saying goodbye gets," Lucy added. "People have been asking about you. Not just today but at the office, too. They think you're taking some time out after everything that's happened."

"For what it's worth, thank you. I know you can never forgive me for bringing this hell to your door." Violet's throat constricted, the burn travelling up to her nose and finally her eyes. "I wish I hadn't ended things with Dean the way that I did. I'll never get to say that I'm sorry. He'll never know how much I cared about him – even loved him in my own screwed up way."

She felt the warmth of Lucy's smile in her voice, marginally relieving her woe. "If this ordeal has taught me one thing, it's that anything is possible.

Dean is here, I can feel it. I *believe* it, Violet."

Violet turned her gaze to Lucy, held it there a few seconds. Then: "I have to go. Me being here is dangerous for both of us, especially now the heat from the cops has died down."

"But Jenna said that she only wanted Joe. I made her promise not to hurt you, even threatened to out her organisation to the world."

The declaration came as an unexpected comfort to Violet. Such a small token but enough to give her hope that there was a chance of absolution.

"That you can still treasure our friendship makes life all the more bearable, but we both know that you'll take this to the grave. Jenna knows it, too. The world is dangerous enough, without creating a mass hysteria."

Lucy contemplated her a moment and then, rather than prolonging the dispute, she gave a sorrowful nod. "Where will you go?"

Violet shrugged while looking back at the decorative gravesite. "Anywhere I want. I've got a bag full of stolen cash that could keep me off the grid until the day I drop dead from boredom."

"Are you serious?"

Violet nodded. "Courtesy of Joe – his parents left him a comfy inheritance. I don't know how he moved so much money around, but Gypsy saw him load it into his car on the night that he abducted me."

"So, will I ever see you again?"

"One day, I hope. Time is the best chance of healing that either of us has."

"Just..." Lucy choked up a little, sniffing back the tears. "Just don't let all of this be for nothing, okay? We've both lost people..." she focused on Dean's resting place once more, "but the best way to honour them is by treasuring what we have left. Dean wouldn't want us hating each other, and Isabelle wouldn't want you to keep punishing yourself for things beyond your control."

"I know that now. Izzy and I might not have shared the same blood, but we were still sisters. Always will be, just like you and me. I love you, Luce."

The girls clung to one another in embrace, each sobbing for the other. An anguish that would bond them eternally, no matter the damage it had caused. The affection was short-lived but it blanketed them long after they'd divided.

"Listen, I'm not going to say goodbye." Lucy smiled. "I know you, and you're smart and stubborn enough to figure this out."

"Stubborn, maybe. Smart... we'll see."

Lucy's brows flexed with worry, and Violet was quick to assuage it. "Jenna requested somewhat of a liaison. A one-on-one thing, neutral grounds. Not exactly above board as far as the Clan's protocol goes. I'm sure it's to discuss a truce, and I'm even more certain that I won't like the terms."

"You're not considering going? Violet, you could be walking into a trap."

"So could she. Before coming to say my goodbyes, I went to make amends with Beverly. To forgive her in the hope that it grants her some peace of mind. I owed it to Isabelle more than anything."

"I understand. You did the right thing." Lucy gave her an encouraging smile.

Violet added, "I told her about meeting Jenna. I guess I just wanted to assure her that she was safe from the Clan and doesn't have to keep looking over her shoulder. I'd never expect anything other than contempt from Beverly, but she acknowledged her part to play in the way my life turned out. Made me see that I'm finally in control of what happens next."

"And... what is that?"

"The options have already been laid out: accept the truce, live a life on the run or take the chance to finish what Joe started. I almost killed Jenna once before, and after today... well, there won't be another."

"It's not just her, though, is it? More will come. They'll keep on coming."

"Yes." Violet nodded. "And I'll be waiting."

***

Violet gazed lazily over the River Derwent. The mild breeze cast ripples over the water's surface so it looked as if it was in a rush to get somewhere. Last time she'd been at Darley Park, her thoughts had been just as unsettled. In fact they were bordering on tempestuous, but now there was just a lukewarm stillness. Not for a scarcity of emotions, but for an understanding and harmony with those that trickled through her.

So immersed in rumination was she that she hadn't seen the figure approaching from the footpath to her right. Violet continued to observe the river as the woman sat down on the bench with her coat belted around her swollen belly. Dressed from the neck down in black, Violet imagined the Grim

Reaper beside her and almost chuckled at the relevance.

"Thank you for agreeing to meet me," said Jenna, in a rather neutral tone considering the events of their last encounter.

"What can I say?" Violet answered. "I was curious, and I figured this would be the last chance that I got to apologise."

Jenna turned her head at the same moment Violet glanced across at her. It was the first time she'd seen the woman in natural light. She wasn't attractive, and her masculinity was even more salient without fear or dismay to interrupt her linier features. Violet wouldn't label her as the enemy, nor did Jenna seem to perceive her as a monster. Right there, right then, they were just two women having a conversation. A normality that they both knew would never last.

"I wasn't in my right mind when I came to your house that night," Violet wanted to explain. "We both know what a manipulative piece of shit Joe was, but it's no excuse. It shouldn't have happened and it won't happen again. Joe never told me where your base of operations is. There won't be any retaliation on my part."

Jenna linked her hands together on her lap, not having to deliberate long before her tone thawed a little. "Well, apology accepted. By rights, my people should never have taken their eyes off the Carters. We do acknowledge the responsibility that we hold towards Isabelle's death, however indirect."

Violet shrugged. "We could play this game all afternoon, it won't change anything. Ever since discovering the truth about my past, I've been wishing that I'd never made it into the outside world. I'd never have known Izzy, but at least she'd be alive."

"That's actually the reason why I'm here..." Jenna hesitated.

Violet smiled cynically to herself. "Let me guess, you've been chatting with the big dogs and now they want me back behind bars. Am I close?"

"If it was up to me then I'd give you the benefit of the doubt and let you get on with building a life for yourself. I've been studying the metasapien for over twenty years; I know a predator when I see one. But every decision has to go through a council, and I have little sway over them."

Violet nodded swiftly but appreciatively. Jenna went on, "As promised, we cleaned up the mess left behind at the mill and cottage. Procedure would have seen to it anyway, but you eliminated multiple threats that would have been detrimental to us all if the wrong people got involved."

"But proving that I'm not a threat isn't enough, right? My guess is that if anything, I've caused even more hysteria amongst your *people*."

"You have to understand that not reporting any of this would have made me no better than the Carters, and I'm not going down the same route as Rochelle. This is my life. I have a code to follow."

"Believe it or not, I get it. So, what happens now? Is this where you tackle me to the ground and make a citizen's arrest?"

Jenna found humour in the notion, and they shared a moment's laughter before solemnity brought a stifling thickness to the air. Then she said, "If you hand yourself in, quietly and without resistance, then I give you my word that you'll be treated with dignity and provided with as comfortable life as possible. No one else has to get hurt. Mainly, we're curious to learn more about you."

"*Comfortable*..." Violet pondered the word. "In all my years on this planet, not a second have I ever felt close to that. I don't think I know the meaning of the word, and that makes me feel anything but. So, thanks – but no, thanks."

Jenna sighed at the ground, not for herself but for Violet's predicament. "As much as I didn't want to hear that, I was expecting it."

"So, how much of a head start do we have?" Violet enquired. "I assume your invitation extends to Gypsy as well."

"I'm afraid so. But until this one is born..." Jenna's hands moved up to her belly, nursing it like a crystal ball, "I'm taking a postponement from the field work. If you want my advice then don't stop moving. After the fiasco with Joe and Camilla, we're investing in certain resources that mean we'll have eyes all over the country. Despite our mutual understanding, I can never forgive the danger that you caused to my unborn child. That alone will be a permanent motivation."

"And I can't forgive the fact that half of my kin are being used as lab rats. Joe had a tendency to speak in riddles, but there was always some strain of truth in his words. There had to be, and I've got a pretty close idea of what goes on at this base of yours."

"Then, we both know where we stand with each other."

With nothing left to say and an ongoing silence between them, Violet rose from the bench and began to walk away.

"Violet... is your friend, Gypsy, the only one left? Or are there others?"

Violet turned partially. "If I told you that it's just us, would you believe me?"

"No. But nonetheless, I have to ask."

"And if I were to ask you if my biological parents are still alive?"

Jenna's expression gave away nothing. But her silence gave away everything.

Digging her hands into her pockets, Violet followed the river for what would be her last meander through Darley Park.

EPILOGUE

The moon hung above her with a magical aura that seemed to brighten the entire sky. Violet wouldn't have needed a torch, even without the acute night vision. With summer approaching, the air was starting to lose its bite. She'd already had to remove her jacket and now, with sweat drizzling down her back and soaking the underarms of her top, she could finally pause for respite.

Violet's shoulders heaved with the exertion of her panting, though it wasn't all from the drudgery of shovelling through six feet of earth for the last hour and a half. More than that, it was the dread fingering her spine and the lead weight in her gut that almost brought her crashing down. She scrunched her mud-caked fists while staring down at the slab of pine beneath her feet. There was no plaque, probably because it was cheaper to do without – then again, it's not like anyone would ever read it.

Violet kicked aside a scattering of dirt and then lowered onto her knees, placing her ear to the wood with her hands splayed either side of her head. Realistically, she didn't expect to hear anything; but her motivation behind this violation of afterlife privacy was preposterous in itself.

"I don't know how," Violet whispered, "but I can feel you in there, Izzy. I tried to walk away... I tried *so hard*... but it always comes back to this. To us, right here and right now. I know what I have to do."

She scooted off the coffin into the trench that she'd dug around its perimeter, the tall earth walls creating a sense of confinement that she'd been trying to ignore. Violet extracted a crowbar out of the rucksack that she'd brought with her and hooked the curved end into the groove between the coffin and its lid. Grave robbing wasn't a skill that she'd acquired over the years but, surely, the pine would be no match for her brawn.

There was no give whatsoever, unsurprisingly, and Violet hadn't the first clue how to crack open the screws in each corner of the box. Even if she did have the correct equipment, the absurdity of what she was doing had been so last minute that she couldn't remember grabbing the tools that she did have to hand – nor did she have any recollection of entering the cemetery gates. It could have been a dream, one that she wasn't sure if she wanted to wake from.

All that mattered was the here and now, her and Isabelle, sister to sister. If all else failed then she wasn't opposed to smashing her way into the coffin by force.

Violet scraped and wiggled the crowbar into the nook to get a decent leverage, and then pushed down using her body weight. The wood groaned, and a startled shudder bolted through her. Perhaps because it almost sounded alive, and in a place that was surrounded by death, an overzealous imagination was one of many distractions to contend with.

Finally, Violet felt some movement on the lid and the crowbar slipped into the tiny gap. Without too much strain, she moved a little further down and repeated the procedure to get an even leverage and avoid breaking off sections of the lid. More creaks, some splintering from the screws as they were torn loose and then, with a mighty wrench on the crowbar that left a friction burn on her hand, it was prised open with a crunching boom.

Whatever musty stench of rot that might seep from the air-tight container didn't deter Violet. Being up close and personal with the viscera of animals and putrescent carcasses had desensitised her, both mentally and physically. If anything, it was the knowledge of where – or more specifically, *what* – the smell expunged from that would test her gag reflexes. Isabelle hadn't been embalmed, and it was Beverly's connections that had allowed her to bypass the costs of a funeral director and set everything up last minute.

Free of reluctance or foreboding, Violet threw down the crowbar and flung back the coffin lid. She hadn't given much prior thought to what she might find. The ground had been frozen over the winter months and soil climates as such that decomposition wouldn't have been accelerated in any way. The pale, serene face of a girl that she'd once loved was a fantasy. The best she could hope for was some sunken, maggot-infested resemblance to what occupied her memories.

When Violet allowed her gaze to descend, all it found was the taffeta lining of the coffin. For several moments her mind was as empty as the box, eyes frozen in stupefied disbelief. No skeletal grin or wispy hair; no brown, prune-like skin clinging to bone. No body. No Isabelle.

Then, as if her thoughts had been building like a queue of traffic, the lights changed to green. She began to pat down the grubby lining as if searching for a fingernail rather than a full-bodied human, even climbing inside the coffin.

"No... no..." The word dripped from her like a habitual leak.

How? Where? Why?

"Isabelle! Where are you?"

If this was a dream then it had quickly turned into a nightmare. The feeling of losing Isabelle was all too familiar, and not just to the eternal darkness. Violet could have been in that cemetery a hundred times, whether in memory or imaginings. Same place, same time, same crucifying circumstances. A sort of déjà vu that scratched away at the back of her mind.

Violet slumped to her knees, fingers clawed around the edges of the coffin, scraping the wood as fiercely as the sound abraded her eardrums. As her head lolled back, she screamed loud and shrill. For if ever there was a time to wake herself, then it was now.

– THE END –

ABOUT THE AUTHOR

Rae Louise is a horror author based in Staffordshire, UK. She started writing fiction in her teenage years, with her first novel, *The Fear*, published in February 2017. Rae edited the paranormal biography, *Diary of a Gonzo Ghost Hunter*, and contributes to a popular horror website in her spare time. She enjoys creating gothic fantasy artwork and watching films with her pet degu.

Thank you so much for reading one of our **Sci-Fi** novels.
If you enjoyed our book, please check out our recommended title for your next great read!

Culture-Z by Karl Andrew Marszalowicz

In the year 2190, mankind has made great strides forward in the worlds of technology, science, and greed. However, when all three get together one last time, this oblivious generation may not exist much longer.

www.ingramcontent.com/pod-product-compliance
Lightning Source LLC
Chambersburg PA
CBHW010446100726
47904CB00008B/2499